Desire Swelled in Him

*at the sight of the woman in the fur onstage.
He thought of Stephanie wearing the coat,
the satin lining caressing her thighs and
stomach and back. In his mind he saw her
turning to him, her eyes heavy-lidded and
her mouth full with passion, shrugging the
heavy coat back to reveal naked shoulders,
then dropping it into a heap on the floor.
Without shame she would stand before him,
promising a loving release from his blissful
torture.*

*All he could think of was pulling her to him
and kissing her until she was breathless and
yearning for his touch, but that was
something he could never do.*

D0121853

Dear Reader:

There is an electricity between two people in love that makes everything they do magic, larger than life. This is what we bring you in SILHOUETTE INTIMATE MOMENTS.

SILHOUETTE INTIMATE MOMENTS are longer, more sensuous romance novels filled with adventure, suspense, glamor or melodrama. These books have an element no one else has tapped: excitement.

We are proud to present the very best romance has to offer from the very best romance writers. In the coming months look for some of your favorite authors such as Elizabeth Lowell, Nora Roberts, Erin St. Claire and Brooke Hastings.

SILHOUETTE INTIMATE MOMENTS are for the woman who wants more than she has ever had before. These books are for you.

Karen Solem
Editor-in-Chief
Silhouette Books

Secret Fires

Kristin James

Silhouette Intimate Moments
Published by Silhouette Books New York
America's Publisher of Contemporary Romance

Silhouette books by Kristin James

Dreams of Evening (IM #1)
The Amber Sky (IM #17)
Morning Star (IM #45)
Secret Fires (IM #69)

SILHOUETTE BOOKS, a Division of Simon & Schuster, Inc.
1230 Avenue of the Americas, New York, N.Y. 10020

Distributed by Pocket Books

ISBN: 0-671-46857-X

First Silhouette Books printing October, 1984

10 9 8 7 6 5 4 3 2 1

America's Publisher of Contemporary Romance

Printed in the U.S.A.

To Sharon,
for all her help throughout the years

Chapter 1

STEPHANIE TYLER STRETCHED HER LEGS OUT ON THE lounger and settled back to enjoy her morning coffee. Heat waves shimmered in front of Camelback Mountain, the most distinctive of the barren mountains surrounding Phoenix and the Salt Flat River Valley. "Valley of the Sun" was what the travel agents now liked to call the area comprised of Phoenix, Scottsdale, Tempe and their environs, once separate towns but now sprawling into each other like children outgrowing their common bed. It was certainly an apt name, Stephanie thought, whatever its commercial intent, for temperatures in the summer soared over the hundred mark almost daily. Although it was June, the first gentle month of summer in other places, it was already blazing in Phoenix. That was why she had scheduled her appointment with Howard Perry for 9:30 in the morning; she liked to get trips outside the house done before the afternoon.

Thinking of Perry, she sighed and for the hundredth time wondered what he wanted to say to her. An overlooked team-owned insurance policy or pension plan for Ty? A paper releasing the team from responsibility for his death? A lawsuit was something Perry's conniving mind might conceive of as a threat. He would cover all the angles. Ty had said the first rule to remember in dealing with Howard Perry was to distrust him. At the time he had been embroiled in bitter contract negotiations. Neil got along with Howard amicably, but Howard and Ty's personalities had been poles apart. Howard Perry was all business and practicality; Ty all talent and fire. They didn't mix well.

Stephanie shook her head, dismissing the thought of Howard Perry. She wasn't going to let him spoil the precious morning peace of her garden. Her eyes turned to the high oleander hedge which shaded her back yard and separated it from her neighbor's. In front of it several hardy irises bloomed in a graceful, nodding arrangement of purple, pink and white, the product of careful tending and profuse watering. The pint-sized pool was a fresh blue rectangle, and the fragrant lemon and lime trees made a splash of waxy green against the white wall of her office.

Her office. That was a joke. It had been weeks since she'd done a lick of work. Stephanie swung her legs off the lounge chair and stood up. If such disagreeable thoughts were going to intrude on her morning contemplation, she might as well go to Howard's office. She stacked her empty dishes on the metal tray which lay atop the wrought-iron table and carried it inside to her kitchen. There she set the tray on the counter and went back to the den to lock the sliding glass door to the backyard before going to her bedroom.

Her house was older and smaller than the sprawling wood-and-glass home in which she and Ty had lived, but it suited her. She hadn't been able to remain in Ty's house after his death, and the settled charm of this older neighborhood appealed to her. There was something comforting about the white stucco, red-roofed house surrounded by lemon and lime trees. It had been the lovingly cared-for home of a retired couple for almost twenty years, and the love seemed to have settled into the walls. That had been what Stephanie needed at the time, a place to curl up and be comforted. But even if it had not touched her heart, the beauty of the Mexican tile entry and the one-room guesthouse in the rear, perfect for a freelance writer's office, would have sold her on the house. Stephanie had never regretted moving here from the house that Pete Cherneski, the team's middle linebacker, had dubbed "the Castle."

Stephanie whisked off her light caftan as she entered her bedroom and dressed quickly. She had decided to wear a pale blue linen skirt with a matching sleeveless shell and jacket. The jacket's jaunty collar and buttonless front were decorated with wide white piping. The effect was simple, crisp and dressier than the sort of clothes she usually wore. She added geometric silver earrings and a simple silver chain, then slipped into low white sandals. She stepped into her small bathroom to apply light makeup and a touch of lipstick. Next she brushed back her straight red-brown hair and secured it with decorative clips on either side, so it wouldn't straggle and cling to her face in the heat.

She was not particularly concerned with fashion, though she possessed a certain innate flair which made her casual clothes and hairstyles eye-catching. Her face was unremarkably oval, with a well-formed mouth, nose and cheekbones; attractive but not compelling. What gave her features interest were her eyes. Accented by the slash of straight, dark brows above, her eyes were wide-set and a mixed gray-blue color, alive and warm, controlled by her emotions. She looked upon the world with a lively curiosity, and when she was angry or happy or surprised her eyes glowed or burned or darkened with the feeling.

Stephanie smoothed her skirt and turned to look at herself from all angles in the mirror. She decided she looked appropriate for the business offices of the Arizona Apaches. Howard Perry prided himself on the team's businesslike approach to professional athletics. Satisfied, she picked up her purse and started out to her carport. It was unlikely that she would bother to check her reflection again all day, and that lack of concern about her looks was a large part of her appeal.

Though the stadium lay south of Tempe on Interstate 10, a site designed to lure fans from the southern city of Tucson, the Arizona Apaches' business offices and practice field were in the northern section of Phoenix. The closer she drew to the four-story gold-glass building off Black Canyon Freeway, the tighter her stomach knotted. She hadn't been to the offices since Ty had died, and it was a jolt to face Ty's home ground again.

She pulled into the parking lot beside the building. Its gold mirrored glass reflected the sun blindingly. The security officer stepped out of his booth to question her, checked a list for her name and raised the metal bar. Stephanie slid past the gate and found a parking space. She stepped out of her car, smoothed her skirt, then lifted her chin and strode toward the front doors.

Inside the building the ultramodern halls were carpeted in dull gold, and the walls were boldly decorated with designs of white, gold and orange, the desert colors of the Apaches football team. No expense had been spared on this dream-child of the Ingram brothers, who had taken a family fortune based on copper mining and parlayed it into a staggering multibillion-dollar enterprise dedicated to tourism. Land speculation, resort hotels, a chain of restaurants and an enormous amusement park in the Salt Flat River Valley formed the broad base of the Ingram empire. Their bold filigreed "I" emblem could be seen all over Arizona and had spread into New Mexico, Colorado and Texas as well. Finally they had amassed the excess millions necessary to indulge in their favorite toy, a professional football team. With the hard zeal they brought to every other enterprise, they had set out to make their fledgling team competitive and profitable, and they had succeeded. They hired a talented coach and a business-oriented general manager and gave them free rein. The result was a team that had won the championship of their league within four years and the Super Bowl the year after that.

Stephanie was familiar with the building and ignored the receptionist at the main desk downstairs, going straight to the elevators. The elevator took her to the top floor, where the executive offices lay. There a polished secretary took her name and moments later ushered her into the spacious corner office of Howard Perry. Perry rose to greet her, a carefully calculated smile broadening his lips. He was a medium-sized man whose supremely ordinary looks concealed a razor-sharp brain and cool nerve.

"Stephanie, my dear, how nice to see you. I hope you're doing well."

"Yes, very. And you?"

"Fine, just fine. Winette and the kids are up north this week visiting her parents and beating the heat."

Stephanie strove to look interested in the whereabouts of his wife and children as she sat down. "How nice. I'm sure they'll enjoy it."

"Let me get straight to the point, Stephanie." Howard sat back in his chair, placing his forearms on the desk and forming a careful steeple with his fingers. He stared intently at his hands for a moment before turning his gaze back to her. "We're involved in a project that I think will please you a great deal."

"Please me?" Stephanie repeated, already lost.

"Yes. The Apaches Wives' Association has been

raising funds for the past year to set up a foundation in Kenneth's name."

"In Ty's memory?" She smiled. "That's very nice." Was this why he had called her to his office? She couldn't imagine Howard Perry involving himself in the Wives' Association's charities.

"They've raised a tidy sum. Karen Randall was the chairwoman, and you know what a go-getter she is. They sold a cookbook and had a dance and I don't know what all. Anyway, they came up with seventy thousand dollars, which Russell and Winslow Ingram matched. That makes one hundred and forty thousand dollars, a pretty healthy basis for the Kenneth R. Tyler Cancer Foundation."

Stephanie was amazed. "It's quite a lot. I never imagined . . . I mean, Julie said something to me— Julie Koblitz—about their raising money for Ty, but I didn't dream it would be so much."

Perry beamed unctuously. "The Ingrams are always generous where their players are concerned. And they were very fond of Kenneth. They were saddened by his loss."

It was on the tip of Stephanie's tongue to remark that the Ingrams were primarily saddened by the loss of Ty's talent, but she bit back the words. She had no illusions about the Ingrams' generosity, but it would sound bitter and ungrateful to say so at this point.

"The wives are turning the fund over to St. Anthony's Hospital, and we thought it would be nice to have a ceremony where we present the check to representatives of the hospital. It will be during halftime of the first exhibition game, the first weekend in August. Now, where you come in. . . . It seems appropriate, since it's in Kenneth's name, to present you with a plaque commemorating the foundation of the fund. His profile will be etched on the metal plate, and below that will be the 'Kenneth R. Tyler Cancer Foundation' and the date."

"I see," Stephanie responded flatly. She did indeed. Howard Perry was seizing the opportunity for a little publicity.

"Barbara Lang is coordinating the ceremony. Her office will get in touch with you closer to the date. I just wanted—"

"Wait a minute. I haven't agreed to attend."

Howard blinked. "Pardon?"

"I said, I haven't agreed to attend. Frankly, I find your trading on Ty's premature death more than a little macabre."

"Stephanie! Where did you get the idea we're 'trading' on Kenneth's death? We're simply—"

"You're *simply* using this fund to obtain more publicity for the Apaches," Stephanie snapped.

"Stephanie!" He appeared shocked. "I . . . I never dreamed you'd fight a foundation in your husband's memory."

"I have nothing against the foundation. It's fine. But what you're talking about is using Ty's death and the Wives' Association's charitable efforts to make the Apaches organization look good. 'See, we're not just a successful team or a profitable corporation. We have a heart too.' It's disgusting."

Perry stared at her as if she were a rare form of animal life, interesting but bizarre. "Kenneth and I had our differences, but I hope you aren't holding that against me or the company. It was only natural. We were on the opposite sides of the bargaining table. That didn't mean I didn't respect him as a man and a talent."

"As a talent, perhaps. But you didn't know him as a man." Old anger surged in her. "You don't know any of those players as human beings. To you they're machines or animals, something you buy and sell, something you squeeze every last ounce of energy, talent and courage out of, then toss aside when they can't perform for you. I don't like this game. I didn't like it when Ty played it. I spent too many evenings before a game watching him tie himself into knots to get any enjoyment out of watching him play. It's profit to you and vicarious enjoyment to thousands of people who haven't the energy or ability to play themselves. But to those men on the field it's sweat and broken bones and torn ligaments and an incredible amount of physical pain and mental anguish."

"It's also quite a few dollars to them."

"That's always your argument, isn't it? If they don't want to play, they don't have to. They're getting paid good money. Well, the fact is they don't know how to do anything else. It's all they've been trained to do their whole lives. Football was worshipped by their parents, teachers and fellow students."

"A lot of them love the game," Howard interjected mildly.

"You use that against them too. What they don't realize is that when they consistently abuse their bodies, when they tape themselves up and dope themselves with painkillers and go out to play with injuries that aren't allowed enough time to heal completely, they're going to pay for it somewhere down the line. I've met forty-year-old ex-football players who shuffle along like old men because their knees will hardly bend. I've seen players with scar tissue on their fingers and elbows and knees so thick they can't move them. I—"

Perry held up a hand. "I realize you've interviewed a lot of malcontents for that book you wrote with Dave Blonsky's wife—what's her name?"

"Sondra," Stephanie supplied tightly. "I have a little more personal experience than that. I was married to a football player for almost three years."

"Kenneth Tyler was the best wide receiver this team had—maybe the best playing in this country at that time. He was talented, likable, flamboyant, but he wasn't typical. He lived on drama and nerves. Most men couldn't keep up his lifestyle, especially the life he led before he married you."

"I think I know my husband better than you. What's the purpose of this lecture on Kenneth Tyler?"

"I'm just saying that you can't judge football by him. He had a tendency to exaggerate. He told a good story. He was temperamental. I'd seen him before a game too. He was a bundle of nerves who spent most of the time before the game vomiting. But that's the way he psyched himself up to play. He enjoyed talking about the hard things in football, but he didn't say a lot about why he did everything the hardest way possible. Or about his love for football. Or how much garbage Gene Cheyne and Jim Cooper and this organization took from him. He was given a lot of leeway, but I doubt he mentioned that."

Stephanie closed her eyes and mentally counted to ten. She still had trouble controlling her temper, a problem she'd had since Ty's death. "I'm sorry, Howard. I know Ty wasn't all sweetness and light. Nor is the game of football all bad. And this discussion has gotten way off the track. We were talking about the ceremony at halftime. I don't like it. It's commercializing something that began as a noble impulse, and it's using Ty's death to promote your product. It's the Wives' Association's money, and they're free to give it to the hospital in any manner they choose. But I won't be a part of it."

"That's your final word?"

"That's it." Stephanie rose, her mouth forming a brittle grin. "I'm sorry to have blown off steam in front of you."

A genuine laugh burst from Howard's throat. "My dear, your little tirade was a dream compared to some of the things that have been said in this office. I hope you change your mind."

"I won't."

Stephanie crossed to the imposing wooden door and opened it. Her knees trembled slightly, part of the aftermath of her anger. She couldn't remember how many times she'd blown her stack like that in the last year and a half. Funny, when you considered that in the past she'd had a fairly equable personality. Ty's death had brought her emotions to the surface, and it seemed that she hadn't yet recovered.

She walked out, closing the door quietly behind her. Howard Perry shook his head in bemusement, then picked up his telephone receiver and rang his secretary. When her crisp voice answered, he growled, "Get Neil Moran on the phone. I've got a job for him."

As Stephanie walked to her car she glanced toward the mountains to the east. For a moment she considered driving out to Neil's house, but discarded the idea. She had used his comfort and aid too often in the past. He must be thoroughly sick of it by now, no matter how good a friend he was. She couldn't run to him every time she was swept with painful memories of Ty. For the past few months she'd managed very well on her own, and she had to continue to do so or she'd never be able to rebuild her life.

Stephanie pulled out of the parking lot and turned her car toward home. Poor Neil. She'd soaked a lot of his shirts with her tears. She remembered the evening when Dr. McIlhenny had gotten back the CAT scan and taken her aside into an empty eye examination room. At first they had thought Ty's problem was something to do with his eyes and had put him in the eye wing of the hospital. When they had realized it wasn't his eyes, but still didn't know what it was, they simply left him there. Stephanie remembered sitting in the room looking at the various machines and posters on the wall. She doubted she'd ever forget the strange black hanging dotted with white stars, like a map of constellations. She had sat down on a padded stool with wheels, which left the neurologist only the examination chair to perch on. He looked both foolish and grave. Stephanie felt only scared.

"Mrs. Tyler, I ordered a CAT scan on your husband.

I wasn't satisfied with the earlier tests." He spoke with the detached manner of a frequent observer of death and grieving. "Mr. Tyler has a very fast-growing brain tumor."

Stephanie had stared at him, unable to absorb the news, while he went on with his clinical analysis of the tumor in Ty's brain. *Ty's brain.* This man was talking as if it were an inanimate object or something belonging to someone else. But it was Ty he was talking about! Ty's brain that was being destroyed! The neurologist must have seen the sudden, confused panic in her face, for he came off the high chair quickly and reached down to touch her arm. "Mrs. Tyler, is there someone you can call? Someone to be with you? Your parents? Mr. Tyler's?"

"No, they live in California. My parents. Ty's mother's in Iowa. She's—I—we hadn't told her Ty was ill. We didn't want to worry her. You see, Ty's father died just a year ago. . . ." Her voice trailed off.

"A friend?" he suggested.

"Yes. Neil. I'd like to call Neil."

"I could have one of the nurses call him for you."

"No. I'd rather do it." She rose, feeling strangely disconnected from herself, and went to Ty's room. He lay in the bed, a long, silent mass beneath the sheets. Tubes ran into his arms and nose and out from under the sheets. His eyes were closed, his face flaccid. He didn't look like Ty at all, except for the mockery of the bright golden hair against the pillow. Stephanie took some change from her purse and walked down the hall to the pay telephone. She didn't want to make the call from Ty's room, no matter how unconscious he looked. She stepped into the dubious protection of the phonebox jutting from the wall and dialed Neil Moran's number. Neil had been at the hospital almost every day since Ty entered—helping Stephanie, taking her down to the cafeteria and forcing her to eat, talking to Ty as if Ty could respond to him. It was ironic that he hadn't been there when the doctor chose to tell her about Ty's brain tumor.

A lump filled her throat when Neil's familiar voice answered the phone, and for a moment she couldn't speak. Finally she whispered, "Neil?"

"What? Stephanie? Is that you?"

She cleared her throat. "Yes. Could you come to the hospital?"

"Has something happened to Ty?"

"No. Well, yes. Nothing's happened, exactly, but they—Dr. McIlhenny told me he has a brain tumor." There was a stunned silence at the other end, and she went on tremulously, "Neil, I need you."

"I'll be right there."

He must have driven down from his hill like a maniac, for it was only minutes later that he charged out of the elevator. Jaw set, hands clenched at his sides, his face stamped with cold determination, he looked for all the world as if he were running onto the field to turn the game around, except that there was a white touch of fear around his eyes that she had never seen there before. Stephanie didn't know whether to laugh or cry. Instead she jumped to her feet and ran toward him and let him engulf her in his hard arms.

She clutched at his shirt and buried her face against his chest, sobbing out broken, incoherent words as she cried. His long, supple fingers smoothed her hair and patted her back. His cheek caressed the top of her head as he murmured her name. For a brief, delicious moment she felt protected. Then reality returned and she pulled away shakily. "The doctor's still here. Do you want to talk to him?"

He nodded. They returned to the examination room again, but this time the neurologist didn't sit down. Neil remained standing, and it would have put Dr. McIlhenny at a distinct disadvantage to have had to look up at him. Neil was pugnacious, questioning, almost rude. The doctor explained again about the tumor and Neil, unconsciously positioning himself between the doctor and Stephanie, had snapped, "Is he going to die?"

McIlhenny sighed. "Mr. Moran, this is a very difficult tumor to treat. It's deep in the brain, not on the surface, which usually rules out surgery. I'd like a neurosurgeon to see him before I give you a definite answer, but my suspicion is that it's inoperable. It's put forth roots that—"

"Oh, my God!" Stephanie burst out, raising her hands to her mouth. She felt suddenly sick.

Neil knelt beside her, one arm going around her shoulders. "Maybe the doctor and I better talk alone. Do you want to go to Ty's room?"

"No. I have to hear it." She smiled weakly at Neil. "I'm not a fragile Victorian maiden. I can take it."

He squeezed her shoulders and stood. "When do you plan to consult with the neurosurgeon?"

"I think we should transfer him to Barrow Neurological Institute at St. Joseph's. The neurosurgeon I want him to see is on staff there. He's the best neurosurgeon in the state."

"Considering the size of Arizona's population, that's not saying a whole hell of a lot," Neil countered.

"I'd put him up against anyone in the country. Barrow is an excellent facility. If the surgeon thinks he can operate, Mr. Tyler will be in the best of hands. I don't want to hold out any false hopes, but Mr. Tyler is a very healthy man, and young. A much better candidate for surgery than most."

Neil strode to the door and back, his hands clenching and unclenching. Stephanie knew the look. Like Ty, he wasn't good at accepting things. He was accustomed to competing, to fighting and winning. He found it hard to deal with something he couldn't set himself to beat. His thick black brows drew together, and his tanned face was tight with suppressed anger. The black stare was flat and grim, unfocused. He was struggling to control his rage. "What I want to know," he began softly, his voice building, "is why the hell it took you so long to figure this out. A man comes in here with a tumor and you're testing him for eye diseases, stroke, diabetes—sinus infection, for God's sake!"

"I wasn't called in until this morning," Dr. McIlhenny interjected, understandably nervous at the other man's fierce anger.

"Why not?" Neil thundered. "I've watched you guys run around here for a week, making test after test and not coming up with a scrap of information among you."

"Brain tumors have many, very variable symptoms. Because they affect both the brain and the nervous system, it may seem to the patient that the pain is in his leg or stomach or somewhere else."

Stephanie rose with a weary sigh. "Come on, Neil, it's no good blaming the hospital. When Ty started feeling bad he went to the team doctor. He presumed it was a football-related injury. You know how he bruised his back in the last game. Dr. Reinhardt thought perhaps that was the reason for his nausea and numbness. He thought Ty's whole side was hurt by the fall. Then they suspected that sinus problems were causing his headaches because he broke his nose in a game in college. You know how it is. You guys spend half your life in pain, and it all comes from playing football. Everybody kept looking for something they could trace back to an injury—a pinched nerve, maybe. Who'd expect Ty to have a brain tumor?" Her voice caught on the words.

Neil's bleak face softened. "Honey, I'm sorry. It doesn't make it any better, does it? I just wanted to lash out at somebody. I feel so helpless!"

"I know."

The doctor interrupted gravely. "This tumor is exceptionally fast growing. If they had done a CAT scan at the beginning I'm not sure it would even have shown up."

The doctor had left soon after that, and Neil and Stephanie returned to Ty's room to sit numbly by his bed and stare at him. He didn't open his eyes or speak, and finally, hours later, Neil talked Stephanie into going home to rest. They drove in silence to the huge, echoing mansion where she and Ty lived. Neil had walked her to the door, and she had turned to him with huge eyes. "Will you stay with me for a while? I—I'm scared to be alone."

He had stayed, and she fixed coffee for them. They had talked about the past, the days before any of the three of them had known each other, and gradually they worked their way back to Ty. Stephanie had described the way she had met Ty, giggling, and suddenly her laughter had turned to tears. "I don't know what I'm going to do! Neil, what if he dies?"

"He won't. Ty can't die. Don't worry, Steph, I'll be right here with you. All the way."

Neil had been wrong. Ty could die. He did. He was taken to Barrow Neurological Institute, and the neurosurgeon there had agreed that the tumor was inoperable. He recommended steroid treatments, and in the next breath admitted that they might or might not work. Russell Ingram had flown in an expert from California at his own expense, much to Stephanie's surprise. But even he had agreed with the diagnosis of the other physicians. It was such a swiftly growing tumor, you see. The steroid treatments had worked as much as they were capable of working. Instead of dying right away, Ty had lived almost three more weeks. They were able to take him out of the hospital, with round-the-clock LVNs at home. He was asleep most of the time, and when he was awake his mind was fuzzy. He often mistook Stephanie for his mother or his sister, and sometimes he thought she was Neil's wife, frowning a little as he remarked that he didn't remember Neil's getting married. He died quietly, with a funny little sigh. Stephanie was standing at his side, holding his hand, and she felt the life slip out of him.

Neil had been there too, sitting in an armchair on the other side of the bed. He had kept his word to Stephanie to see her through it. He was with them almost every day. On the weekends, even with the night-shift nurse on duty, he had slept at their house, his long frame stretched out uncomfortably on the living room sofa so that he would be near in case Stephanie called him for help.

It was funny how close he and Ty were when they seemed so dissimilar. Ty was always joking and laughing, a flamboyant, controversial character who had trouble living by the rules. He was flashy, charming, foolhardy and enormously talented. Neil called him a "natural," a man who played by instinct and who was so skillful that his success was inevitable. Neil, on the other hand, was not as naturally talented but far more hardworking. He succeeded on drive, mental ability and his ice-cool nerve, surpassing other quarterbacks in the league who had more powerful or more accurate arms. Neil's personality, though he showed frequent flashes of humor, was quieter and calmer than Ty's. He was good-looking, but not a charmer. He was steady, intense and deep. He was reliable, a "team player" who could always be counted on to pull everyone together.

Despite their differences, Neil and Ty were the best of friends. Neil had stuck with him through everything, even those horrible days before anyone realized Ty was ill, when Ty had changed personality, becoming sarcastic, moody, irritable and even violently angry. Neil hadn't turned away from his friend, though Ty cursed and threatened him. Once Ty had actually taken a swing at him, but Neil, the stronger of the two, had only wrestled him to the ground and restrained him until the anger passed.

After Ty's death Neil had continued to help his friend's widow. He had taken care of the funeral arrangements and managed to keep away most of the press, sensation seekers and Ty's friends and admirers. He listened patiently to Stephanie's litany of should-haves and what-ifs, always reassuring her that she had done everything she could have to save Ty. Most of all he had given her a shoulder to cry on. Numb with grief, it wasn't until several months later that Stephanie realized how much it must have cost Neil to give her comfort so unstintingly when he himself was grieving over the loss of his best friend. But that was Neil for you. He considered it natural that his strength should be used to help those who were weaker.

Stephanie drove home mechanically, her mind occupied with the past. It startled her to turn onto her street and realize that she hadn't noticed anything along the way. She pulled into her driveway and simply sat for a moment. Oh, Ty! She rested her forehead against the steering wheel. The sharp pain of losing Ty had long since passed, and now she spent most days without thinking of him at all. She no longer cried at the slightest bit of sadness in a book or movie, nor did she long to strike out and scream with rage. But her talk with Howard Perry had dredged up the sorrow-laden memories. She thought of Ty as he had looked when she first met him—golden hair, golden skin, bright blue eyes, a smile as mischievous and winning as a boy's.

She had come to interview him for the book she was ghostwriting for Sondra Blonsky. Sondra was the wife of a star linesman for the team Ty had played for before he came to the Apaches. She had suggested Ty as a player who would give Stephanie an honest picture of the team. Stephanie had called him, and he had agreed to let her come to his house for an interview. When she rang his doorbell and he opened the door, a spontaneous grin had split his face. "I never expected you to look like this," he'd teased, "or I'd have agreed to talk to you weeks ago."

Stephanie had been unable to resist smiling back at him. She had gone inside for the interview and had emerged an hour later after accepting a dinner invitation from him for that evening. The quality of the notes she had taken during the interview was poor, but it didn't matter. By the end of the evening she was sure she was in love with him, and two months later they were married.

Tears filled Stephanie's eyes and plopped onto the lower rim of the steering wheel. She thought of Ty as he lay in his hospital bed, gaunt, waxen-faced, his fingers twitching aimlessly on the bedcovers, and she cried for all that had been lost.

Chapter 2

NEIL MORAN EASED THE WEIGHTS IN HIS RIGHT HAND down to shoulder level, then straight out and finally lowered them to his side. With the same agonizing slowness he reversed the procedure, lifting the short barbell straight out, back to his shoulder and up. Sweat glistened on his skin and his hair was plastered against his skull. When he returned the weights to their original position by his side, he let out his breath in a burst and bent to set the barbell into its place on the floor of his workout room. He dropped onto the padded bench, rested his elbows on his knees and let his head droop forward. From years of habit he draped a small towel around his neck and used the ends to wipe his face.

The work had paid off. His elbow hadn't felt any more strain than the rest of his arm. The surgery had frightened him, even though it was the new arthroscopic, quick-healing kind, and the long weeks when he couldn't use his arm for anything strenuous had been even worse. He could almost see his muscles atrophying. But then he had begun a carefully programmed schedule of workouts beneath the watchful gaze of Hal Mintner, the team's head trainer. They had paid off. He had had to move slowly and exercise patience, but that was his forte. His consistent ability to exercise control over his body and emotions was one of his most powerful weapons as a quarterback. It was a rare day indeed when pain, fatigue or anxiety were allowed to shadow Neil Moran's game. This singleminded concentration and almost icy calm had earned him the soubriquet of the "Electronic Quarterback" from one sportswriter.

He had applied his concentration and control to rehabilitating the troublesome elbow, and it was beginning to look as if he'd won. Of course he wouldn't know for sure until the arm was put to the stress and strain of an actual game. Sometimes a player had a weak spot that, even if healed, was vulnerable to future injuries. Neil would never forget the day they had carried Len Franklin from the field. One leg had dangled uselessly and his face had been pale and drawn. It was the brilliant runner's third injury to that knee, and mingled with the pain on his face was the bleak knowledge that his career was ended, cut short by a knee that would never be able to stand the pressure.

But at least Neil was in a much better spot than he'd been last season, when he'd started out with an already tender and partially immobilized throwing arm. He rose and strode out of the workout room and across the tiled floor of the hall and breakfast room. He opened the sliding-glass door, one of three sets leading onto the wooden deck, and stepped out into the dry heat. He had turned on the whirlpool hot tub before he began his workout, and it was bubbling away, ready for him. He stepped into the sunken tub and positioned himself so that the jetting water massaged his arm.

A large Irish setter sprinted around the corner of the

house and skidded to a halt at the edge of the whirl-pool. His tongue lolled out one side of his mouth as he wriggled enthusiastically, his tail whipping back and forth. Neil smiled with amused resignation. "Hello, Red-dog."

The animal barked and approached the hot tub. He backed off, only to come close again, and stretched his nose cautiously toward the steaming water. The setter, who loved water and happily splashed in streams and mud puddles alike, was always torn over the hot tub. He wanted the water, but the heat put him off.

Finally, when the heat of the small pool became unbearable, Neil heaved himself out of the tub and dashed across the cement patio beyond the deck to dive into the large rectangular swimming pool. Red-dog loped happily beside him and entered the pool with a splash. Neil was too used to his dog's presence to even turn his head. The Irish setter paddled close behind him and vaulted up the steps and out of the water at the opposite end, where he gave his coat a thorough shaking, then settled down, head on paws, to watch Neil complete his swim.

This was the one part of his morning routine that Neil really enjoyed, and he swept through the water with powerful strokes, luxuriating in the glide of the cool water over his heated skin. He had finished three laps when the telephone rang. With a grimace he climbed out and padded to the redwood patio table to pick up the receiver. "Yes?"

"Neil? This is Howard Perry."

"Howard. How goes it?"

"Not so good at the moment. You were right. She wouldn't go for it."

"Who? Oh, you mean Stephanie? You asked her about the ceremony?"

"Yeah, this morning. She jumped on me with both feet."

"I told you she wouldn't like it," Neil reminded the

other man mildly. "She's been down on football since Ty died."

"Football didn't kill him!"

"No, but you have to turn your anger somewhere, I guess. Who's responsible for a brain tumor? God? Ty? There's nobody to blame."

"But why take it out on the sport her husband played? It seems a bit immature to me."

Neil shrugged, and a spark of humor glinted in his dark eyes. "Howard, anything that conflicts with what you want seems immature to you."

Perry chuckled at the blunt statement. "You're probably right about that. I'm handing it over to you. Talk to Stephanie and see what you can do with her."

"Me? Are you kidding?"

"No. You're the only one who has a chance. You were Tyler's best friend. She likes you, trusts you. Doesn't she?"

"I guess." The tanned face was impassive, black eyes narrowed as they gazed unseeingly into the sparkling aqua water of the pool. He saw Stephanie Tyler's face, tear-streaked, tense and white, as she hurried toward him down the hospital corridor, hands stretched out to reach him sooner.

"Neil!" she had cried, her mouth so downturned and vulnerable it shook him to the core. He had pulled her close to him, wrapping his arms around her tightly as if his very strength could ward off her demons, though there was nothing that could do that. "Oh, Neil, please . . ." she had sobbed. "Please help me. Ty is . . . Ty is dying!"

Yes, she trusted him. It was one thing that made the way he felt about her so difficult. "But, Howard, that doesn't mean I can convince her to come to the ceremony. Why can't you leave her out of it?"

"It wouldn't be as effective. Damn it, Neil, it would reflect badly on the team," Perry uttered the most condemning words in his vocabulary. "It would look as if Tyler's wife were snubbing us, as if she didn't approve."

"Which is the truth," Neil reminded him mildly.

"It doesn't look good. All I'm asking is that you talk to her. I'll understand if you can't get through to her. She's a stubborn girl."

"She's a woman who knows her own mind," Neil corrected jokingly. "Your sexism is showing again."

"Please, spare me. I've spent the past two weeks arguing with female reporters about the interview facilities."

"Howard, I'm sorry, but I can't try to change Stephanie's mind. I refuse to use my friendship with her and Ty."

His words halted Perry for a moment. It was rare for a player to refuse a request from the powerful general manager. Though Neil Moran was indispensable enough to get away with it, he was usually too reliable and team oriented to do so. Howard had never considered the possibility that Neil might refuse his request. "I'm not sure I understand your point," Howard began cautiously. "You wouldn't be asking her to do anything illegal or immoral."

"I won't trade on the memory of my friendship with her dead husband to get to her." Neil's words were clipped and precise.

"Then don't. Go to her as *her* friend. You've done enough for her to qualify as that."

Neil pinched the bridge of his nose and closed his eyes, his thoughts turning inward. His instinctive reaction to Perry's suggestion had been revulsion. He didn't want to prey on Stephanie's emotions, to play on her grief in order to benefit the team. But Perry was right. He didn't have to do that. He could simply offer her his opinion. Just give her the reasonable other side. She would listen to him with a more open mind than she would to Perry, whom she disliked to begin with. No pressure, no talk about "what Ty would have wanted."

It would be a simple discussion, and she could make up her mind freely.

He wavered, picturing Stephanie as he had last seen her over a month ago, in a colorful, full cotton skirt and puff-sleeved peasant blouse. Her straight spice-brown hair had hung unadorned to her shoulders, pushed back behind her ears to reveal dangling silver earrings that matched the silver concho belt around her slim waist. There was something slightly bohemian about Stephanie, a certain flair and free-spirited attitude, though she never strove for the eccentric look which some artistic types affected. She just looked like herself: casual, unique—and utterly devastating to the senses.

It would be wonderful to see her again. It had been a long time since his last visit. He wanted to see her, and Howard's request would make a reasonable excuse.

But, no, he didn't like it. He didn't like struggling for excuses to see her: It was too dishonest. Nor did he want to open up the wounds of Ty's death again just to help out Howard Perry. "No." Neil's voice was flat and uncompromising. "If I see her and we happen to talk about it, I'll give her my opinion, but I'm not going to force it on her. I think a widow has the right to keep the memory of her husband to herself."

Perry sighed. Neil leaned too strongly toward noble ideals to suit him. The year when Neil had been the player's rep had been a tough one. While Tyler had been a troublemaker and a real pain sometimes, at least he hadn't been one to stand on principles. Howard understood and could deal with the motivations of self-interest much better. "All right. I know when it's pointless to argue with you."

"Good." Neil smiled. He'd have to remind Howard of that statement next time his contract came up.

He hung up the phone and wandered to the edge of the pool. He was a tall, well-built man, with lean hips and wide shoulders. His chest, covered by a sprinkling of curling black hair, was a hard pad of muscle, and his arms bulged with a strength disproportionate to his slender frame. His hands were those of a natural quarterback, large, supple and long fingered. His olive skin, tanned dark brown by the Arizona sun, and his black hair and eyes bespoke his Louisiana Creole heritage. His face was angular, the cheekbones broad and high, the jaw wide. It was a tight face, usually impassive, as if the skin had been stretched too tightly across those prominent bones. But fire and ice and sparkle could dance in those black eyes, and when Neil was amused the planes of his face shifted upward and the skin around his mouth and eyes crinkled almost boyishly. Offsetting the cold structure of his features and giving him a slightly rakish look, a small scar bisected one thick black eyebrow, cutting it into two distinct pieces.

There was no denying his handsomeness, no matter how shiver inducing his flat black stare could be. Wealthy, famous and good-looking, he was one of the most eligible bachelors in all of Arizona. He knew most people would be amazed, then laughingly disbelieving, if they knew he had been quietly in love for several years with a woman whose love he had no chance of winning.

But there it was. It was the truth. The moment Ty had walked into that bar with Stephanie Caldwell on his arm, Neil had groaned inside. In that one instant every nerve and emotion in his body had leaped up in a clamor of joy, desire and certainty that he'd finally encountered that mysterious "real love" others had always talked about. And in the same instant he was gripped with the despair of knowing that she was Ty's love. Ty had talked of nothing but her for the past three weeks—during the short periods of time when he was around Neil. Most of the time he had been out with Stephanie. Finally Neil had badgered him into introducing this paragon of femininity to him, and Ty had agreed to meet Neil and his date in one of their favorite bars.

Ty had introduced Stephanie, and she had smiled at Neil, bending forward a little to hear what he said. Neil had hidden the sudden rush of longing as well as he hid his anger or nerves during a game. It was second nature to him by now—and a skill he would use often during the next four and a half years. For instead of fading under the harsh light of reality or the wear of time, his love for Stephanie grew. After an evening in her company he knew he desired her more than he had ever desired anyone, and by the time she married Ty he was equally positive that he was hopelessly in love with her.

It seemed absurd, even to him, that in this day, and with the vast array of women eager to help him ease the pain of unrequited love, he should have remained in love all these years. But he hadn't the surcease of absence from the beloved which was given most rejected lovers. Ty was his best friend, and Stephanie became his friend too. They were often together and shared laughter, fun and disappointments, as close friends do. He tried to stay away, for it ate at his heart to see Ty hold and kiss Stephanie, but it was worse to be away from her. He had to be with her and enjoy what part of her he could have. It wasn't in his nature for his love to fade. He was as steady and devoted as his Anglo-Irish father, and as passionate and intense as his Creole mother. The combination was deadly for any attempt to forget her.

Neil sat down at the edge of the pool and dangled his long legs in the water, idly swishing them about. If it had been any other man but Ty he wouldn't have hesitated to do his utmost to take her away. He was too accustomed to winning, to striving for victory and the prize, to idly sit by while another man married the woman he loved. By nature, trade and long years of training he was a predator, a fighter. But this was one man he could not fight. Ty had been his best friend since their first days together in training camp.

Neil had been drafted from the players' pool which the established teams were required to offer the new expansion team. He had been the second-string quarterback of a successful team and was eager to escape the no-win situation of playing backup to a legend. Brad Chisholm, barring an accident, had had at least four or five superb seasons left before he would retire. At twenty-six, five years out of college, Neil had never gotten a chance to play except in the last minutes of games that had been won by the second quarter, exhibition games and during the rare times when Brad was injured and unable to play.

Kenneth Tyler was the first man he met in training camp, a technically gifted wide receiver whose personality and antics on and off the field had been too much for the staid franchise he had played for. He was as happy as Neil to have been placed in the players' pool and drafted by Phoenix.

Different as their personalities seemed, they had hit it off immediately. On the field they meshed beautifully. Over the course of the next few years they made play after dazzling play, providing the showmanship that sold tickets and saving a few games while the solid base of the new team developed. Once the rest of the team had risen around them, they represented an almost unstoppable force to their opponents, and had won the Super Bowl a year and a half ago. They were friends, and they were the best of coworkers. Neil could no more have betrayed Ty than he could have betrayed one of his own brothers.

So they had gone along, both loving the same woman, but neither Ty nor Stephanie had known of Neil's feelings. Then, in February of the year before, the month after they had captured the Super Bowl crown, Ty had developed his tumor and died almost before they knew what had hit them. By March he was dead and Stephanie was free. But strangely enough, Ty's death seemed to separate them as much as he had in life. Stephanie had depended on Neil as a good friend, trusted him, put her faith in him. He could hardly tell her that he was not what he seemed to be and never had been.

Moreover, he was riddled with guilt. He couldn't forgive himself for that one involuntary leap of hope he'd felt after Stephanie told him Ty was dying—the fervent, throat-tightening thought that now Stephanie could be his. He had suppressed the wish, but like all hidden emotions it had seeped through his being, tainting other thoughts, other feelings, until even his giving Stephanie comfort and support seemed questionable to him.

Neil had come to think that fate would never allow him anything more than Stephanie's friendship. With all that had happened between them, with all the common memories of Ty, would it ever be possible for them to love each other? In brighter moments Neil told himself that it would just take time, that he would have to be patient, as he had been after the surgery on his arm. In darker times he was sure that he and Stephanie would be permanently out-of-sync. He would never know the warmth of her love. She couldn't be brought to love the best friend of her dead husband.

He had gradually cut down on his visits to her, checking up on her fewer times each week . . . then each month. She needed the time alone to come to terms with Ty's death. If Neil were with her constantly, as he had been during Ty's illness, she might decide that she loved him out of sheer gratitude for his support. That was the last thing he wanted. In his own sorrow and guilt he had denied himself the company of the one person he wanted more than anyone in the world.

Neil slipped into the water again and resumed his laps. After two times up and down the length of the pool he stopped and grasped the tiled rim. Thoughtfully he studied the rocks of the mountain rising behind the pool, now bathed in the fierce sunlight. Every time Neil saw Stephanie she was less filled with grief. She was getting over Ty, and if he waited much longer the odds were that another man would sweep her up before Neil had a chance with her.

Perhaps they were ill-fated, and he would spend the rest of his life loving a phantom, a friend who would never love him back. But if there were any hope of winning her love, now was the time to find out. For the first time since he'd known her, he had the opportunity to do what he did best—strive and win. Neil pulled himself out of the pool and strode toward his house to dress.

The bout of crying left Stephanie drained, yet curiously at peace. She went into the house and washed the tears from her face. Then she slipped out of her sandals, jacket and hose. Comfortable once again, she strolled back to the kitchen for a glass of iced tea and picked up the key to the guesthouse.

The guesthouse consisted of one room and a bath, and it had been easily converted into an office. Stephanie loved the place. Simply being in it made her feel better. There was a large, ugly, incredibly comfortable stuffed chair next to a scuffed end table that held books and a table lamp. A desk was piled with books, papers and writing pads, and in the center stood an old, sturdy electric typewriter. The rest of the furniture consisted of two short bookcases which were stuffed with books, a tall metal filing cabinet, and a typist's chair on rollers. The walls were hung with photographs of Stephanie's family and her favorite prints. It was not a pretty room, but it was familiar and cozy, filled with the work Stephanie loved.

When Stephanie entered her office she went immediately to the large chair and flopped down, leaning her head against its back. Her eyes were beginning to ache from crying, and she closed them. There had been a difference in her tears, a letting go of Ty and the memories. She felt . . . released. That was odd. She hadn't realized before that she had felt imprisoned. For a time she sat, thinking of Ty, remembering their fun times, and she smiled. It was the first time in a long, long time that she had thought of him with anything but sorrow. Were her emotional wounds finally healing? Perhaps her outburst of resentment against Howard Perry and professional football that morning had helped sweep away the remaining dregs of grief and anger.

Again she smiled. Poor Howard. No doubt he had been appalled at her distinctly unprofessional behavior. He had probably expected her to receive his proposition gladly, to be thrilled that her dead husband was to be honored. Instead she had delivered a lecture on the inhumane treatment of professional football players by the teams for which they played.

There was a knock on the door and Stephanie opened her eyes, surprised. Few people ever sought her out in her office. That was one of the reasons she liked it. It protected her from the salesmen and casual visitors who might stop at her front door. She rose and opened the door to find Neil Moran outside, muscularly slim in blue jeans and a pale blue, casual shirt. He was turned away, gazing at her minuscule swimming pool when she opened the door, and he swiveled back to look at her, a smile creasing his face.

"Neil!" she exclaimed, her face suddenly glowing.

"Hi, Steph. Am I bothering you?"

"No. Heavens! I wasn't working, just sitting here dreaming." She extended both hands and pulled him inside. "Come in and sit down. I'm so happy to see you. It's been ages."

He followed her and sat in the large, overstuffed chair she indicated. She sat down in the typist's chair facing him and curled her legs up under her. Neil watched her graceful movements, his throat suddenly dry. Whenever he was away from her for any length of time he forgot precisely how lovely she was, how desirable. And each time he saw her again he experienced a renewed surge of love and passion, a fierce longing to reach out and stroke her cinnamon hair or trace the smooth line of her leg. Fortunately, by now the suppression of his desire was almost automatic. He was sure nothing showed on his face except mild interest and pleasure at seeing a friend again.

"You must be psychic," Stephanie told him, smiling.

"Why?"

"I almost drove out to see you this morning."

"Really? Why didn't you?"

"For one thing, I wasn't sure my car could make it up your mountain road," she teased, and was rewarded for her efforts by the slight smile that turned up the corners of his mouth. Neil had such an impassive face that she enjoyed making him smile. "Besides, I figured you'd heard enough of my troubles."

"Stephanie . . ."

"I know. I know." She held up a hand to stop his words. "You're about to tell me that I'm never a burden and you don't mind hearing my troubles and all that. But honestly, Neil, I've taken enough advantage of your kindness." She paused for an instant, then began drolly, "But since you're here . . ."

Neil's smile returned. "Yes?"

"I was upset because I saw Howard Perry today. It stirred up a lot of memories."

The familiar hard knot appeared in his chest. "You missed Ty?"

"No, not really. I began thinking about his death. I remembered Dr. McIlhenny telling me he had a brain tumor, and then that neurosurgeon he called in so calmly telling us that Ty's tumor was malignant and inoperable and he was sure to die."

"I remember." Neil leaned forward to take one of her hands in his. "I'm sorry it upset you."

"No, it was a good thing, really. I thought about Ty and his death all the way home. Then I thought about when I met him, and I cried for a long time. But it was different. I still wound up with a headache and red eyes, but I found out that it doesn't hurt anymore. I feel . . . maybe this is the end of my mourning for Ty. I felt sadness, but it was a soft thing, not hurting. I think I've finally come to terms with his death."

Neil's shuttered face concealed the sudden uprush of emotion in his chest, but he withdrew his hands from hers for fear his very skin would convey it. "Honestly, Stephanie? Then why did you react so strongly to Howard's wanting you to receive the foundation's plaque?"

Her eyebrows vaulted up. "How did you know about that?"

"Howard called me after you left his office. He wanted me to convince you to attend."

"Is that why you came here?" Stephanie jumped up from her chair, her expressive eyes darkening with surprised hurt. "To talk me into going along with Howard Perry's show?"

"No. Of course not. I told him I wouldn't do it. But it made me think about you, and I decided I'd stop by to see you."

"Oh." She dropped back into her chair, somewhat mollified. "But you think I should agree, don't you?"

Neil shrugged. "I don't understand why you don't want to accept the plaque."

"If they really want to honor Ty and do a charitable deed, they can accomplish both without any fanfare. I think it's marvelous that they raised the money, and I'm proud they're establishing a cancer fund in Ty's name. But I don't have to receive a plaque on TV and in front of sixty thousand fans in order for them to set up the foundation. It's a publicity stunt that Howard

Perry cooked up to make the organization look good. He's trading on Ty's death, and I refuse to cooperate with him."

"Honey, it's the first exhibition game. It won't be televised. The stadium won't even be full, and most people will be getting a beer and nachos during halftime. It isn't a big publicity event. There'll be an article and a picture in the newspaper, and that's about it. They get more publicity on the team's charitable deeds out of the second exhibition game, where all the proceeds go to the burn center for children. Of course Howard wants to wring all the public sympathy from it that he can, but that isn't the major purpose of the ceremony."

"No?" Stephanie asked skeptically. "Then what is?"

"For one thing, cynical lady, they actually want to honor Ty. You probably don't know it, but in his bachelor days Ty was pretty good friends with Russell Ingram. Russell invited him up to his ski lodge in Utah a few times. They partied together. Russell flew in that neurological expert, remember?"

"Yeah, I remember. So they were friends, and Russell wants to do something in his memory. Does it have to be so public?"

"It's usually the way you pay tribute to someone. That's the purpose of putting something in someone's name, isn't it? So the public will know him and remember him always? What kind of honor is it if nobody hears about it? The other reason the organization wants to have the ceremony is to give the Wives' Association a little publicity. They've worked hard on the fund drive, especially Karen Randall. Nobody ever hears about the civic and charitable things they do. People think they do nothing but sit around counting their husbands' money. Everyone likes a little pat on the back, and this is one way for the Wives' Association to get it."

"I never thought about that." Stephanie frowned.

Perhaps she had acted too hastily that morning. Of course Howard hadn't explained why they wanted to do it, but still . . . she hadn't given him much chance. She had to admit that she had been prejudiced against the idea before she heard it simply because she and Ty had disliked Howard Perry. "I don't want Howard to use Ty's death or taint his memory with commercialism."

"Tell me something honestly." Neil leaned toward her, elbows braced on his knees. "What do you think Ty would have said about the whole thing?"

For a moment Stephanie stared at him, caught offguard, then she smiled. "He'd have laughed. He didn't care about things like that."

"Right. He wouldn't care either way. I suspect he would have gotten a kick out of Howard Perry's putting on a big public ceremony to honor him after all the times they argued over contracts and all the things Ty did that offended Perry."

Stephanie had to chuckle. "You're right." The anger which had spurted up so readily in Perry's office seemed to have dissolved in her tears. There really wasn't that much going against the idea, and, like Neil had said, Ty would simply have laughed and shrugged it off. He never took himself or others too seriously. It occurred to her that her reaction looked more ungrateful than morally upright. She didn't want to do it, of course, but that was simply because she dreaded standing in front of thousands of people to accept the plaque. Her fear wasn't something she could allow to stand in the way.

She cast a rueful glance at Neil. "For someone who didn't come here to convince me, you've done an awfully good job of it."

He chuckled. "I didn't say I wouldn't convince you. I said I wouldn't do it for Howard and the team."

"Okay, I'll accept the plaque." She felt suddenly lighthearted and jumped up, grinning. "Now let's forget Howard Perry and the team for a while, okay?"

"Fine with me."

"How about lunch? I'll whip us up something if you'd like."

Neil rose too. "I'd love it." He followed her out of the small guesthouse, his eyes on her trim figure in the blue top and skirt. Her warm brown hair brushed against her bare shoulders, tantalizing him with the thought of his fingers doing the same. She still stirred everything within him—thoughts, emotions, passions. He would never be really content without her. No matter what the difficulties would be in overcoming their past, he had to try to win her love.

Chapter 3

STEPHANIE CHECKED HER CABINETS AND REFRIGERATOR and found very little with which to make a meal.

"And they talk about bachelors not having an adequate stock of food," Neil teased.

Stephanie grimaced. "That's enough of your smart remarks. My mother didn't raise any housekeepers. We'll just have to pay a little visit to the supermarket."

They drove to a nearby grocery store in a small, L-shaped shopping center. It was as old as the neighborhood around it. The aisles were narrow, the cash registers noncomputerized and it carried little but foodstuffs. However it was clean and bright and staffed with friendly people. It reminded Stephanie of the grocery store she would have gone to as a child with her mother—had she lived in someplace more old-fashioned than California, and had her mother been a housewife, not a real estate entrepreneur.

Neil confirmed her opinion by commenting, "This

looks just like the store where Mom used to shop. Boy, I loved Wednesdays. That's when she shopped. They gave double stamps or something on Wednesdays."

Stephanie pulled out a cart and they started down the aisle. "What would you like for lunch? Something fancy? Plain?"

"Do you know how to cook anything fancy?"

She shot him a fulminating look. "As a matter of fact I do—but it takes a couple of hours to fix."

"I'll opt for something plain, then. How about a sandwich?"

"That's too plain."

"Oh, excuse me. Well, what do you think fits your requirements?" He smiled down at her, thoroughly enjoying their easy banter. It was one of the things that made it impossible to stay away from her. He liked talking to her, liked being around her. What made it grim was the fact that he couldn't be around her without wanting her too.

Even their glib chatter warmed his blood, and he loitered behind her as they walked along the aisles, watching the movement of her rounded derriere beneath the thin material of her skirt. Her skin was golden, not the leathery tan of so many women who spent all their time in the fierce Arizona sun. Smooth, almost apricot-colored, it beckoned the touch of his fingers. Her shoulders and chest above the elastic band of her top presented an enticing amount of bare flesh. She turned and smiled up at him, and he had to shove his fists into the pockets of his jeans to keep from jerking her to him and kissing her. She said something and he nodded, not hearing a word. She stretched forward and up to reach a jar of mayonnaise on the topmost shelf, balancing on one tiptoe. Her skirt slid up, revealing several inches of her long, slender legs. Neil watched with hooded eyes, his black gaze glittering and hungry. He ached, imagining the feel of that hard, lithe body pressed against his, her legs firm and insinuating, her hipbones sharp points against him and only the rounded breasts pillowy soft against his chest.

Stephanie glanced back at Neil and halted in midmotion, startled by the fierce expression on his face. Had she said something wrong? Reminded him of some forgotten sorrow about Ty? "What's the matter?"

"What? Nothing. Why?"

"You looked—I don't know, almost angry."

"Thinking about something else, I guess." He recovered quickly, reforming his expression into a tight smile.

"Something about Ty?"

"No. I wasn't thinking of him at all. I remembered something I have to do at home. Nothing important."

Stephanie didn't believe his explanation, but she dropped the subject. Neil obviously didn't want to talk about it. She put the jar of mayonnaise into the grocery cart and started forward, reverting to an earlier subject. "I've decided on tuna salad. How does that sound? With a couple of those big, fat homegrown tomatoes from the produce section. And a melon salad on the side. Cantaloupe is one thing I actually have at home."

"At least you stock the essentials." They continued through the store, with Stephanie shopping in her usual haphazard way—picking up whatever caught her eye and often backtracking for a missed item. The third time she wheeled the cart around to search for something Neil burst out laughing. "I can tell you're an expert shopper."

Stephanie grimaced. "I learned from my mother. She was anything but Mrs. Homemaker. I didn't know what a coupon was until I was grown up."

"I take it you eat out a lot?"

"Yes, always have. I'm a junk-food addict." She grinned up at him, her eyes gleaming mischievously.

"You know what terrible habits I have. I don't jog or play tennis. . . ."

"Or do exercise of any kind."

"My favorite occupation is lying on the couch reading novels."

"And your second favorite is lying on the couch watching TV."

"Neil! I'm not *that* lazy. My second favorite is sitting in a movie theater."

"Oh, excuse me. I didn't mean to malign your character."

Stephanie laughed and unexpectedly slid an arm around his waist, resting her head lightly against his arm. "I like being with you. Why haven't you come by more often lately?"

Neil's pulse speeded up. The skin of his arm was tinglingly aware of her hair brushing against it. She was so warm, so vibrant—and her gesture was utterly platonic. He forced his voice to a lightness he didn't feel. "I was trying not to wear out my welcome."

"Come on, Neil, I mean it. It's been at least two months since you came by."

"Six weeks," he corrected.

She turned amazed eyes on him. "Good Lord, you *are* meticulous."

He realized then how much his words had revealed. It was pure luck that Stephanie had interpreted them only as an indication of his precise, detail-oriented mind instead of as the statement of a lovesick man who'd counted each painful day. Damn! After this long you'd think he could control his tongue better. He shrugged, as if unable to excuse or explain his ways, knowing that the less he said about it, the better. "I thought you needed to be alone, that's all."

"I was depending on you too much? You're probably right."

"No, not that. I figured you might appreciate being by yourself some."

"I was afraid you'd gotten tired of my crying on your shoulder."

"Surely you know better than that." He struggled for the right words to assure her that she never bored or tired him. "I liked your crying on my shoulder."

"I always knew you were perverted," she quipped and glanced down at the grocery cart. "I think I have everything we need for lunch. No doubt I've left behind at least two necessities of life, but I won't remember them until I put away the groceries."

They wheeled the cart to the shortest check-out line, the brief moment of gravity over.

After a tedious wait at the check-out counter they loaded the groceries into the car and drove the few blocks home. Together they carried in the sacks and put the food away. Then Neil, with the ease of a longtime friend, casually searched her cupboards for dishes and set the table while Stephanie prepared a light lunch. Stephanie plunked down the serving bowls, and they sat down to eat. For the first few minutes they said little, but when the pangs of hunger were somewhat assuaged they began to talk desultorily. "How's your love life?" Stephanie inquired casually, and was surprised to see a strange, unreadable look flicker over Neil's face.

It was gone in an instant. He shrugged. "Like always, I guess."

"Are you still dating Jill?"

"Who? Oh. No. We broke up a long time ago, not long after Ty died." He halted, dismayed. "I mean— oh, hell, honey, I'm sorry."

"About what? Mentioning that Ty died? It's okay. I can talk about him now without crying. It's funny. When somebody you love dies, you know you'll eventually reach the point where you can remember him and smile instead of bursting into tears, but you can't imagine how. Finally you realize you've reached it, and it seems almost disloyal that you don't hurt any longer. Has it been that way for you?"

"Yeah. I know what you're talking about." Neil carefully dipped out another portion of melon salad, keeping his eyes on the bowl as he talked. "Does that mean you've started dating again?"

"Dating? I'm a long way from that. A friend of mine wants me to come to the opening of a community theater she's started, but I'd feel strange without a date, so I told her I couldn't— Say!" She paused and looked at Neil.

He raised his eyes to meet hers. "Say what?" He had a funny feeling, part excitement, part sickness, that he knew what was coming.

"Would you go with me? Claire's a nice lady and a good friend. I'd hate to miss the opening, because she's worked so hard on it, but I don't want to go alone. I wouldn't want to interfere with your social life, but if you aren't doing anything . . . Neil, I'd really appreciate it."

"How could I refuse such a flattering invitation—'I have to have a man who isn't a date, and you'll do'? When is it?"

"Oh, Neil, I didn't mean it that way. It's just that you're a good friend, and you won't expect . . . I mean, it wouldn't be like a real date. . . ." She floundered to a stop.

"You're getting in deeper and deeper," he teased, grinning. "Okay, I'll take pity on you. Of course I'll go with you, and I won't even try to take you out on a lonely country road to park afterwards."

Stephanie smiled. "You're a terrible tease. Did anybody ever tell you that?"

"A few times. Usually people who think I'm the epitome of the straight-arrow, All-American jock. When's this wild date of ours?"

"A week from Saturday."

"Why don't we throw caution to the winds, and I'll take you out to dinner before the play?"

"I'm not sure I can stand the excitement. Besides, who knows, you might decide you wanted 'compensation' if you paid for a meal."

His grin was exaggeratedly wolfish. "You know me. If I pay for dinner I expect a dessert."

"Like ice cream?" She opened her eyes wide in innocence.

"I had something a little hotter in mind."

Stephanie smiled and stood up to take her plate to the sink. "I don't think I'll ever figure you out."

"Why not? I thought I was pretty simple."

"About as simple as a maze. Like you said, you're the All-American type. Serious, loyal, steady, dependable, honorable."

"You make me sound like a Boy Scout."

"They're very attractive qualities. I'm not downgrading you. There were lots of times when I'd have given anything if Ty had had something of your down-to-earth way of viewing the world. I'm simply saying that no one would suspect you of having a positively wicked sense of humor. People thought Ty perpetrated half of your jokes on other players. Another thing. You're the last guy on the team I'd pick as a swinging bachelor. By all rights you ought to have a wife, three children and a home in the suburbs. Yet here you are, thirty-two and still unattached. You haven't even been divorced."

"I know. It's a disgrace I've had a hard time living down."

"Be serious. Aren't you the marrying kind?"

"Of course I am. In a lot of ways I'm old-fashioned. But I think it's because of that that I haven't married."

"You mean you want a virgin?"

"I said I'm old-fashioned, not delusional. What I mean is I don't fall in or out of love lightly. Once I get married I intend to stay that way the rest of my life, so I have to wait for the right woman. I don't want to get stuck with the wrong one."

"And no one good enough has come along?"

"I didn't say that. But maybe she didn't want to marry me."

"Give me a break. What woman in her right mind would turn you down? You're handsome, wealthy, fun and very, very kind. She'd have to be crazy."

His eyes became flat and remote, and his voice, formerly teasing, took on a faintly wistful tone. "Not if she were in love with someone else."

"Are you serious? I'm sorry. I didn't mean to dredge up any bad memories." Stephanie frowned, suddenly concerned that she had hurt him. "Let's forget it, okay?"

"Okay." They were skirting far too close to the truth for safety. If he were to have any hope of winning Stephanie's love in the future, he couldn't cloud it with pity or remorse. "Why don't you tell me about your work?"

"What work?" Stephanie responded with a sigh. "I haven't worked in weeks."

"Why? What's wrong?"

"I can't come up with a subject. I've been through all my clippings"—she waved a hand toward her office— "and nothing appeals to me. It's getting bad. The book I finished after Ty died will be out in a few months, and I don't even have an idea for a new one yet."

He frowned. "Writer's block?"

"I guess so. I've never had it before, so I'm not sure. But I do know that I've filled about three trash cans full of beginnings of books. When I couldn't pick a topic for a nonfiction book, I tried my hand at a novel. It was a worse disaster than the rest of my efforts. So now I'm back to nonfiction. But nothing grips me." She sighed. "I have to find a topic before I start running out of money."

"I'd let you ghostwrite my autobiography, but I'm too dull. Who wants to read about a quarterback who hasn't been investigated for drugs or gambling?"

Stephanie chuckled. "You're probably right. Maybe you ought to get involved in something scandalous so I could write about you."

"Thank you, but I'll decline that one."

"It's such a helpless feeling. It's not like the days when I'm too lazy to write. Then I can talk myself into doing it anyway—threaten, bribe, whatever. But this is a blank, a total inability to think or write. Do you think it's lack of discipline?"

"You're very disciplined mentally."

"That's what I thought—until now. Now I'm beginning to wonder. What seems really strange is that when I was so torn up after Ty died I was able to finish that book. I made myself do it. One time I sat at the typewriter writing about the death of the youngest child, and tears were running down my face while I typed. But I kept on. I told myself I had to, and I did."

"Maybe that's why you can't now."

"You mean I burned myself out? It's a possibility. Maybe I used up all my discipline and talent and power then; maybe I drained myself."

"Those things replenish themselves. All you need is rest, and they'll rebuild. Why don't you stop worrying and give yourself a chance to recoup?"

"You really think so?"

"Yes. If there's one thing I'm an expert on, it's waiting patiently. I sat around for weeks after my elbow operation, not using it. I wanted to test it out. It was like the urge to scratch a mosquito bite, you know? But I knew if I tried to use it too early I'd hurt rather than help. Your body needs time to heal. Why not your mind and emotions? You spent every reserve during Ty's illness and afterwards. Now you're depleted, and you need to vegetate for a while."

"I might as well. That's all I'm doing anyway, but I'm making myself miserable worrying about it."

"Right."

Stephanie flashed him a smile. "Want to do it with me?"

"What?"

"Relax."

Longing coiled in his abdomen, and his hand tightened around his glass. "Sure. What did you have in mind?"

"Well, we could swim."

"In that bathtub you call a pool? No way. You want to go back to my place?"

"Then I'd have to actually swim. Too strenuous. How about a movie?"

"I know. How about an afternoon excursion to Sedona?" Sedona was a small community of artists that was a two-hour drive from Phoenix. Backed by the red cliffs of Oak Creek Canyon, it was a scenic location for many small boutiques and art galleries.

"Okay. That sounds like fun."

Stephanie stacked their dishes in the dishwasher, and they left. They roared up Black Canyon Freeway in Neil's comfortable four-wheel-drive vehicle, passing the team's offices. Stephanie leaned her head back against the seat, cool in the air-conditioned car despite the blazing summer heat. Funny, she thought, how much she had missed male companionship the past few months. It was odd to have Neil's masculine presence looming beside her, to smell the faint trace of aftershave and hear the deep rumble of his voice, to see the long, capable fingers curl around the gearshift and the muscles of his forearm move beneath his skin as he shifted gears. Yet it was also comforting—no, not comforting exactly. There was a tinge of excitement to it, and the pleasure was more distinct and deep than mere comfort.

She had hardly been anywhere with any man since Ty's death. At first Neil had been with her, but the past few months even he had stopped coming by. Much as she liked her female friends, there was something nice about having a man around. She didn't know if it were security, ego or some obscure form of chauvinism, but she knew she was enjoying this day and Neil's company more than she had enjoyed anything in a long time. At last she seemed to be emerging from her shell of sorrow.

Neil glanced at Stephanie, then back at the road. His mind barely registered the desert scenery of rock and cacti around him. Instead he pictured Stephanie clad in a glittering silver dress with thin straps. She stood smiling at him, her lips barely parted and slightly moist, waiting for his touch. He brushed his hands over her hair, delighting in the silken texture, and lingered over the smooth golden flesh of her shoulders before he pulled the straps of her dress down with agonizing slowness. The top of her gown fell to her waist, the straps shimmering loops on her wrists, like bracelets. He gazed at her, drinking in her high breasts, rounded and white against the darker skin of her chest. The circles of her nipples were the color of her lips, and in the center of the aureoles the nipples pouted with desire.

Her lids were half closed, her lips soft and full. Her tongue crept out to moisten them, and desire sizzled through him like a fallen wire, sparking and jumping, out of control. "Take off your dress," he told her, and, as always in his dreams, she obeyed, eager to arouse him. She skimmed the dress down her slim hips and let it fall, caressing her long, streamlined thighs as it went. She wore nothing beneath it, and he gazed at the full glory of her body. Passion was thundering in him, swelling, aching. God, he wanted her. He trembled for her. She caught her lower lip between her teeth and he shuddered.

"Neil?" Stephanie asked, and he started guiltily. Good heavens, what was he doing, letting himself drift into such fantasies around her? If he didn't get them both killed, he'd embarrass them with his too-evident arousal.

"What?"

"Are you here?" Stephanie teased. "For a minute there I thought you must be in outer space."

"Oh, I'm sorry. Just thinking about, uh, the quarterback camp. Trying to get some of the plays down."

"I'd have thought you had everything down pat long ago."

He shrugged. "I forget details."

They began to talk about mutual acquaintances and individual interests. Stephanie asked about the surgery on his elbow, and he described his daily routine of workouts, which made her groan. "Where do you get all that willpower? I wouldn't last two days."

"I should hope not, or the program wouldn't get me back into shape."

Stephanie smiled, her eyes on Neil's hand, resting lightly on the gearshift. She noticed the fine sprinkling of black hairs across the backs of his hands and above his knuckles, and the sight brought a peculiar little ache to her abdomen. Stephanie glanced up a little guiltily at his face. She had felt a flash almost of desire. Were her passions reawakening after all this time? Surely not for Neil! He had been such a good, close friend to her, so kind and helpful after Ty's death, that it seemed almost a betrayal of that relationship to feel anything but friendship for him.

Neil was watching the road, not her, and she was grateful, for she was afraid he might have read her thoughts in her face. She studied him for a moment, taking in the smooth, sculpted structure of his face, the prominent cheekbones and thickly lashed eyes, the ink-black hair sweeping back from his face. He was handsome, there was no doubt about that. And there

was a definitely sensual undertone to his carefully
controlled face, a suggestion of a passionate nature
kept ruthlessly banked. The hot black eyes . . . strong,
sensitive fingers . . . magnificently well-toned body
. . . yes, Neil was unquestionably sexy as well as
handsome.

Stephanie was sure that Neil had had his share of
women over the years. She remembered his statement
at lunch that he had been in love with a woman who
hadn't loved him. She wondered how much of that was
true and how much a joking way to slide away from a
subject he didn't want to discuss. It was hard to tell with
Neil sometimes. Ty had been an open book: volatile,
emotional, never hiding anything. But Neil was not. He
was deep and silent, easily hiding his emotions with
barbed remarks and humor. Stephanie suspected that
there were more twists and turns to him than anyone
expected.

Had there been such a woman? Had he really loved
her that much? Why hadn't she reciprocated? The
obvious answer was that she was married. Stephanie
wondered if she had ever met her. Whoever it was, Neil
had certainly kept her identity from Stephanie. She felt
a small pang of jealousy. She had thought she was
Neil's good friend. Why wouldn't he have told her
about it? Confided in the woman closest to him? No,
that was silly. Why should he have confided in her? Ty
was the one he would have discussed it with, if he had
talked to anyone about it. Knowing Neil, he had kept it
locked within him.

Besides, Neil's love affair with a married woman
wasn't the question. The point she should be concerned
with was whether she had in fact felt a spark of physical
attraction to a man whom she had heretofore regarded
as a brother. It seemed unfaithful to Ty and unfair to
Neil, who had helped her so unstintingly and would no
doubt be dismayed to learn that his efforts had earned

him her unwanted desire. Poor man, he would probably be sickened by the idea of sleeping with his best friend's widow. That was all she was to him. Not a person in her own right, but someone who had belonged to his friend and was therefore an obligation to him.

She felt the same way about him, didn't she? It had been easy to accept his help because he had no interest in her. He had been Ty's friend and therefore was safe to lean on. She had had nothing to give any man, so Neil had been the only one from whom she could take comfort. There were no strings attached, no fears or doubts or guilt. Neil had been safe. Surely he still was.

Stephanie turned away to gaze out the side window at the stark desert beauty. What she had felt wasn't desire for him. It was simply unsettling to be alone with a man again, even one as familiar as Neil. Her senses and emotions, frozen by Ty's death, were coming to life and, seeing Neil's masculine hand, she had reacted to the maleness. It wasn't Neil himself who had inspired the funny upsurge of feeling. Any man would have. She should be glad it had happened with Neil, for she wouldn't have any trouble maintaining her equilibrium or mistaking her feelings for more than they were.

Before they reached the mountains of Flagstaff they turned north at Junction 179 and soon reached Sedona, named for the wife of an early settler. The beauty of the red sandstone buttes flanking the town was breathtaking. The sun slashed across the jagged rock formations, throwing them into a magical pattern of light and shadow. They spent the remainder of the afternoon browsing among the shops and galleries, thoroughly intrigued by the unique works of art, some beautiful, others arresting and a few haunting.

Stephanie purchased a small sand painting for her father and lingered over a jewelry display, entranced

by a necklace, earring and bracelet set. The necklace
was a gold circle with a piece cut out, and on the two
ends were pieces of pale pink rock crystal cut into the
shape of sea shells. The bracelet was a miniature of the
necklace, and the earrings were two semicircles carved
with the whorls of seashells. Stephanie fell in love with
the set immediately, but forced herself to turn away
from the case. Ty had made a lot of money but had
spent it carelessly, and after his debts and the estate
and inheritance taxes had been paid there had been a
relatively small amount left for Stephanie. It had been
enough to purchase her small house, an important
thing for someone subject to the vagaries of freelance
writing, and to support her for several months. But she
hadn't been joking when she said that soon she would
be entirely dependent on what she could make with her
writing. And since that wasn't going too well at present,
she'd better not make any extravagant, unnecessary
purchases.

Neil watched her, imagining the pale pink shells
against the skin of Stephanie's throat, cool against her
warmth, a reflection of her free, unique beauty. After
they left the shop and went to another he made an
excuse and went back to the silversmith's store to
purchase the set. She wouldn't accept it as a gift from
him now, but sometime, somehow, he would find a way
to give it to her. He folded the small package and thrust
it into a hip pocket of his jeans, then rejoined
Stephanie.

When they grew tired they rested and ate supper at a
small, attractively decorated restaurant. Plants lined
the walls and hung from the wooden ceiling beams,
turning the place into a cool green oasis in the midst of
the hot desert and rock. Afterwards they drove back to
Phoenix. Stephanie was silent, enjoying the gathering
dusk. Neil didn't break her quiet, seemingly lost in his
own thoughts. When they pulled up in front of

Stephanie's house he walked her to the front door, declined a drink and strolled back to his car. Stephanie experienced a momentary touch of loneliness, then smiled. She would see him again in a little more than a week, when they would attend the opening of Claire's theater.

Chapter 4

STEPHANIE SPENT THE FOLLOWING MORNING GIVING HER
house a thorough cleaning, following Neil's advice not
to even try to work on a book. Afterwards she sat down
to read, but was unaccountably restless. Soon she was
up and roaming the house aimlessly. She considered
visiting one of her friends, but most of them worked
during the day. Claire was busy preparing for the
opening of the theater. Julie Koblitz came into her
mind, and Stephanie grinned. Of course. Julie had no
job besides the volunteer activities Karen Randall lured
her into. More than once Stephanie had heard Julie
remark that her chief occupation was shopping. It was
likely she would be home.

Stephanie dialed her number and was pleased to hear
Julie's Boston-bred voice answer the phone. When
Julie realized who was calling, she burst into an excited
babble of conversation and invitations. It was several
minutes before Stephanie was able to ask if it was okay
to drop by for a visit. "Heavens, yes!" Julie exclaimed.

"That'd be super. Darren's down for his nap, and the other two are in summer camp, thank God. We can have some peace and quiet for a change."

A few minutes later Stephanie was on her way to Julie's fashionable North Scottsdale home. The Koblitzes lived on one side of a small cul-de-sac, a quiet, isolated place that Julie described as perfect for her three boys to play in. The house was long and low, a modernistic design of stone, wood and glass which opened across the back to give an unspoiled view of the McDowell Mountains. Stephanie parked in the ample drive. As she got out of her car and started up the pebbled sidewalk, Julie burst out of her front door and hurried forward, her hands stretched out in greeting.

"Stephanie! I was beginning to think you'd forgotten me." Julie embraced her vigorously. "It's so good to see you. You look marvelous, as always."

Julie was a small, energetic brunette given to hyperbole and enthusiasm. In her own way she was as athletic as her husband, spending much of her time in their pool or on the tennis court. She was dressed in her usual attire of shorts and a sleeveless top. Her feet were carelessly thrust into thong sandals to protect them from the heat of the sun-soaked cement. Indoors, she went barefoot. Her skin was deeply tanned from her outdoor activities, and her pale blue eyes were an attractive contrast to her skin. She had been the first player's wife Stephanie had met after she started dating Ty, and she remained Stephanie's favorite. Since Ty's death they had seen each other only a few times—more from Stephanie's choice than Julie's, for Stephanie had found it hard to be with many of the people she associated with Ty.

Today, however, Stephanie didn't experience the usual painful reminder of Ty, and she smiled with genuine pleasure at the smaller woman. "Julie, I'm sorry I've been so bad about coming to see you."

"Don't worry. I understand. Come inside. Darren's

still snoring away, thank goodness. I fixed coffee, and we can have some delicious, gooey coffee cake Maxine brought me yesterday."

"Maxine Fulton?" Stephanie asked as they strolled up the sidewalk and into the cool house. "How is she?"

"Over her depression, thank goodness. I think the shrink she's been seeing has really helped her. And Rusty's getting his contract renewed for three years at a whopping salary didn't hurt. Coffee?"

"I'd love a cup."

Julie went into the kitchen and returned with two mugs, which she set down on the low coffee table beside the crystal sugar bowl and creamer. She went back to the kitchen for slices of the rich cake while Stephanie added cream to her cup. When Julie returned she handed Stephanie a small plate of cake and flopped down, turning sideways to throw her legs over an arm of her chair. Feet dangling comfortably, she forked a piece of cake into her mouth and closed her eyes in a pantomime of ecstacy. "Delicious."

"So tell me what's been going on," Stephanie prompted, and Julie readily began to recount all the current gossip about the team players and their wives and girlfriends, having to backtrack now and then to fill Stephanie in on an important aspect of one story or another.

When Julie finally ran down, Stephanie asked, "What about Neil and Jill Byerly? He told me the other day that they'd broken up."

"Oh, yeah. A long time ago. Well, she was the kind who couldn't take being second best."

"Second best? What do you mean?"

An almost guilty look flashed into Julie's eyes, but it was gone as quickly as it had come. "Oh, you know. Football's his first love."

Stephanie sensed that her friend's response wasn't what she had originally meant, and she was puzzled by

Julie's unusual attempt to hide something. Did Julie know about this other woman Neil claimed to have loved? If so, she apparently wouldn't reveal it, even to Stephanie. "Who's he been dating since?"

Julie crinkled up her eyes thoughtfully. "Nobody. I mean, no one particular girl. For a long time he avoided all the parties. He was real torn up when—" She paused uncertainly, sneaking a glance at Stephanie.

"When Ty died," Stephanie finished for her. "It's okay to talk about it."

"For months Neil was moody. He avoided people. Last season he had a lot of trouble with his game too. He injured his elbow again—and it hadn't been good to begin with. He had difficulty adjusting to the other receivers. I mean, he was used to Darrell and Asa, but he used Darrell only in short situations, and he just didn't click with Asa like he did with Ty. You know how it is. He and Ty understood each other so well I think Ty could have run the pass patterns without even being in the huddle."

Stephanie smiled fondly. "Probably."

"Anyway, Neil stayed away from social gatherings. When he did attend one, he was by himself or with a different girl each time."

"When you said Jill couldn't take being second best, it sounded like she left him."

"I think so. At least, that's what I heard."

"Do you suppose he was very upset by it? I mean, was that the reason he dated different girls?"

"I don't think so. He never seemed that crazy about Jill, if you ask me. I think he just likes to be alone when he's troubled." Julie paused. "I take it you've seen him recently?"

"Yeah. Yesterday, in fact." Stephanie went on to relate Howard Perry's request and her initial refusal, then Neil's visit.

"Then you'll be at the ceremony?" Julie beamed, confirming Neil's opinion that the occasion meant a lot to the Wives' Association. "I'm so glad."

"Well, when Neil pointed out how hard you'd worked, I realized I couldn't refuse."

"We really did. I was in charge of assembling the recipes for the cookbook, and I thought I was never going to get it all together." She paused, her face sad. "Everyone liked Ty a lot. We wanted to do something special for him."

Tears burned in Stephanie's eyes. "Thank you, Julie. It was a wonderful thing to do, and I appreciate it."

Julie, who was unable to stay on any sad topic for long, moved on to something else. "Listen, I'm having a coffee next week for a bunch of the wives. Why don't you come? I know everyone would love to see you."

"Oh, no. I'm not part of the group anymore."

"It's not an official Wives' function, just a bunch of us getting together to talk. You know."

"I don't fit in any longer. I'm not one of you now. It's very kind of you to try to get me involved in things again, but it wouldn't work. It would be awkward."

"We're still the same people. We can be friends, can't we?"

"You and I can. At least, I hope we can. But we were good friends. Most of the wives weren't really my friends. We were thrown together by circumstances, and once those circumstances were gone we became merely acquaintances again. You know what I'm talking about. How many of the wives would be friends if their husbands didn't play on the same team? That's the common bond that holds you together. I was never an active member of the group to begin with, and now that the tie is gone . . ."

Julie sighed. "Maybe you're right. But at least promise that you won't stop seeing me."

"Of course not."

"Good. Why don't we go to a movie or something

soon? I know! Training camp starts in a few weeks, so Bob will be gone, and the kids don't return from camp until August the eighth. Why don't I pack Darren off to the babysitter's, and you and I can go to dinner and a movie?"

"Great. Call me about it later. Now, tell me about the boys. You haven't said a thing about them."

Julie proceeded to recall their various accomplishments over the past few months. Darren was his usual vigorous three-year-old self, and he promised to grow into his father's size and skill. Brad, the middle boy, was a true athlete, but his body size apparently had been inherited from Julie rather than his huge father. Ironically, Travis, the eldest, was already tall and well-built at ten, but was constantly giving his father apoplexy by turning down athletic activities in order to read or play a musical instrument. His latest interest was drawing, and Julie laughingly related that Bob had practically cried with despair.

It was a pleasant visit, interrupted finally by Darren's awakening from his nap and bounding into the room to join them. He turned a little shy when he saw Stephanie, but was soon bringing her toys to examine and recounting the many excitements of his life. Stephanie admired what he brought her, smiling at the sturdy boy in his khaki shorts and green knit shirt. Tanned and healthy, he was larger and stronger than most boys his age, and his flashing grin was almost irresistible. There was a painful tug at Stephanie's heart. Once she had fondly dreamed of having Ty's son—for who would inflict a 5'7" mother and 6'4" father on a girl? She'd grow up to be a giant! She had imagined him being like Darren, tall and straight, with Ty's shock of bright hair and his cobalt blue eyes, athletic and charming even as a child. Now it would never be.

Stephanie looked away, and Julie caught the sudden flash of sorrow in her eyes. Quickly she ordered,

"Darren, that's enough now. Go play in your room for a while."

Darren began to protest, and Stephanie interrupted. "No, please, it's all right. I really need to go."

Julie frowned. "Will you promise to come by again?"

"I promise. Call me about dinner and the movie, okay?"

"Sure." Julie walked her to the door, Darren bouncing around them, and they exchanged good-byes. Stephanie hurried through the heat to her car and turned to wave again. Julie was framed in the doorway, waving with one hand, the other restraining the enthusiastic Darren from dashing out after Stephanie. Stephanie smiled at the picture they made and started her engine.

As she drove home her mind returned to the subject of Neil and Jill Byerly. She hadn't consciously thought of it when she decided to visit Julie, but as she had asked about Neil and his former girlfriend Stephanie had realized that deep down she had visited Julie in order to hear the latest gossip about him. Julie knew everything that went on, if anyone did. Funny, Stephanie wasn't usually so curious about her friends. Why had she wanted to hear the details of Neil and Jill's breakup? She couldn't remember being curious about Neil's lifestyle or girlfriends before.

She frowned, recalling the funny flash of feeling she'd had yesterday as she watched Neil's hand on the gearshift of his car. What was the matter with her? Neil was her friend! More than that, he was Ty's friend. She couldn't possibly be interested in him. She couldn't feel desire for him. She had been devoid of desire for or interest in men for so long that it was a shock to feel anything for any man. Had she, in her isolated sorrow, suppressed her passion so much that now it was seeping out and tainting her relationship with the only man who was her friend?

Perhaps she ought to take it as a sign that she should

get out more. Maybe Claire was right, and she ought to date again. Many of her friends, Claire among them, had tried to fix her up during the past few months, but she had repeatedly turned them down. Now she realized that she might have been wrong. She obviously needed to see other men again if she were going to start yearning for Neil Moran. Otherwise she might end up embarrassing both Neil and herself and destroying their easy friendship.

When she reached her house Stephanie marched straight to her phone and dialed Claire's office. Claire, sounding slightly harried, answered on the third ring, and Stephanie immediately apologized for interrupting her.

Claire laughed in her odd, throaty way. "Listen, darling, you probably just saved a deliveryman's life. I was ready to choke him with my bare hands. So what's up? Coming to my opening night?"

"Of course. Would I miss that?"

"Bringing anyone interesting?"

"Just a friend."

"A woman?" Claire's voice vibrated with disgust.

"No. A male friend."

"Aha, that's better."

"*Just* a friend," Stephanie repeated firmly. "That's what I wanted to talk to you about. You remember all the times you've offered to arrange a blind date? Well, I'm ready."

It turned out to be a fiasco from beginning to end. Claire set Stephanie up with an attorney named Ron Porter. He was of medium height, reasonably good-looking and able to converse easily. He also bored Stephanie almost to tears. As soon as he arrived at her door she knew she had made a mistake. Her stomach was sick with nerves, and she greeted him with the awkwardness of a teenager on her first date. She invited him in for a drink, and they sat on the edges of their

seats, sipping desperately at the cocktails she had
made. He talked about his work and his hobbies,
neither of which particularly interested Stephanie. She
downed her drink quickly, hoping that leaving would
cut off his conversation—or at least change the topic.

Unfortunately it didn't. He continued in the same
vein all evening, pausing only once to inquire about
what Stephanie did for a living. They ate at an excellent
restaurant, but the food couldn't make up for her
boredom. She felt not the faintest stirring of desire,
even though he began to casually touch her arm, her
shoulders and her legs until finally, when dinner was
over, he slipped one arm around her. It was all
Stephanie could do to keep from rudely shrugging it
off.

She had been a fool to get into this situation, she told
herself. It wasn't that he was terrible; she imagined that
a lot of women would consider Ron Porter quite a
catch. But for her the evening was utterly lifeless. She
found herself comparing him to Neil, and he came up
sadly lacking. When he smiled it didn't change his face
the way Neil's smile pulled a remote, almost stern
expression into warmth. Nor was there the quiet,
waiting power in his body that Neil had, the tensile
strength of long fingers and corded arms. She felt none
of the camaraderie she did with Neil, the kind support,
the similarity of humor.

She realized with a jolt that she was comparing her
date to Neil, not her dead husband. Why? Logically it
should have been Ty. Stephanie gnawed at her lower
lip, completely lost now to Ron Porter's conversation.
She didn't understand the way she'd been acting
recently—unable to work; curious about Neil's lovelife;
deciding to date, then thoroughly hating it; experienc-
ing that strange, vague moment of passion in Neil's car.
Everything she did seemed confused and aimless, yet
she felt happier than she had at any time since Ty died.
It didn't make sense!

The date lasted far too long for Stephanie's comfort, and she was relieved when at last it was late enough for her to say she needed to go home. Reluctantly she invited him in for a drink. She hated to spend any more time in his company, but it would be rude not to. Carefully she chose a single chair instead of the sofa where Ron plunked himself down, and sipped her crème de menthe, smiling vaguely in a pretense of interest in what he told her. When he set his drink down on the coffee table and moved toward her, she knew she had made a mistake in continuing the evening. He'd taken it as an invitation to something more.

Ron knelt on one knee before her chair and took her face in his hands. Stephanie went utterly cold inside, and her palms began to sweat. How did one handle a situation like this? It seemed so long since she had had to fight off a suitor. "Ron, no . . ." Awkwardly she clutched her tiny liqueur glass, wishing she were free of it so she could raise her hands to ward him off. He cut off her words by pressing his lips to hers. Stephanie remained stiff as a board beneath the pressure of his mouth. He didn't take the hint, however, and moved his lips against hers, seeking to open them. She was chilled with disgust, both at him and herself, and she raised her hands to push him away, forgetting the glass she held.

He pulled away with a yelp and stared in consternation at the thick green liquid staining the front of his shirt. Stephanie jumped to her feet, torn between laughter and tears. What an embarrassing, impossible situation! "Please, Ron, I think you'd better go. I—I'm sorry about your shirt. I forgot—oh, this is so juvenile!"

Ron Porter's mouth thinned grimly and he jerked his suit coat from where it lay over the couch. "Good-bye, Stephanie."

"Good-bye." She watched him leave and close the front door firmly behind him. Her lips twitched, and she sank down into her chair, giving way to laughter. Well, she'd certainly found out one thing. She wasn't ready yet to venture into the world of dating. She'd better stick to safe evenings out with a friend like Neil.

Neil swung into the front seat of his car and started the engine. It wasn't precisely the kind of car to take a woman to the theater in. He had bought it because the dirt and gravel road from the asphalt county road to his house was narrow, full of dips and rocks and treacherous when wet. He liked it that way, because it discouraged casual sightseers from driving by to peer at his home or knock at his door asking for autographs.

He hoped Stephanie wouldn't be offended at their inelegant form of transportation. Then he grinned. Stephanie wouldn't be offended at all. She had been much more embarrassed by Ty's Ferrari. She'd ridden in Neil's car many times, and while she liked to make cracks about it they were in the same spirit in which he made remarks about her little swimming pool, indicative of affection, not dislike. The only problem was in his mind, just like his nervousness. The way he was acting you'd think he was a kid going on his first date with a school cheerleader. His palms were sweating on the steering wheel and there was an icy block in his stomach. He was having the shakes about taking out a woman he'd known for four years! It was absurd.

It was also scary. Even though Stephanie had asked him only because she considered him safe—God, that hurt like a knife—it would be the first time they had gone out on a date. It was also the first step in his campaign to change their relationship from friendship to love.

The past week had been one of the worst since he'd known Stephanie, comparable only to those first few aching weeks after he met her. She was never far from his mind, no matter what he was doing. She invaded his sleep, his exercise periods, his business dealings, his conversations. He thought of her constantly, envisioning her clad in a bathing suit, dressed in a backless evening gown or completely naked. He dreamed of the body he had yearned for, for so long, yet never actually seen, and imagined her opening her arms to him, beckoning, welcoming. . . .

Neil ground his teeth as he pulled to a stop at the main road. There he was again, daydreaming about Stephanie and getting himself excited to no purpose. It wouldn't be an easy evening if he started out already aroused by his own thoughts. He drew three deep breaths, then turned onto the road into town. As he drove he concentrated on the Apaches' blue play book, which he had been studying recently in preparation for training camp. If anything could vanquish his desire, surely it would be thinking of "double reverses" and "gold 67 turn-ins."

He was reasonably calm by the time he reached Stephanie's house. She opened the door at his knock, smiling a greeting, and once again he was shaken by the force of his feeling for her. She was beautiful. No, not beautiful exactly. But infinitely appealing and desirable, with that long-legged, slim build that made a man ache to measure her length with his hands. Neil was agonizingly aware of the warmth flushing his neck and jaw.

"Hi, come in," she greeted him, extending both her hands to him as she would to any dear friend. He clasped her hands briefly and hoped she didn't notice the blazing heat of his skin. She turned and led him down the short hall into the living room. Entranced, he followed, watching the movement of her legs and buttocks beneath the long skirt.

She wore a long tube dress that skimmed gracefully down her body to her ankles, touching her breasts and hips, but not adhering to them. The neckline cut straight across the tops of her breasts, and thin spaghetti straps went from the bodice over her shoulders. The top had an irregular pattern of dark blue and white stripes running diagonally across her body. The skirt was solid blue. Separating the two was a diagonal chain of huge white daisies running from one side of her waist to the opposite thigh. It was simple, and neither prim nor overtly sexy. But even the sight of her bare shoulders and throat was inflammatory to Neil's oversensitized nerves. As he followed her he was aware of an almost overpowering urge to hook a hand in the back of her dress and pop the fragile straps from their moorings.

He closed his eyes briefly, struggling to remain calm. Her effect on him was frightening. She chatted as she strolled into the living room, blissfully unaware of his torment. "Would you like a drink before we go?"

"No, thank you." His voice came out raw and hoarse.

She turned, brows drawing together in concern. "Are you all right?"

He cleared his throat. "Of course. You took my breath away, that's all."

Her silvery laughter bubbled out. "Neil, when did you turn so smooth?"

"And here I thought I always was."

Stephanie picked up her purse and a long rectangular shawl done in the same pattern as the dress. He took the wrap from her and draped it around her shoulders, his fingertips grazing the smooth flesh over her collarbone. He could see the clear outline of the bone beneath her skin, and the vulnerable hollow of her throat, faintly pulsing. It was a contrast of softness and rigidity as subtly arousing as the hovering scent of her perfume.

"Where are we going?" Stephanie asked as he escorted her out of the house to his car.

"How about the Golden Eagle?" The restaurant was located on the top floor of a downtown bank building.

It was known for its excellent continental food as well as its breathtaking view of the city.

Stephanie drew in her breath. "Oh, lovely! You're very sweet."

"You mean I'm not macho?" He cast her a wounded look, and Stephanie giggled. She couldn't remember when she had felt this good—free, happy and vaguely excited.

Their meal was delicious and the view stunning. Stephanie was used to the whispers and stares of other diners when they walked into the restaurant. Both she and Neil had long ago become adept at ignoring them. They talked as they always did: joking and bantering, perfectly at ease. Yet there was an odd glitter in Neil's black eyes that stirred her formless excitement, and her insides quivered whenever he looked at her.

Time passed swiftly as they talked, and Stephanie was startled when Neil glanced at his watch and announced that it was time to leave. He paid the bill, and they walked out to the bank of elevators. Several other couples gathered there as they waited, and it was a sizeable crowd by the time they stepped into the elevator. As the people shoved in Stephanie pressed closer to Neil, and she was suddenly, heartstoppingly aware of the warmth and power of his long, muscular body. His lapel rubbed against her bare arm, sending gooseflesh up it, and she breathed in the spicy scent of cologne and warm flesh that was Neil's alone. His breath ruffled her hair, tugging faintly at the sleekly pulled-back hairdo.

Someone behind her shifted, and she swayed a little closer to Neil. Her leg came in contact with his, and she felt the jump of his hard muscles. Stephanie was curiously breathless and very relieved when the elevator reached the ground floor and the doors slid open. She stepped out and hurried toward the car, absurdly shy with this man she'd known for so many years. Neil's long hand rested on the small of her back, his fingers reaching from one side of her waist to the other. Stephanie's knees felt like spaghetti and she wondered what he'd do if she sagged against him for support. Whatever was the matter with her?

He handed her carefully into his car and followed her directions to the theater. Stephanie said little except to tell him when and where to turn, not trusting her voice to achieve any more. She wondered if she were coming down with a summer cold. She never had colds, but why else would she feel so oddly hot and then cold and lightheaded?

They had to park quite a distance from the theater and barely managed to slide into their seats before the lights went up onstage. The troupe was putting on a romantic comedy often used by community and dinner theaters. In the opening scene the heroine kissed the hero lightly, and he, misinformed as to her identity, turned it into a deep, fervid kiss. A white-hot flame stabbed Neil. His passions were too raw tonight; even passive voyeurism excited him. He hoped Stephanie hadn't felt the surge of heat in his arm, which lay against hers on the armrest. He had no idea that Stephanie was so affected by the kiss that she wouldn't have noticed any change in his temperature. Her entire body had flushed, and she rebuked herself for being so juvenile as to be embarrassed by a public kiss, especially one in a play.

The play went along innocently enough for a while, humorous and light, without any heavy kissing. Neil began to relax and enjoy the funny story, but midway through the play the male lead gave a fur coat to his "dumb blond" girlfriend, and Neil's thoughts went shooting back to the week before the Super Bowl the last year Ty had been alive. It had been held in Chicago in a brand-new indoor stadium, but the weather outside had been snowy and frigid. When Stephanie com-

plained about the cold, Ty had swept her out to the
store and bought her a blue fox fur coat.

That evening Ty, Stephanie, Neil and Jill had arranged to meet for drinks in the hotel bar. Ty came
down by himself, explaining with a grimace that
Stephanie was running late. Minutes later Stephanie
arrived, jokingly wrapped up in her new fur. She was
flushed and sparkling, her pink cheeks and spicy hair
glowing against the muted softness of the fur. She
refused to take it off, smiling and cuddling against Ty's
side. A black ache of yearning had sprouted in Neil.
The next day Ty confided with a grin that later, in their
room, Stephanie had revealed that she had nothing on
beneath the coat. The knot of yearning in Neil had
exploded into searing lust.

At the sight of the fur onstage now, desire swelled in
him again. He thought of Stephanie wearing the coat,
the satin lining rubbing against her soft white body,
stimulating her nipples to hardened points, caressing
her thighs and stomach and back. In his mind he saw
her turning to him, her eyes heavy-lidded and her
mouth full with passion, shrugging the heavy fur back
to reveal naked shoulders, then down her arms and into
a heap on the floor. Without shame she would stand
there before him, letting his eyes drink their fill,
promising a loving release from his blissful torture.

He swallowed. This was crazy. Crazy. He adjusted
his program to hide his lap. How was he to face
Stephanie at intermission? All he could think of was
pulling her to him and kissing her until she was
breathless and yearning for his touch. But that was
something he couldn't do, even if they weren't in a
crowded theater. Stephanie would be shocked and
furious. She would regard it as a betrayal of their
friendship. He had to go slowly . . . but how could he,
when everything that happened, every look at her,
drove him almost insane?

Chapter 5

INTERMISSION CAME AND THE LIGHTS WENT UP IN THE theater. Stephanie, avoiding Neil's gaze, busied herself with picking up her purse and shawl. When the girl had pulled the fur coat out of the box it had reminded her of the coat Ty had bought for her in Chicago before the Super Bowl. They had quarreled fiercely over it, because Stephanie had thought it a ridiculous extravagance for a woman who lived in a city where the lowest temperatures were in the forties. Ty had insisted on buying it, and she had been huffy for the remainder of the afternoon.

She had made them late to meet Neil and Jill by having a crying storm and consequently needing to repair her makeup. She had felt guilty for getting mad at Ty. It was ungrateful and shrewish, particularly since Ty was nervous as a cat about the game anyway and needed nothing extra to upset him. To make amends she had sent Ty down to the bar before her and slipped out of her clothes and into the fur coat. Downstairs in

the bar, she had hustled Ty through an obligatory drink
and back upstairs. Inside their room she had turned and
dropped the coat. Ty had stared, bug-eyed, then roared
with pleased laughter. It had been one of the best times
they made love.

The memory of her former daring made Stephanie
blush; she wasn't quite able to meet Neil's eye. What if
he realized what she had been thinking! Neil waited for
her to get her purse and shawl, then guided her out to
the lobby. While he purchased refreshments Stephanie
glanced around and found Claire. Her friend, stunning
in a silver lamé dress, stood in the middle of the lobby
chatting with theater-goers. Claire was thirty-six,
tanned dark brown from years in the Arizona sun, with
platinum blond hair and a whippet-thin figure. Breed-
ing and money showed in every line of her body. She
had been married to a wealthy physician and had
received a healthy settlement when they divorced two
years ago. This, coupled with the fact that she received
an income from trust funds established by her grand-
parents in Illinois, enabled her to live quite well
without a job. She was, however, too full of energy and
too anxious to get over her divorce to remain idle for
long, so she had turned to a girlhood interest, the
theater, and soon became involved in establishing
another amateur theater in the Phoenix area.

When Neil returned with the drinks Stephanie smiled
and took his hand, her earlier shyness forgotten.
"There's Claire Webner. I want to introduce you to
her."

"The friend we came to support?"

"Exactly." She pulled him toward Claire, and the
other woman, seeing her, waved enthusiastically.

"I'm so glad you came!" Claire exclaimed when
Stephanie and Neil drew near enough to talk.

Stephanie introduced Neil to Claire, and with a spark
of humor noticed the way the other woman's eyes swept
over him, assessing and approving. Claire was an

inveterate matchmaker, and she continually harped at Stephanie to date again. She had been the one who set up the date with Ron Porter. Stephanie knew that Claire was delighted to see her with a man and would doubtless call her soon, full of eager questions about him. She would be dreadfully disappointed, Stephanie thought with a smile, when she discovered that Neil was merely a friend.

They exchanged a few pleasantries about the play, then drifted away to let Claire greet the other patrons who had lined up behind them. Stephanie and Neil sipped their drinks and made trivial conversation. Stephanie sensed an awkwardness between them that wasn't usually there. Neil seemed unusually jumpy tonight, almost like Ty, who hardly ever sat still because of his nervous energy, and there was a wild glitter in his eyes. It was the other side of Neil, the part she'd never seen except on the playing field when he came out passing to Ty and Asa Jackson, never missing, brilliance zinging from his fingertips. This was the Neil whose fires were barely banked; who ran with the ball despite the despair of Gene Cheyne, the coach; who challenged Ty to a race at three o'clock in the morning after a night of partying.

The look on his face set off a little spark of fear in her stomach and an accompanying leap of excitement. How well did she really know Neil Moran? Sometimes she felt as if she'd known him since childhood. At other times she sensed something locked away deep inside him, and she knew she didn't understand him at all. It was a relief when the intermission was over and they were able to return to the quiet of the dark theater.

Neil had managed to regain some degree of control over his emotions during the intermission, and now he set himself to endure the rest of the play. At any other time he would have found it funny and delightful, but with the fever burning within him he found it difficult even to listen to the lines, let alone enjoy them. For most of the last act he was all right. But toward the end all the characters were brought together in a climactic scene at a discotheque. The secondary male character, who was in love with the "dumb blond" girlfriend, danced romantically with the female lead, ironically named Stephanie, in an attempt to make the other two characters jealous. As they moved slowly to the music the man bent his head to nuzzle "Stephanie's" neck, and Neil's breath began to come faster. His hands clenched as he forced them not to move when the actor's hands began to roam over the woman's back and hips. He hardly noticed the hilarious outrage of the male lead. All he could see was the man kissing and fondling the actress. Stephanie. The passion he had been striving to repress burst into full flame. His fingers tingled to touch Stephanie, to glide over her back, her buttocks, her stomach, her thighs. He yearned to bury himself in her and lose himself in an oblivion of pleasure. Stephanie, Stephanie. He bit down hard on his lower lip to keep from groaning out her name.

This was insane. He was going wild watching another man and woman kiss. A make-believe kiss, at that. There was no real passion on the stage, only in his heart and body. He ached to kiss Stephanie—wildly, deeply, his tongue filling her mouth and tasting her sweetness. He wanted to taste and touch her everywhere, to rip away her dress and view the reality of her nakedness about which he'd dreamed so often. He could almost feel her breast in his hand, soft and full, her nipple prickling into a delicious bud beneath his circling thumb. She would lean back against his other arm, moaning with pleasure, lips sultry and moist from his kisses, and she would slide up and down, rubbing herself against him, seeking fulfillment.

Neil closed his eyes. It took him the rest of the play to gain full command of himself. When the play ended he knew he had to take Stephanie home and leave her as quickly as possible. He simply couldn't trust himself around her tonight. He was likely to blow everything by coming at her like an animal.

He said little on the drive home, and Stephanie shot him an anxious sideways glance. Was Neil angry? He seemed so remote and hard. She cast her mind back, trying to remember if she'd said or done anything to upset him. But he had seemed strange even when he arrived. And it wasn't only him—she had felt definitely peculiar herself. Whereas in the past she had always been perfectly at ease with Neil, tonight she had felt some very disturbing sensations. When one actor had been nuzzling the character named Stephanie onstage she had almost felt his lips on her own neck—no, not his lips. To be truthful she had imagined Neil's hot breath and searching mouth on her skin. Had he sensed that? Was that what made him so tense and silent? Did he think she might try to turn their relationship into a nonplatonic one?

Stephanie couldn't think of any way to reassure him on that point. Even to bring up the subject would be highly embarrassing. What if he hadn't thought that at all, and she implanted the idea in his brain? If she handled it wrong it could ruin their friendship. She assured herself that the treacherous feelings she was having would vanish soon. They were simply part of reawakening from her grief. She was giving her blossoming emotions a safe outlet in Neil; she could dream about Neil knowing that he wouldn't press her to transform her fantasies to reality. Later she would no doubt be able to transfer her desires to other men, and her feelings for Neil would return to their normal state.

When they reached her house Neil walked her to her door and left abruptly, almost rudely. Stephanie watched him return to his car, then stepped inside, closing and locking the front door. Aimlessly she wandered into the den. She was restless. It would be useless to try to sleep. She tossed her purse and patterned wrap onto a nearby chair and opened the glass doors to the patio. The full moon washed the backyard with pale light. Stephanie smiled. Maybe the moon was the reason for her strange emotions. People claimed that a full moon brought out one's craziness. She strolled across the cement patio to the side of the pool, where she slipped off her sandals. Hiking up her skirt above her knees, she sat down and dangled her legs in the cool turquoise water.

Why had she never noticed the sexiness of Neil's smile before? Had his thick black hair always been so inviting? She thought about his broad-shouldered body, arms bulging with tight, hard muscles, so different from Ty's willowy runner's frame. He wasn't at all like Ty physically. Ty's coloring had been fair. His body hair was sparse and so blonde it could hardly be detected. Neil, on the other hand, was dark as a villain—or a romantic hero. She had seen him often enough in swimming trunks to know that his chest was covered with curling black hair, thinning down in a V to his navel. She wondered what it would be like to feel the prickle of his chest hair against her naked breasts.

Something scraped against the gate at the front of the yard, and Stephanie jumped at the noise, jarred from her thoughts. Annoyed at her nerves, she turned and her breath froze in her throat. A dark form stood inside the gate, watching her. She couldn't move, but her heart began to race within her chest. Then she reacted instinctively, swinging around and pulling her legs out of the water. She jumped to her feet to run to the house as the dark shape of a man left the shadows and the moonlight hit his face.

"Neil! What are you doing? You scared me half to death!"

He said nothing as he strode rapidly toward her. His face was unreadable, a mask of shadow and reflected moonlight. A shiver ran through Stephanie, part apprehension, part anticipation. She had no time to think before he stopped inches in front of her. His eyes were dark hollows, his cheekbones slender shards of light. His mouth was dark and full, softened from its usual precise lines. His eyelids drooped, and he reached out to grasp her shoulders. "I couldn't do it," he said thickly, pulling her toward him. "I couldn't leave without—"

The words died in his mouth as their lips met. A ball of ice and fire filled her chest. So different . . . she'd never expected . . . His mouth moved against hers, digging in hungrily, and his breath was a hot blast on her cheek. Stephanie began to tremble, and her hands stole up around his neck. A tremor racked him. His hands left their painful grip on her shoulders to slide around her back, pulling her against the rigid bone and muscle of his chest.

Stephanie was dazed, lost in the moment, awash in sensory perceptions. She felt his heat, smelled the tang of his flesh, tasted him on her lips. His mouth widened, pressing her lips apart. They opened readily, and his tongue swept in, hot and fierce, firm yet velvety smooth. Neil made a noise deep in his throat, and his fingers sank in, grinding her against him. He kissed her desperately, as if he would consume her, moving his mouth only to change the angle of the kiss. His breath was heated and rasping, almost panting, and the sound stirred her unbelievably. She curled her fingers into the cloth of his suit coat. He groaned and moved his body over hers, imprinting her with his desire.

Stephanie clung to him, long-slumbering desire bursting into life throughout her body. She was filled with brilliant, whirling St. Catherine's wheels, spinning her wildly upward. Neil's hands were everywhere on her body, searing her with the astounding heat of his passion. He shoved his fingers into her hair, wrecking the sleek knot and sending the strands tumbling in a cascade through his hands. The pads of his fingertips dug into her scalp, holding her head immobile as his tongue plundered her mouth. Stephanie had never experienced such wild, unleashed passion, and the thought of his furious hunger was as exciting as the purely physical sensations his hands and mouth were awakening in her.

"Stephanie, Stephanie," he mumbled, pulling his mouth away and sliding it across her cheek to find her ear. His teeth teased at the soft lobe. She felt the tremendous strength surging in him and knew that only the remnants of his iron control held it in check and kept him from hurting her. She touched his neck and the soft skin of his throat, and his flesh quivered beneath her hand. Neil, mindless, beyond his own command—it was an amazing, unbelievable idea.

His hands slid between them, and he cupped her breasts, his thumbs pressing against her nipples. Stephanie sucked in her breath, startled. He was nuzzling her neck now, murmuring choked, unrecognizable words as his hands slid down and around to squeeze her buttocks, thrusting her even harder against his burgeoning desire.

Suddenly the fierceness of his hunger frightened her. The man in her arms was a stranger—hardly calm, controlled Neil. It was scary to have the familiar turn unfamiliar, despite the delightful sensations he was stirring within her. Even the intensity of her own response was frightening. She shivered and went stiff in his arms.

"No, Neil, please," she whispered. For a moment he didn't stop, and she was swept with a helpless terror. She simply wasn't ready for this! Then he froze, still holding her tightly against him, his face buried in her neck. A shudder ran through him and he relaxed his arms. Stephanie slid back to a flat-footed stance, his arms encircling her loosely. She looked up at Neil. His eyes were closed, his face covered with a faint sheen of sweat.

"I'm sorry," Neil said through clenched teeth. "You're right." He opened his eyes and drew a shaky breath. He was moving too fast, pushing her. She hadn't even thought of him as a lover before, and he was practically throwing her to the ground and taking her in a fury of desire. He had felt her initial response —or had he only wished it?—but then he'd rushed it, pawing her like a schoolboy. It had been foolish to come back and kiss her, because now he was even more aching and unfulfilled, yet he had to leave without satisfying his passion. For a moment he doubted his ability to do it. Then he pulled away abruptly. "I'll go now. Good-bye, Stephanie."

Silently Stephanie stared after him, shaken and breathless. When he disappeared through the gate she looked around, as if surprised to find herself there, and wandered slowly back into her house. What a strange, crazy situation! She locked the sliding door to the patio and mechanically went about her preparations for bed, her mind whirling with a confusion of thoughts, images and emotions. She felt jittery and jumped-up, too excited to sleep, yet she was still too much in the grip of her emotions to think clearly. She lay down in bed and turned off the lights, her mind retracing the moments by the pool, her blood racing once again as she recalled Neil's passionate kisses and exploring hands.

Imagine that. All these years Neil Moran had been hiding a very passionate nature beneath that layer of cool. She smiled to herself, recalling the heat and urgency of his caresses. What had come over him? Had the play they'd seen affected him too? That much? Everything was topsy-turvy. Neil, her good, kind friend, suddenly wanted to be her lover. Or had it been a fluke, a combination of a sexy, romantic play and a full moon?

As strange as his kissing her had been, even stranger was the way she had reacted to it. She had exploded into passion before the intensity of it had frightened her. His consuming kisses had lit an answering flame in her. For Neil? It seemed ridiculous. But even now a quiver of desire ran through her as she remembered his smooth, searching lips and dexterous fingers. No one, not even Ty, had ever sent such shock waves of pleasure through her—and just by kissing her! She hated to think what she'd have done if he'd really made love to her.

How could she face him? Would he regret what had happened? Would he avoid her for fear she would expect more of the same? It wrung her heart to think she might not see him again. But no, surely that intense a passion wouldn't completely die in the course of a few hours. Would he want to date her? Would he try to seduce her into his bed? Her eyes sparkled at the thought.

This was crazy. It was all pure speculation, she told herself. She had no idea how Neil felt about her or what he really wanted. All her preconceptions about him had come tumbling to the ground tonight. She obviously didn't know the man at all, despite their years of friendship. So how could she hope to guess what he thought or what he would do? The best thing to do was to get some sleep. Firmly she turned over and willed her mind to stop running. But her brain stubbornly continued to cover the same ground over and over, and it was hours before she finally fell asleep.

The next morning she awakened, not sleepy as she usually was, but fully alert. She almost jumped out of bed and hurried to shower and dress. She hummed as she made a quick breakfast of coffee and toast, then sat down with her food and the morning newspaper. First she turned to the sports page, something she hadn't done in months. The rookies were already in summer training camp; they left two weeks before the majority of the team. That meant there was only one more week before the special camp for the quarterbacks and receivers.

Neil would leave Phoenix next week. Even if he wanted to pursue what had begun last night, he

wouldn't have time. In a few days he would be in
California, and it would be over a month before he
returned. What lousy timing. She wondered if he were
thinking the same thing. Or was he looking forward to
leaving as a way to extricate himself from a difficult
situation?

Stephanie frowned and stood up. She had to stop
thinking about Neil Moran. Either he would call her or
he wouldn't, and there was nothing she could do about
it. She must not allow it to upset her work. Today was
the day she had targeted for returning to her writing.
She put her dishes in the sink and refilled her mug of
coffee. Then, setting her chin, she marched outside to
her small office. Forcing herself not to think about Neil,
she pulled out a drawer of the gray metal filing cabinet
and thumbed through it. She took out three folders that
looked promising and sat down to look through the
newspaper clippings inside. When she found a clipping
that caught her interest she took it out and set it aside.
When she had four such clippings she returned the
folders to the file cabinet and took up a pad and pen to
sketch a brief outline of the story she saw in each
article. She wasn't overly concerned with finding the
perfect idea, for she had decided not to try a book yet,
but simply to get her feet wet again by writing a short
article. Soon two of the clippings emerged as the most
workable ideas, and one of the two was perfect for a
magazine, oriented to the Southwest, to which she had
sold articles before. She opted for that one and settled
down to serious work.

After an hour of thought and jotting down important
questions, her next step was to do research on the topic
at the library and the newspaper. She hesitated, thinking that if Neil called or came by she'd miss him, but
she tightened her lips and told herself not to be silly.
She wasn't even sure she wanted to get involved with
the man, so why worry that he might not find her at

home? If he wanted to see her he'd come back. She knew Neil wouldn't give up after one attempt.

Her work at the library went well, and she followed it up the next day by going to the "morgue" of the newspaper to find other newspaper articles on the subject. She found little there, but that fact didn't discourage her. Research was often slow in the kind of work she did. Now that she had done the preliminaries she could start interviewing the people she needed to see, always her favorite part of the job. As she drove back to her house she found herself humming. This would not be the best or most controversial or closest to her heart of any article she'd written, but at least she was getting back to writing.

The phone was ringing as she came in the door, and she grabbed for it. "Hello?"

"Steph? It's Neil."

"Neil!" Her voice came out more excited than she had planned. "How are you?"

"Fine. I wanted to know if you'd be home this evening. I found something that might interest you."

"Oh? What?"

"An idea for a book. I think it would be fascinating, but I don't want to tell you about it over the phone. I want you to read it yourself."

"Sure. I'll be here all evening."

"I'll come over in . . . say, an hour."

"Would you like me to fix dinner?"

"No, thanks. I've already eaten." He hesitated for a beat. "Stephanie, I hope I didn't scare you off the other night."

"Oh. No, I . . . well, that is . . . only a little."

He chuckled. "Shall I say I don't know what came over me? That you drove me insane with desire?"

Stephanie relaxed, joining in his laughter. At least they were able to talk about it. Perhaps they could keep their old relationship from dying if nothing were to come of what had happened the other night. She wondered if that were Neil's purpose in coming tonight: to get their friendship back on track, explain the slip-up and request a return to normality. Her heart sank at the thought.

"We can talk when I get there. All right?"

"All right."

When Stephanie hung up the phone she glanced down at her ancient shorts and blouse and hurried to her closet for a change of clothes. It was silly, she knew, to worry about looking good for Neil, who had seen her looking all kinds of ways. But she couldn't stand to meet him tonight in an old, grubby outfit. She pulled out a simple denim dress that was smart and stylish but sufficiently casual for an evening at home. She ate a quick dinner of fruit and cheese as she speculated on what Neil had found.

He arrived on time, and Stephanie jumped up to open the front door for him. She smiled a little shyly, remembering his kisses and her response. What did he think of her now? Her senses were abnormally heightened. She was aware of everything about him, from the curve of his jaw to the color of his shirt. He was dearly familiar, yet somehow new and unknown at the same time. "Hello, Neil."

"Hi." He paused before moving inside, as if he too were uncertain. He held out a newspaper, folded back to a story. "Here. This is the story. I found it yesterday in the Tucson newspaper. I thought I'd better bring it by because I'm leaving town tomorrow."

"Tomorrow? But I thought the passing camp didn't start until next week."

"It doesn't. I'm going to Louisiana for a few days to visit my parents. Karen's getting married this Saturday."

"Who?"

"My sister, Karen. She lives in New Orleans and is a research chemist."

"Oh. I forgot you had a sister. I only remember you talking about your brother."

"Charles. Yeah, I'm closest to him."

"Well, come in. Would you like something to drink?" He refused, and they sat down stiffly in the den, he on a chair and she on the sofa. Stephanie glanced at the folded newspaper he had given her. "Do you get the Tucson paper?"

"Yeah, I own some property there, and I like to keep an eye on what's going on, so I get the Sunday paper. They live near Tucson."

"Who?"

"The people in the story." He pointed to the folded paper.

Stephanie glanced at the article in the middle of the folded square. There was no picture, and the small headline read: "Willoughby Heiress to Wed." She looked back up, puzzled. "A wedding story?"

"Just read it. I promise, there's a lot more to it."

Obediently Stephanie turned her eyes back to the article. It stated briefly that Marianna Willoughby of Tucson was to marry Wesley Hammond of Caulfield, Massachusetts. The article went on to say that the prospective bridegroom was a distant relative of the Willoughbys, and that the bride was the daughter of Bernard Willoughby of Tucson and Angela Drake of Beverly Hills, California. Something tugged at Stephanie's memory, and she unconsciously straightened, reading the article with new interest. Angela Drake had been one of the biggest movie stars of the fifties and sixties. And hadn't her child been involved in something? What was it? The story held nothing further, and Stephanie frowned at Neil, lost in thought. Finally she snapped her fingers and exclaimed, "Kidnapping! Angela Drake had a daughter who was kidnapped a long time ago, didn't she?"

Neil grinned. "Right. I wasn't sure you'd remember. You were just a kid then."

"But it was big news. I was eleven or twelve, I think. She—Angela Drake, I mean—was married to a wealthy guy from an old family. Right?"

"Right. The Willoughbys. Their background is New England, textile mills originally, I think. Anyway, they're filthy rich. And Angela wasn't exactly poor."

"No. The kidnapper asked for half-a-million dollars, didn't he?"

"Something like that. A real fortune at the time. They paid it and got their daughter back alive. Then the police caught the kidnapper and tried him."

Stephanie clapped her hands together excitedly. "Rodriguez! The Rodriguez case. It was almost as famous as the kidnapping. They convicted the wrong man. A couple of years later the maid confessed that she had lied. It was really her boyfriend who had kidnapped the girl, and when he dumped her, she went to the police. There was a lot of civil-rights agitation over it because the man who was wrongly convicted is a Mexican-American."

Neil nodded. "It was a fascinating story, including the hunt for the real kidnapper. They finally got him about four years later. But there's more to it than the kidnapping. You notice that there isn't a picture of Marianna Willoughby with the news story about her wedding?"

"Yeah, it seems strange, since this must be a big society event."

"She hasn't been photographed since the kidnapping."

Stephanie's brows went up. "Really? Because they're afraid of another kidnapping?"

"Apparently. Have you heard of the 'Fortress' outside Tucson?" Stephanie shook her head. "It's Bernard Willoughby's home. He bought it right after they got Marianna back, and he and his daughter have lived there ever since. He and Angela split up about two years after the kidnapping, but Bernard got custody of the girl. Angela Drake comes to visit her now and then. Otherwise she doesn't see her. Marianna literally doesn't leave the house. Or at least not the grounds. Apparently they were terrified that something might happen to her, especially when it was discovered that the real kidnapper was still on the loose."

"Poor girl. She sounds like Sleeping Beauty."

"Right. And now the prince, this Wesley Hammond, is kissing her awake."

"A distant relative," Stephanie mused. "How many men do you suppose she's met, living that way?"

"Not many, I imagine. Interesting thought, isn't it? Is she really in love with the guy or is he just the only man she's ever been around besides her father and the servants?"

"This one's got everything: glamour, suspense, wealth, crime, even legal issues." Stephanie felt a rising excitement in her chest, something she hadn't experienced in a long time. "Neil, I think you're onto something. What do you know about this 'Fortress'?"

"It's why I noticed the article to begin with. The name Willoughby set off bells in my mind, so I read the story. I couldn't think why the name was familiar, and then I remembered an article I had read about the house when I first moved to Phoenix. It was in a regional magazine."

"*Arizona Leisure?*" she suggested. "*Tucson* magazine?"

"*Southwest Style,* I think. About four years ago. Anyway, this article described the 'Fortress.' First of all, the place is out in the middle of the desert and difficult to reach by road. There's an electrified fence around the estate, with a guard at the gate. At night they let out a pack of Dobermans to roam the grounds —trained attack dogs. Then there's a second fence, a ten-foot-high brick wall. Inside that are the yards and the house, which has the latest alarm system. There's also a chauffeur who's a trained bodyguard. Tucson stores send saleswomen out there to show Marianna the latest clothes. The house has indoor and outdoor swimming pools, stables, a tennis court, a game room with a pool table, everything. There's even a small movie theater."

Stephanie stared. "How bizarre. I can't imagine never leaving your house. She must have led the most peculiar life." She leaned forward, propping her elbows on her knees and resting her chin on her clasped hands. "I'll go to the library tomorrow and see if I can find a copy of the article you're talking about." She flashed a grin at him. "Neil, this could be the best book I've written yet."

"I thought you'd like it." He returned her smile and they fell silent, suddenly awkward again now that they'd discussed the idea for her book. Neil studied his hands. "Steph, about the other night . . ." She swallowed. Her stomach squeezed itself into a ball. "I hope I didn't come on too strong." Intently he rubbed one thumb along the opposite forefinger. "I don't want to scare you."

"It's all right. Don't worry."

He faced her squarely. "I'm not saying I'm sorry I did it. I wanted very much to kiss you." A faint smile eased his tense expression. "In fact, that's exactly what I'd like to do right now."

Stephanie's indrawn breath was shaky. She felt as if she were stepping into space. "Why don't you?"

Before she could regret what she'd said, his hands whipped out and latched onto her wrists. He pulled her out of her seat and into his lap. She looked up at him, eyes wide, as he settled her sideways on his lap, one arm curling around her shoulders. With the other hand he tilted her chin, and then his mouth came down to fasten on hers.

discovered that she wasn't ready? "I'm not sure I'm capable of dealing with a man anymore."

"Anymore? You mean you don't plan ever to fall in love again?"

"I'm not sure it's possible. I've been drained of emotion for so long."

"I'll give you some of mine," he joked dryly. "Look, Steph, don't make a tragedy out of this. If things don't work out between us it won't be the first time I've struck out." Neil paused. He hoped she had no glimmering of how hard it was for him to speak lightly when what he really wanted was to bind her to him forever. But after the heavy scene he'd pulled the other night he had to hide at least part of his feelings or he'd frighten her away. "All I want to know right now is whether you . . . felt anything night before last. Or was it just me?"

Stephanie's eyes flew open wide. "You've got to be joking! Surely you must have realized—I mean, well, of course I enjoyed it. I liked it so much it was scary. That's why I cut it off. I don't want to get involved too quickly or too deeply. Ty's death left such a hole in my life, and I don't want to hurt you or me by jumping in and trying to fill it up. Do you understand what I'm saying?"

"I think so. Getting involved with another man frightens you. Ty's death made you very vulnerable."

"Yes." She let out her breath in a sigh of relief. "I should have known you'd understand." She smiled shakily and held out her hands. "Let's take it easy for a while, okay?"

"Okay." He took her hands and stood up also. He brought first one hand, then the other to his lips, kissing each finger in turn. Stephanie's knees were like butter by the time he finished. "I better leave now or I'll go overboard again."

Stephanie giggled. "I would never have imagined

you and me developing into a romance. Isn't it strange, our being attracted to each other now after we've been friends for so long?"

He smiled. "Yeah, it's strange." He bent to place a final kiss on her lips, a quick, hard one, as if he dared nothing more. "I won't see you until the exhibition game where you get Ty's plaque. I'm flying straight to camp from Louisiana."

"I see."

"I'll call you from camp."

"Really?" Spontaneous pleasure lit her eyes. "Good. I'd like to hear from you."

"Count on it, then." He stood staring down at her for a moment, then turned abruptly. "I'll let myself out."

She listened to his steps down the hall. He opened the door and she heard the click as he locked it, then closed it behind him. It would be several weeks before she saw him again. The thought brought an ache to her chest.

Stephanie occupied herself over the next few days by delving further into the story of the Willoughbys and the kidnapping case. She went to the library to locate the article in *Southwest Style* about their house in the desert. Even more intrigued after she read it, she visited the morgue of the newspaper again. Over the past few years she had become friends with Phyllis Black, the woman who ran the morgue, now sanitized as "the library." Phyllis allowed Stephanie to study their clippings file on Bernard Willoughby, which contained information about him from the past few years. There were only a few articles in the manila file about his business dealings. His conglomerate had purchased this company or been involved in the takeover of that one. She soon reached the conclusion that he was a high-powered businessman and that his fortune had come from a great deal more than textile mills.

Next she referred to the newspaper articles at the

time of the kidnapping, which were set up on microfilm. Stephanie rolled through the papers until she
found the date she wanted, then settled down to read.
By the time she left the building that evening her eyes
were aching and her head swimming from all the
reading of microfilm.

At home she took a couple of aspirin, then lay down
on the couch to mull over what she had learned. There
had been pictures of Marianna Willoughby, a pale,
skinny seven-year-old with a gap-toothed, winning
smile. Stephanie's chest had contracted painfully when
she saw them. How horrible to think that this merry,
pretty child had undergone the terror of kidnapping
and then years of isolation because of it. For the first
time she was curious about how Marianna looked now.
What did she wear? What did she think about? What
did she do in all that lonely splendor? Stephanie was
becoming more and more fascinated by the moment.

The articles had revealed not only the day-by-day
facts of the kidnapping, but had also delved into the
family's history. Angela Drake, curvaceous and lovely,
with pale blond hair cut in a swinging, shoulder-length
bob, was described and given credit for her past movies
and marriages. There was a heartwrenching photo of
her walking out to her car from their huge Beverly Hills
home, pale and plain with the strain of waiting for word
of her missing daughter. The Willoughbys were described as an old New England family and the textiles
mentioned, but the article made it clear that Bernard
Willoughby had greatly expanded his family's fortune
by moving into the relatively new electronics field. He
was also rumored to have his fingers in several other
pies, including an airline and a chain of hotels. He had
taken the Willoughbys from "old wealth" into the
realm of the super rich. If Angela looked strained and
worried in the pictures, Marianna's father looked
ghastly. Deep lines were pressed into the skin beside
his mouth, and he seemed years older than his stated

forty-five. Stephanie could readily see that his worry might have made him build an inviolable castle around his returned princess.

Stephanie dreamed about the Willoughbys that night and the next morning called her editor in New York to discuss the idea. Lucia, the editor, was ecstatic, and a call to her agent elicited much the same response. Thus encouraged, Stephanie decided it was time to get down to some serious research. She packed her suitcase, threw it in the car and drove to Los Angeles. The newspaper files there would have a much more complete record of the kidnapping and Rodriguez trial, since both had occurred there.

She spent the rest of the week in L.A., wading through microfilmed stories until her head was splitting, and taking copious notes. She researched magazines of the period for articles about the kidnapping and trial. Before long her brain was swollen with information, and on Saturday she decided to return to Phoenix to sort it all out and develop a rudimentary outline of the book.

Stephanie was exhausted by the time she drove into her driveway Saturday evening, and she straggled into the house carrying a suitcase that seemed twice as heavy as it had when she left. She set the bag down in the kitchen, kicked off her shoes and went to the liquor cabinet to mix herself a long, cool gin and tonic. After turning on the air conditioning and a fan as well, she flopped down on the couch and propped her tired feet on the coffee table. What a week! She knew she had the makings of an excellent story, but at the moment it was so jumbled in her mind that it hardly made sense.

She sipped her drink as she let her mind wander where it would. The phone rang, its piercing bell startling her even from the distance of the kitchen. Stephanie sighed. She really wasn't in any mood for talking tonight. However, she rose and padded to the wall phone in the kitchen. "Hello?"

"Stephanie, where have you been?" Claire's voice came over the line. "I've been calling you all week."

"I was in Los Angeles researching a story."

"Oh. Well, I suppose I'll excuse you. But I have to tell you it was a real trial not being able to reach you. Here I was just bubbling with news about the play—and questions about that gorgeous male person you were with Saturday night—and I couldn't get hold of you to gossip! It was terrible."

"Sorry," Stephanie retorted dryly. "I hope you didn't lose any sleep over it."

Claire chuckled. "No. So tell me, who was he?"

"Neil Moran. Come on, Claire, you've met him before, haven't you?"

"Believe me, honey, I'd remember him. I'm sure I haven't. Another football player?"

"Yes. But don't get any ideas. He's just a friend."

"You must be crazy! How can you be 'just friends' with a guy like that?"

"Easy. He's a very nice person."

"He also has sexy black eyes and a body that's unbelievable."

"Claire . . ." Stephanie closed her eyes, amused despite herself.

"I'm telling you, if you don't latch onto that one you might as well resign from the feminine sex."

"He's a friend of Ty's from way back. He's the quarterback for the Apaches."

"Why didn't anyone ever tell me jocks were so handsome? I always thought they had necks a yard wide and flattened noses. Think you could introduce me to any more of the team?"

"You're incorrigible." Stephanie chuckled. "As if you need more men in your life. The last I heard you were dating three different guys."

"All duds." Stephanie could hear the sounds of Claire lighting a cigarette and inhaling. "I tell you, being a swinging single leaves a lot to be desired, particularly when you don't start until you're thirty-five. Have you ever tried meeting men? No, I take that back. You don't have to. You sit quietly at home and tall, dark, handsome men come beating down your door."

"Not exactly."

"Close enough. But I can tell you, for the rest of us there's a lot of potluck involved. The only men who really seem interested in me and who have anything going for them are guys I knew before I got divorced—and they're all still married. The rest of them are dull or snobbish or strange-looking or have absolutely no sense of humor."

"You don't need to tell me. I recognize the quality of the men you know from the guy you set me up with."

Claire laughed. "I'm sorry. I thought Ron would turn out to be pretty interesting."

"Well, someday I'm going to matchmake for you, just to get back at you."

"Please don't. I can find enough weirdos on my own. Besides, you need to concentrate on *your* love life."

"I'm trying."

"Really?" Claire countered skeptically. "Not if you consider Neil Moran 'just a friend.'"

"Maybe I'm thinking about reclassifying him."

"That's the most intelligent thing I've heard you say in months."

"How was your opening?"

"That's not the most subtle change of topic I've ever heard," Claire commented, but went on to talk about the good reviews and full houses the play had had. Stephanie was happy to hear her friend so enthusiastic and happy. Claire's divorce had been difficult. Her husband of fourteen years had left her for a younger woman, and both Claire's self-image and cheerfulness had been hard hit. The theater project had really helped pull her out of her despair.

Finally Claire wound down on the subject of the play, and they made an appointment to meet for lunch the following Thursday. Claire added a playful warning that Stephanie had better come prepared to divulge what was going on between her and "the quarterback." Smiling ruefully, Stephanie said good-bye and hung up. It would be difficult to tell Claire what was going on when Stephanie herself wasn't sure she knew. She found Neil very attractive. She couldn't deny that. She had responded to him physically more than to any other man she'd ever met, including Ty, yet she couldn't shake a lurking sense of guilt nor the fear that she might feel the same about anyone at this point in her life. What if it were simply another phase of her grief that drove her into Neil's arms? She didn't want to rush into anything that she might regret later, particularly with a man who was a good friend, for it could easily destroy their friendship and leave her with nothing.

She strolled back to the living room, worrying over the problem of Neil, when the telephone rang again. Stephanie made an exasperated noise and returned to the kitchen. This time it was Neil's voice on the other end of the line, and her stomach began to flutter. She hadn't expected him to call so soon after he'd left. "Hello, Neil, how are you?" She managed to sound far calmer than she felt.

"Fine. I just got back from the wedding reception."

"Oh? How did it go?"

"Not a single slip-up—unless you call the flower girl's dumping her basket as well as her flowers a slip-up."

Stephanie smiled. "No, that's just part of the program where flower girls are concerned. As I remember, at my wedding my cousin's little girl took each flower petal out very selectively and dropped it. It took her about thirty minutes to walk down the aisle."

"I remember. Ty and I had to stand there without fidgeting while she sauntered along." Neil unfastened the bow tie of his tuxedo with one hand and opened the top button of his shirt, then lay back on the bed, setting the phone on his stomach. He gazed at the familiar water stain above his bed and idly wondered how many times he had lain here as a teenager and whiled away the hours on the phone with the current love of his life. The clutch of eagerness in his chest now wasn't all that different from what he'd felt then. Despite the activities his family had arranged, there had been an empty ache inside him during his whole visit. He had wanted to call Stephanie every day, but had managed to hold off till now, reminding himself that he mustn't rush her. But today at the wedding the empty feeling had been overwhelming. Seeing his sister in her white gown, hearing the vows, repeating the responses of the wedding mass, he had been able to think of nothing but Stephanie. He wanted her with him. Wanted to see her standing here in his old bedroom, slowly turning to view the old trophies his mother had saved and kept on display on the shelves. Wanted to stretch out on the old cracked leather sofa in the gameroom and hold her in his arms as he'd done at adolescent parties. They would tour the somnolent little town—thick with humidity, shaded by huge old oaks dripping with lacy Spanish moss, filled with lazy Cajun accents—and he would show her every spot that held a part of his life—the high school, the football stadium, the drive-in hamburger joint.

Most of all he wished he could have shared with Stephanie the intimacy of the wedding ceremony, and the laughter and high spirits at the reception afterwards. Hell, he might as well admit it—he'd dreamed through half the mass of marrying Stephanie here. After the reception he'd raced home and dialed her number, and the sound of her voice answering the phone had sent excitement sizzling along his nerves. Even the mention of her wedding hadn't doused the warm glow he felt at hearing her voice.

"How's your work going?" he asked, just to hear her talk.

She told him about her trip to Los Angeles and how interested she had become in the girl, the family and the kidnapping. The trial and falsely imprisoned Julio Rodriguez had captured her imagination also. Neil smiled to hear the enthusiasm in her tone. Thank heavens she was finally recovering from her grief and apathy. He wished he could be with her to share her excitement. He thought about the sparkle in her gray-blue eyes, the glow that warmed her skin, flushing the gold of her cheeks with an apricot stain. He knew that if he saw her he would have to pull her into his arms and kiss her. Just thinking about it made the ache of yearning start deep within him.

"So that's been my week," she finished. "What about you?"

He brought his mind back to their conversation. "Oh, not much has been happening. I've been visiting relatives and my old friends who still live around here. I went by the old spots where I used to hang out. Last night I went to confession."

"Confession! That must have been the highlight of that priest's week."

He laughed. "It was no worse than the ones I made in high school. Except those didn't cover as long a period of time."

"Somehow I can't quite picture you in the confessional booth."

"It's your WASP mind. Every good Cajun boy goes to confession. Although I have to admit that Mama had to threaten me with the bad brown spoon before I went."

"The what?" Stephanie giggled.

"The bad brown spoon. It was what she used to keep me in line with when I was a kid. God, I thought that wooden spoon was a yard long."

"I bet you were a tough one to keep in line."

"What makes you say that?" he asked in an injured tone. "I was a very upright individual."

"Tell that to someone who hasn't heard about all the practical jokes you and Ty played during training camp. I can just see you as a kid, little black eyes gleaming with mischief."

"You have a very distorted picture of me," he assured her gravely.

"Uh-huh." Her voice conveyed supreme disbelief.

"Hey, Stephanie," he began, his tone suddenly serious, "I miss you."

Her breath caught in her throat. "I . . . I miss you too."

"A lot?"

Her breath came out in a little rush of a laugh. "Yeah, a lot. You trying to feed your ego?"

"That's not what needs feeding at the moment." He paused. "I have the feeling that camp is going to be worse than ever this year."

Stephanie didn't know what to answer. She had never carried on this kind of conversation with Neil before. It warmed her out of all proportion to the words, and she felt silly and giggly, like a teenager with a crush. Yet it was strange too, almost scary. It wasn't what she was used to with Neil, who had been a rock in her life until now. "I don't—I don't know what to say. This is crazy."

It was all he could do to bite back the words he wanted to say. If he stayed on the phone much longer he'd be spewing out his love for her. Neil cleared his throat and tried to clear his mind. "Yeah. But isn't it fun?"

"Yeah."

"I have to go now. I'll call you from camp."

"Good. I'd like that."

They said reluctant good-byes, and Stephanie hung up the receiver. For a long moment she stood with her hand still resting on the wall phone. Suddenly it seemed an eternity until training camp would be over and Neil would return.

Stephanie threw herself into her work, researching, outlining, setting up interviews with the people involved in the case. One of her major problems was tracking down all the people she wished to interview. The kidnapping had happened over fifteen years ago, and many of the people involved had moved. The detective who originally worked on the case, for instance, had retired and left the area. And finding a man whose last name was as common as Rodriguez in L.A. was positively mind boggling. She started with the attorney who had represented Rodriguez at the trial and on appeal and went on from there, getting leads and suggestions with each new discovery.

She had little free time, but she was so grateful to be interested in something again that she didn't mind the tiredness. Besides, her work kept her from missing Neil. At night she was exhausted enough to fall into bed and sleep without lying awake thinking about the future and how Neil might be involved in it. She went out to lunch with Claire and let her friend grill her about Neil. Later that week her parents called, her mother to inquire whether she was working again and her father to ask if she was dating yet. She laughed at how typical it was of both of them. To her surprise Neil called two or three times a week. He didn't speak again of missing her or wanting her, but stuck to recounting the amusing incidents and hard work he was involved in. She began to look forward eagerly to his calls; each night about eight she would start anticipating the ringing of her telephone. When it didn't happen she was disappointed. She told herself that it was because she had so little social life, with her time being consumed by her work.

Largely because of her book, the weeks didn't drag as she had feared. Before long it was the fourth week of camp, and the day of the ceremony honoring Ty loomed before her. It was scheduled for Saturday evening, during halftime of the first Apaches exhibition game. As always the Apaches would fly in for the game and return immediately to camp.

On Thursday evening Stephanie went to the stadium, where she met Barbara Lang, the coordinator of the program. The owners of the team, Russell and Winslow Ingram, were there, as well as Karen Randall, the president of the Wives' Association, with a representative of the hospital. Barbara placed them all on the platform, explained where Coach Cheyne and Neil Moran would stand, and walked them through their parts in the ceremony. Afterwards Barbara informed Stephanie that she was expected to view the game from the owners' private box. Barbara herself would be there sometime during the first half to answer any questions she might have.

Stephanie nodded and left as quickly as she could. She hated the idea of accepting the award, even though she had agreed with Neil that it was better to do so. But she didn't like the thought of standing in front of so many people, and she dreaded even more spending an entire game in the owners' box. Why couldn't they just have given her a seat with the players' wives? She would have been far more comfortable. However, as she drove home she realized that despite her dislike for the ceremony she was elated at the prospect of seeing Neil again. It would be only for the few moments of the ceremony, of course, but the expectation of even that small taste of his presence excited her.

On Saturday she was too nervous to work and spent most of the day roaming restlessly about the house. She took a long bath and tried several different hairstyles, finally settling for a conservative knot on the nape of her neck. She applied her makeup carefully and polished her nails. Then she waited until she could leave without arriving at the stadium ridiculously early.

When that time finally came she stepped into the ice-blue linen shift she had chosen for the occasion. Its sleeves were puffed and ended just below her elbows. The waist tied with a wide, textured belt, and the only ornamentation was the large buttons that closed the slanted opening that ran from the high round neck to one shoulder. It was simple and conservative, suitable for a widow receiving an award in her husband's name, yet it was lovely enough to satisfy her desire to look good for Neil.

When she finished dressing she drove to the domed stadium where the Arizona Apaches' games were played. In the huge parking lot she followed the yellow signs to the section reserved for those people sitting in the expensive box seats. A uniformed parking attendant asked her name, then directed her to an assigned parking space. She walked across the asphalt, so hot that her slender heels punched holes in it, to the elevator at the near end of the stadium. There another uniformed guard stopped her. The owners of the private boxes had keys to operate the elevator, and the names of their guests were on a list which the guard held. Stephanie showed the guard her identification and he smiled politely, pulling a key on a long chain from his pants pocket and inserting it into the keyhole on the wall beside the elevator. He told her the number of the Ingrams' box and gave her directions for finding it after she stepped off the elevator.

The elevator carried her upward silently and whooshed open onto a hallway far different from the concrete ones above and below it. The corridor was hushed, its silence augmented by the plush carpeting on the floor. The walls were painted a.pale, creamy yellow and were hung with large paintings of Arizona scenes. All the doors were painted the brilliant orange of the Apaches. A discreet rectangle beside each door stated its number.

Stephanie strolled along the hallway, glancing at the

pictures. The Ingrams' box would be halfway down the south hall, the guard had said, right on the fifty yardline. Despite her dislike of spending the game there, Stephanie had to admit that she was curious to see what surely must be the plushest in the ring of private rooms between the upper and lower tiers of the stadium.

Stephanie's steps slowed and she began to check the small numbers beside the doors. 109. The Ingrams' door should be only four away. When she came to the appropriate door she checked its number twice, smoothed her skirt and knocked softly. A moment later the door was opened by a casually dressed, graying man. He smiled and shifted his drink to his other hand in order to shake hands with her. "Hi, I'm Brett Kingsley."

"Stephanie Tyler."

From behind him a voice boomed out, "Stephanie! Come in." Brett Kingsley stepped aside for her to enter, and Stephanie drew a deep breath and moved into the room.

Chapter 7

THE LARGE ROOM WAS A JUMBLE OF NOISE AND PEOPLE. Stephanie looked around, unable to locate the voice that had called her. Then she spotted Russell Ingram standing by the plate-glass windows on the far side, smiling at her, one hand raised in a gesture of welcome. He excused himself to the people he was standing with and came toward her. "Brett, I see you've met our guest of honor. Stephanie, you're as pretty as ever. I always told Ty he was a lucky dog to have found you."

"You're Kenneth Tyler's widow?" Kingsley asked. "Well, I'm very pleased to meet you. I was a great admirer of your husband."

"Yes, Ty's death was a great loss to us all," Russell agreed. "Stephanie, let me introduce you around." He looped one arm around her shoulders and pulled her away with him.

Stephanie glanced around the room as she went. There were two rows of plush swivel chairs across the front of the box, staggered and raised so that every seat had an excellent view and was easy to reach. There would be no stumbling across other people's knees to sit down here. Along one wall was a darkly paneled wet bar, well stocked, with a bartender waiting to make drinks of the guests' choice. Now and then he cast a careful eye over the large table in the corner where an array of finger sandwiches, cheeses, fruit and various appetizers was laid out for nibbling.

The back area of the room was furnished with several comfortable chairs grouped around a long coffee table and a loveseat and matching chair. These seats were for those who weren't interested in the game at any given moment, allowing them to chat convivially without interfering with those in the front seats who wished to watch the action on the field. The carpet was a deep, muted orange, thicker than that in the hallway, and the paintings were considerably more expensive. Cut-glass ashtrays were scattered around, adding to the elegant atmosphere. Above the plate-glass windows, slanting down at a comfortable angle for viewing, were two television sets so that the occupants of the box would not have to miss the instant replays and stop-action shots. Tonight, however, the screens were blank, for the first exhibition game of the season was not televised. The stadium loudspeaker, muted to an acceptable level, was piped in.

As she relaxed Stephanie could see that the room wasn't as full as she had first thought. There were no more than ten or twelve people clustered together in small knots around the room. She could see the coach's wife, Susan, perched on the arm of the sofa, talking to Howard Perry's wife, Winette, and Leona Ingram. All three were dressed in the latest fashion: Leona in a bright red dress with a split skirt and a red-and-white striped jacket; Susan in a collarless dress with a plain white bodice and gaily striped skirt; and Winette in a subdued short-sleeved suit of gun-metal gray with wide, turned-back white piqué sleeves. Very properly, neither Susan nor Winette's outfits were quite as expensive or outstanding as that of the owner's wife. Susan Cheyne had even managed to look less glamorous than she really was; normally she was far more attractive and better dressed than Leona.

Thank heavens she no longer had to function in that highly political atmosphere, Stephanie thought. It was like being a military wife, where the husband's rank determined how the wife dressed, talked and acted. She had always tried to be polite and friendly, but she had never fit in. Susan Cheyne looked up and saw Stephanie. She smiled, rising, and carefully cued Leona by saying in her low, cultured voice, "Stephanie, my dear, how good to see you."

Leona and Winette turned smiles upon her too, greeting her by name. Russell left Stephanie in their care while he went to fetch her a drink, acquiescing to Stephanie's request that it be a mild one since she didn't want to make a mistake during the ceremony. Susan questioned her about her work, and Stephanie was happy to have an answer after these months of inactivity. She marveled at Susan Cheyne's memory. The woman always knew everybody's names and usually recalled their jobs, hobbies and children's names as well. It made her quite popular with the coaches and players' wives, although she was also careful never to let her dignity slip. She was a perfect match for Gene Cheyne, who managed the players with equal skill, knowing when to cajole, threaten or praise, often managing to mix all three together. The players feared and respected him even when they railed against his edicts.

Russell returned with Stephanie's drink and a woman on his arm. Stephanie presumed she must be his latest girlfriend. Russell had been divorced for five years, and he enjoyed his bachelorhood. "Stephanie, have you met Serita Crenshaw?"

"No, I don't think so. Nice to meet you." Stephanie

extended her hand, and Serita shook it limply. Serita was several years younger than Leona, Winslow Ingram's wife, and considerably flashier. She was dressed in black silk trousers and a sleeveless shell topped by a white jacket. The jacket sported a narrow stand-up collar and extremely wide, tapering lapels that were black-and-white-striped, like piano keys. Huge, black, shiny buttons fastened the jacket at the waist. It wasn't an outlandish costume, and it bespoke as much wealth as the others, but neither was it conservative. This woman obviously did as she pleased. Serita greeted Stephanie casually and accompanied them as Russell escorted Stephanie around the room, introducing her to Brett Kingsley's wife and two tanned, chain-smoking men whom Stephanie gathered were business acquaintances of the Ingrams.

Finally Russell stopped beside the general manager, Howard Perry, and turned Stephanie over to him. Russell drifted off with Serita, and Stephanie turned to Howard. He wasn't her favorite person, but at least she knew him better than she did the Ingrams and their cronies. Howard smiled. "I'm glad to see you reconsidered."

"Neil's very persuasive."

"You can say that again. Although I don't know that persuasive is exactly the word I'd use. Usually he's a little more forceful than that." Howard motioned toward one of the swivel chairs in front of the windows. "Would you like to sit down? The players are coming onto the field."

Stephanie stepped up to the glass to watch the team desultorily entering the field to warm up. The sight of the familiar white, yellow and orange uniforms sent an ache through her chest. Instinctively she looked for a jersey numbered 86. She was surprised when she couldn't find it. Usually every available number was used in the first exhibition game because of the large size of the roster before the big cuts were made. She spotted Neil's number, 14, and leaned forward intently. Howard offered her a pair of binoculars, and she put them to her eyes, adjusting them until Neil's crow-black hair popped into focus. His features were clear and seemed unnaturally close to her. She felt a little guilty, as if she were spying on him or eavesdropping, watching him when he couldn't see her. But you could hardly call it spying when he was standing in front of over 50,000 people.

That was something she had never fully understood —Neil and Ty's ability to play in front of huge, even hostile crowds. Ty had in many ways been a ham, and even though he'd been incredibly nervous before a game, once he was on the field the fans made him feel better. It was easier to comprehend his playing before so many people. But Neil wasn't the showman Ty had been. He didn't play to the crowd or use its excitement to pump up his own adrenaline. Rather, he played as if the stands didn't exist and that only he and the twenty-one other players were on the field. That sort of coolness and concentration amazed Stephanie.

She studied Neil's face, the smooth skin stretched tautly over his cheekbones, the fierce black eyes, the handsomely modeled mouth set in determined lines. Stephanie lowered the binoculars and realized that her stomach was dancing in excitement. She was stirred merely by the sight of his tall form, his masculinity emphasized by the broad-shouldered, low-waisted style of the football uniform. She wished he weren't flying immediately back to camp tonight, though she told herself it was probably better that he was. Neil had promised not to rush, but her willful emotions weren't complying. They were sweeping her along at a breakneck pace.

The players ended their warmup exercises and streamed off the field. Susan Cheyne came over and invited Stephanie to visit her private box. Stephanie followed her out and Susan took her several doors down, explaining that both Howard Perry and her husband had their own private rooms where family and friends gathered for the game, although she and the Perrys always dropped by the Ingrams' box for a little chat first. The Cheynes' room was smaller than the Ingrams' but decorated with Susan's impeccable taste, so it seemed cozy and warm. There was no bartender or huge table of appetizers here, although the low coffee table held a silver coffee service and a scrumptious-looking dessert. Stephanie shook hands with the Cheynes' three sons, amazed at how much the eldest had grown since she had last seen him. Susan laughed and agreed, then introduced Stephanie to Gene's sister and her husband, visiting them from Minnesota, and a couple who were close friends. Stephanie smiled at them all, more comfortable here than she had been in the Ingrams' box, and settled down in a plush swivel chair for a short chat with Susan.

When the players ran back onto the field, however, Stephanie reluctantly excused herself and returned to the Ingrams' box. It would seem rude to spend any more time in Susan's domain. Back at the Ingrams', she slipped into an empty seat and concentrated on the game. Neil played the first quarter, and she watched anxiously, hands clenched together as they had been when she watched Ty play. She hoped that Neil would play well and the team would win, but most of all she hoped that he wouldn't get hurt. Neil displayed his usual skill, and she noted with pleasure that his elbow seemed to move freely and without pain. Exhibition games, however, lacked sizzle and excitement. Rookies were substituted freely, and the purpose of the game was more to evaluate the players than to win. After Neil left the field Stephanie lost all interest in the proceedings.

At one point Barbara Lang entered the room and took Stephanie aside to repeat what would happen during the ceremony. A few minutes before the half ended, Russell and Winslow escorted Stephanie to the underground level of the stadium and through the long, bleak concrete corridors. Eventually they entered the area of the dressing rooms and then took the half-flight of steps leading up to the tunnel. As they emerged from the semidark tunnel the light of the stadium was dazzling, and Stephanie blinked as her eyes adjusted to the stadium lights. They moved off to the left just as the half ended. Players from both sides, monstrous in their padded uniforms, streamed past them into the tunnel. Barbara Lang and Karen Randall, Boojie Randall's wife, joined them from the stands. Gene Cheyne and Neil, idling behind the rush of players, stopped beside them instead of continuing into the tunnel.

Cheyne nodded at Stephanie, and Neil offered a quiet hello. His dark eyes burned into hers, and Stephanie was intensely aware of him and his happiness at seeing her; it was as if he had kissed her. She looked at him for a long moment, then tore her gaze away. She noticed Karen Randall eyeing her speculatively, and knew that soon there would be gossip about her and Neil all through the Wives' Association. That meant all through the team too. She wondered how Neil would react to it. Stephanie glanced back up at him, so foreign and large in his padded uniform, and discovered that his eyes were still on her. She decided that the gossip probably wouldn't bother him at all. Neil simply walked right through gossip, speculation and criticism as if they didn't exist.

They waited for a moment. Barbara whispered to Coach Cheyne, and he signaled to the Ingrams. The group walked along the outside track, where the cheerleaders usually marched, to a small raised platform in front of the fifty yardline. They climbed the narrow steps and positioned themselves as Barbara had instructed. A man waited for them there. Stephanie recognized him from the rehearsal as the representative of St. Anthony's Hospital. First Winslow stepped for-

ward and made a ponderous but mercifully brief statement about Ty, his death and the money the Wives'
Association had raised. Karen gave Winslow the check,
and he in turn passed it to the hospital administrator,
who gave a brief thank-you speech. Russell read from
the plaque and handed it to Stephanie. She smiled and
nodded her thanks, more moved than she had thought
she would be.

She was surprised to see Neil step up to the micro-
phone. Barbara hadn't mentioned this in the run-
through the other night. Neil spoke of his friendship
with Ty and their rapport on the field. There was a
crack in his voice as he ended and moved back. Next
Gene Cheyne went to the mike and made a statement
with his characteristic brevity and punch. He described
Ty's great ability and his flashing personality, the way
he could spark up the whole team or ease the pain of
defeat with his quips. "He was a great player, one of
the best I've seen. But all of us lost more than a good
player. We lost a friend and a man who enriched our
lives by passing through them. There'll never be another one like Kenneth Tyler, and for that reason the
Arizona Apaches are retiring his number. Eighty-six
will play only in our memories."

Cheyne turned to Stephanie, who stood rooted to the
spot, staring at him. Her entire chest was an ache, and
tears spilled out of her wide gray-blue eyes. She saw
Neil out of the corner of her eye and turned to him. He
held out a white jersey, slightly stained and dingy,
emblazoned with the huge orange number 86.
Stephanie took Ty's jersey with trembling hands, not-
ing the added glitter of tears in Neil's fierce black eyes.
The stadium thundered with applause and cheers. A
sob escaped Stephanie's lips as she clutched the jersey
to her chest.

The others turned and filed off the platform. Neil
grasped Stephanie's arm to help her down the steps.
She needed it, because her vision was blurred. "You

didn't tell me you were going to do this!" Her words were barely audible in the blast of noise from the stands. She began to cry in earnest. Neil looped an arm around her shoulders and walked with her down the track and into the tunnel. By the time they reached the cool silence of the underground hallway Stephanie's sobs had stopped. Barbara Lang, always prepared, popped up with tissues to wipe away the ravages of her tears. Huskily Stephanie -thanked the Ingrams and Coach Cheyne, then turned to Neil. He took her hands in his and squeezed them gently. "You okay?"

"Yes, I'm fine. I'm not sad, really. It was just so touching. Thank you."

He paused. "I'd like to see you after the game."

"I thought you were flying back immediately."

"We are. But I'd like to at least talk to you a bit. Could you wait for me by the exit?"

"Of course."

The Ingrams were waiting for her and Cheyne had already headed into the dressing room. Soon the teams would be streaming out to take the field again. Neil gave her hands a last squeeze and turned away. Stephanie joined Russell and Winslow, and they walked back to the elevators and the elegant suite above. She paid little attention to the second half as she sat at the back of the room, sipping a strong drink which Russell had ordered for her. She folded and refolded Ty's jersey, remembering him: his unbelievable catches, his laughter, his humor, his crooked smile. They were right—there was no one else like him. How she had loved him! The saddest part was that despite her surprised tears this afternoon, there was only a sweet, soft feeling for him inside her now. The raw ache, once so hard to bear, was gone. Her love was a memory, gentle and sentimental but no longer real.

She was jolted from her thoughts by the end of the game. Everyone around her began to rise and move about, getting a last drink while they waited for the crowds to leave the parking lots. Stephanie put aside her empty glass and made the rounds, saying her polite good-byes. By the time she finished and took the elevator to the ground floor the huge crowd was thinning out. She walked to the outside tunnel from the dressing rooms. There were a few children and adults standing around with pads and pencils in hand, waiting to get autographs from their favorite players. There were also two or three women whom she didn't know waiting to one side. She wondered if they were wives, girlfriends or simply fans.

Finally a player emerged from the tunnel, a rookie, Stephanie surmised from his eager young face. Stephanie knew Neil would be one of the last to leave no matter how quickly he showered and dressed, because the quarterback was always detained by reporters. Stephanie had noticed in the newspaper that the sports reporters this year were creating a duel between Neil and the second-string quarterback, Tommy Simpson. The reporters claimed that Neil's less-than-excellent performance last year had thrown the job open to competition. Stephanie knew that Cheyne would never go with an inexperienced quarterback instead of the one who had taken the team to the Super Bowl two years ago simply because Neil had had medical problems which were now cured, and she was certain the reporters knew it equally well. But it gave them something to write about during the dull preseason, when football fans were eager for news and the games were unexciting. So Neil would be kept even longer than usual to rehash the important plays in light of the press's fictitious contest.

The players emerged from the tunnel in a trickle, at first mostly rookies and lesser-knowns who weren't asked for in the press room. Then Bob Koblitz, Paul Anton and Boojie Randall, all veteran offensive linemen, came up the steps, flight bags thrown over their shoulders. Bob saw Stephanie first and waved, and

Boojie and Paul glanced over also. They smiled and made their way across the asphalt to her, after being detained for a moment by a fan. Obviously a little uneasy, they spoke haltingly of Ty and how glad they were that he'd been honored that day. She could see the question they didn't have the nerve to ask lurking in their eyes—what was she doing waiting by the players' entrance? Finally they nodded good-bye to her and moved away just as Neil trotted up the steps. He glanced around over the heads of the fans who immediately surrounded him. When he caught sight of Stephanie he flashed her a smile.

He signed autographs while Stephanie gritted her teeth and smiled and nodded to the other players who stopped to speak or waved to her. Asa Jackson, a warm, emotional person, reached out to envelop her in a bear hug. "Lady, I gotta tell you," he said, "that man was a runner. He was almost as fast as me. And I'll tell you the truth, he could catch them better. He is missed."

"Thank you, Asa." He left, and Stephanie looked over at Neil, who was pulling loose from the clot of admirers. Then he was in front of her, bending down to cup her face in his hands and kiss her lightly on the lips.

"God, I've missed you."

Stephanie's smile was shaky. She felt as if every eye in the place—those of fans and players—was on them. Nervously she took a step backward. "I missed you too. In fact, I felt guilty because the only reason I wanted to come to the ceremony today was to see you."

Something flashed in his dark eyes. "I thought you could drive me to the airport to catch the plane. That way we could be together a little."

"Sure. My car's in the B lot."

"My, my, how we've moved up in the world," he joked, curling an arm around her shoulders. As they walked toward the parking lot Stephanie was awkward and silent, certain the other players were watching

them. What did they think about Ty's widow walking
off with his best friend? She was used to seeing these
men only in connection with Ty. Being before them
now with Neil made her feel as if she were betraying
her husband. Neil, aware of her stiffness, gave her
shoulders a little shake. "Hey, loosen up. What's the
matter?"

"I . . . I feel so stránge being with you with the other
guys around. I mean, they think of me only as Ty's
wife."

He frowned, and she could feel a slight stiffening of
his body. "What does it matter?"

"It's strange, that's all. I don't know how to act."

"You'll get used to it," he assured her.

"I'm not so sure." Stephanie sighed. "Things just
aren't easy."

"Ah, but the challenge is half the fun."

They reached the car and opened the doors. Stale
heat rushed out, and Stephanie slid in carefully to turn
on the engine and let the air conditioner run. The
steering wheel was too hot to touch, and they sat in the
front seat for a few minutes, letting the inside of the car
cool before Stephanie put it in gear and headed for Sky
Harbor Airport. Since the airport was on the southern
side of Phoenix, as the stadium was, it didn't take long
to reach it. There was a stiff silence between them as
they rode. Stephanie couldn't understand it. They had
talked easily on the phone whenever Neil had called.
She guessed that it was the emotional impact of the
ceremony that afternoon that made the air between
them heavy and charged.

"Why didn't you tell me they were going to retire
Ty's number?" Stephanie asked, groping for something
to end the silence.

He shrugged. "It would have spoiled the surprise."

"I wouldn't have been as reluctant if I'd known what
they planned."

"I know. But Gene insisted on keeping it secret. He

didn't want it to leak to the press. And Howard thought it would have more impact if your reaction was spontaneous."

"Good old Howard, always the showman," Stephanie murmured. "He wanted to make sure I'd cry."

"Now, Stephanie, you're being unfair to him."

"Maybe." She sounded unconvinced. She turned the car into the airport drive and headed for short-term parking. "You know, I felt peculiar this afternoon after the ceremony. I sat and thought about Ty—everything I could remember about him. And it was as if he'd become—"

"Damn!" Neil exploded. Stephanie slammed on her brakes and whirled to stare at him, her mouth dropping open in surprise. Neil's face was thunderous and dark, and his voice cut through the air like a whip. "Don't you think about anything else? Is that what you plan for our relationship—a nonstop rehashing of your life with Ty?"

Stephanie turned her eyes back to the road, hurt tears forming. She didn't know how to react. This outburst was so unlike Neil. Automatically she pressed her foot down on the accelerator again and carefully pulled into a parking space. She turned toward Neil. "I'm sorry. I didn't mean to talk about him all the time."

"But you just can't help yourself. Is that it?" Neil's eyes were burning. He grasped her shoulders and hauled her roughly across the seat to him. "Do you intend to love him forever?"

He made an impatient noise and his mouth came down on hers, startling her even more. Neil's lips were fiery and demanding, prying hers open to his seeking tongue. The kiss was as passionate as on that first night, but there was a hard, angry taint to this one that hadn't been there before. It was as if he wanted to control her, to force her to accept and enjoy his lovemaking. His hands slid up to hold her head, searing her wherever they touched. He ground his mouth against hers, pressing her lips against her teeth and filling her mouth with his tongue.

"Stephanie, Stephanie," he groaned as his lips left hers and trailed across her face and neck. One hand came down to cup her breast, moving over her skin through the material. He raised his head. His eyes were fierce pinpoints of desire that held her transfixed. "I want you, and I'm alive. Why can't you take what I can give you and forget him?" He pulled her across his lap, twisting her so that she lay half reclining against his chest. Stephanie stared up at him, pinned by the incredible force of his will.

He bent his head to kiss her again, his mouth dominating hers, teeth and tongue and lips demanding surrender. Stephanie was almost faint from the demanding intensity of his kiss. One iron arm supported her, leaving his other hand free to roam her body. His fingers moved firmly, slowly over her, following the contours of her breasts, waist and hips. He traversed the smooth linen covering her thighs and came up under her skirt, his roughened fingertips rasping over the fine mesh of her hose. "I'll make you forget him," he grated out, and his lips left her mouth to prowl over her throat, nipping and teasing at the soft skin.

He left the teasing exploration of her thighs and returned to the soft curve of her breast. As he kissed her throat, his hand curled around one breast. He brushed the tip with his forefinger until it tightened and pushed against the cloth of her dress. With a groan he buried his face in her neck, and his arms went around her like tight steel bands. "Stephanie, you're killing me. Tell me you don't love him still. Tell me."

Stephanie swallowed, unable to speak. Coherent thought had fled at his assault upon her senses. Emotionally she had been pulled in all directions today, and this surprise attack by Neil left her trembling with aroused desire, yet stunned and resentful of his anger and force. "Neil, I—I can't—" she began shakily, hardly knowing what she was saying.

Neil made a disgusted sound deep in his throat, and the skin around his mouth tightened. He released her, practically shoving her back from him. "Damn it, Stephanie, how long do you intend to keep a ghost for a lover?" He jerked open the car door. "I'm not interested in a *ménage à trois*, especially with a dead man." In one lithe movement he was out of the car, slamming the door shut behind him. Stephanie watched him lope across the parking lot, her hands unconsciously clasped together at her throat. Her heart pounded violently. What was the matter with Neil? She had seen tears in his eyes too, when they retired Ty's number, yet just now he had shouted at her as if he hated Ty. Stephanie hadn't realized that Neil was capable of such volatile behavior.

Not that she was any better. She was furious at what he had said and the way he had jerked her to him and kissed her. He had no right to treat her like that! Yet she couldn't suppress a thrill of excitement when she thought of the passion underlying his actions. She had never seen Neil lose control of himself like that. It must have taken a powerful emotion to break through his icy reserve. A delicious shiver darted through her. Suddenly, perversely, she was very anxious for Neil to come home from camp.

Chapter 8

THE TELEPHONE RANG THE NEXT MORNING AS STEPHANIE was preparing breakfast. The thought of Neil flashed into her mind and she almost jumped on the phone. "Hello?"

"Stephanie? This is Julie."

Stephanie's shoulders slumped. Why had she thought it was Neil? No doubt he was busy looking at the game film this morning. She tried to keep the disappointment out of her voice. "Hi, Julie. What are you up to so bright and early?"

"The question is more what are *you* up to?" Julie teased. "Honestly, Stephanie, you could at least have given me a hint about you and Neil."

"What about me and Neil?" Stephanie's voice turned guarded.

"Don't try to be coy with me. Bob saw you two last night."

"Neil and I are friends," Stephanie said automatically in her own defense. "I waited for him after the game to thank him for Ty's jersey."

"Uh-huh, tell me another one. Why are you hiding it?"

Stephanie paused. Why was she trying to hide it? Why was she defensive and awkward about Ty's teammates knowing she had dated Neil? She sighed. "I don't know. I suppose I feel guilty, as if I were somehow betraying Ty. I'm afraid his teammates will think badly of me. What if people assume Neil and I had something going before Ty died?"

Julie made an exasperated sound. "Believe me, honey, nobody'd think that."

"Why?"

"Neil's far too loyal."

Stephanie laughed. *"He's* far too loyal! That's a fine thing for my own friend to say!"

Julie realized how her remark sounded and laughed too. "You know what I mean. The guys are more familiar with Neil. A lot of people wouldn't have any idea what you'd do, but at least they're sure of Neil."

"I hope you're right."

"So tell me, how did this start? What's going on with you two?"

"I'm not sure anything is," Stephanie admitted frankly. "We went out once, and he called me a few times from camp. We aren't into anything hot and heavy, Julie."

"How disappointing." Julie emitted a fake sigh. "Promise me you'll call me when you are."

"If we are," Stephanie corrected. "Neil was angry when he left yesterday. I may not see him again."

"Don't be silly. I can guarantee that won't happen. Why was he angry?"

"I'm not sure. He blew up all of a sudden and said I was still in love with Ty. He seemed angry that I loved Ty."

"Jealousy and nervous tension. Speaking as one who's had vast experience with football players undergoing training camp, I suggest you forget the whole incident. They're always a little on edge until Cheyne makes the cuts, no matter how secure their jobs are. Don't you remember the way Ty was?"

"Unbearable," Stephanie agreed with a fond chuckle. "I was grateful he had to live in California instead of at home during camp. But Neil seems so calm that I don't think of him as feeling the pressure."

Julie's words cheered Stephanie and they talked for a while longer, setting up a date for dinner and a movie during the last week of camp. After Stephanie hung up the phone she ate a quick breakfast, intending to get right to her research into the Marianna Willoughby kidnapping. However the telephone interrupted her meal, and she answered it less merrily than she had earlier. It was Karen Randall, ostensibly calling to chat. Stephanie grimaced. She and Karen had never been close enough friends that they called each other simply to chat. Why, until the ceremony yesterday Stephanie hadn't seen Karen since Ty's funeral. Soon Karen's thinly disguised curiosity reached the subject of Neil. Stephanie had trouble keeping her answers pleasant and she soon made an excuse to get off the phone.

She dumped the remainder of her meal in the garbage disposal, stacked the dishes in the dishwasher and poured a cup of coffee to take into her study. Once there she examined the calendar to see when Neil would be home. Two weeks, he had said. Next Sunday was an exhibition game away from home, and the Sunday after that was a home game. That meant she might see Neil the next day, Monday—provided he still wanted to see her.

Finally she settled down to work and was soon immersed in typing up the notes of her interview with Rodriguez's attorney. Through him she had gotten

Julio Rodriguez's present address and had written to him requesting an interview. She had been ecstatic to receive a letter the previous week agreeing to her request and giving her a telephone number where she could reach him. Stephanie returned to her calendar and jotted down several dates that were possibilities. Then she called the number and set up an appointment with Rodriguez for the following Thursday.

As she worked Stephanie was continually interrupted by the ringing of her telephone. Each time it was one of the team wives wanting, like Karen, "to chat" or inviting her to a coffee or cocktail party. Stephanie refused each invitation as politely as she could, struggling to keep a firm grip on her irritation. It was exactly this kind of gossiping and nosiness that had put her at odds with many of the team wives. They were like a huge family, riddled with secrets, gossip, feuds and jealousies.

She hadn't liked it when she was married to Ty, and she wasn't about to get involved again, especially with herself as the main topic of conversation. Stephanie was essentially a private person, and she didn't relish having her affairs discussed all over town. The last straw was a call from a reporter who wanted to know if it were true that she was "seeing" Neil Moran. It was all Stephanie could do not to snap back a sharp retort. But that wouldn't have helped Neil any, so she made a polite disclaimer that she and Neil were "just friends," which neither she nor the reporter believed.

After she hung up she stared at the phone for a moment. No doubt it would soon ring again. It was hard enough to get any work done with the memory of the scene with Neil yesterday constantly intruding. The interruptions from the telephone were making it impossible. Decisively she unplugged the phone from the wall. She'd have to trust that she wouldn't get any important calls. Once again she settled down to work, and this time it went a little easier. Before long she was thoroughly immersed in it again, and even the thought of Neil didn't tease her brain.

She was surprised when midway through the afternoon a knock sounded on her study door. She went to answer it and was flabbergasted to find a gorilla on her doorstep. In one hand he carried a bunch of silver helium balloons. Stephanie's mouth dropped open inelegantly. It took a second for her stunned mind to register that the gorilla was really a person in a gorilla suit and that he probably came from a service that specialized in bizarre birthday and anniversary greetings. She burst out laughing. "Who on earth . . . ? It's not my birthday or anything."

The gorilla pointed silently at the balloons. Stephanie glanced up and saw that each balloon had "I'm Sorry" printed on one side and "Forgive Me" on the other. Neil. A giddy excitement gathered in her chest as she extended her hand to take the small folded card which the gorilla held out. On the inside it read: "Can you forgive me for acting like an ape? Neil." Her smile stretched even wider as she took the balloons from the actor's hand. The gorilla shuffled away, and Stephanie returned to her desk in a haze of euphoria. How like Neil. She tied the strings of the balloons to a desk drawer handle as she contemplated how to answer him.

She hated to phone him at camp. The players were difficult to reach and she would have to leave a message, which she was reluctant to do. On the other hand, a letter would be far too slow. She wanted to let him know immediately. She could respond in kind by sending the same sort of messenger to him, but Coach Cheyne frowned on such shenanigans in training camp. She didn't want to get Neil into trouble. Finally it occurred to her to send a telegram. She called Western Union and relayed the words: "All is forgiven. I've always had a thing for Tarzan. Stephanie."

After her unusual caller the day zipped by. When she finished working she plugged her telephone back in, braving the nuisance calls in order to receive Neil's call—should he phone. In contrast to the afternoon the evening seemed interminable. Stephanie had trouble eating the light supper she cooked, and after that she couldn't keep her mind on the book she sat down to read. Every time the phone rang she seized it eagerly, and each time she sagged with disappointment and got rid of her caller as quickly as she could.

Finally it was Neil who answered her hello. "I got your telegram."

"Neil! I . . . I'm so glad to hear from you."

"I'm sorry about the way I acted last night."

"Forget it. You're under a lot of pressure during preseason."

"That wasn't the reason, but I'm glad you excused me."

"What was the reason?"

"The mean reds, I guess."

Stephanie could picture his shrug and smile. His eyebrows would rise, the scar in his brow giving him a devilish look, and a single, unexpected dimple would appear in his left cheek. "The what?" she chuckled.

"I can tell you aren't a country girl. That means a foul mood. You know, times when you feel mean and out of sorts for no reason."

"That's called stress nowadays."

He chuckled. "Well, whatever you call it, it doesn't excuse it. Hell, I was jealous, plain and simple. It's a frustrating thing, competing with a dead man, especially when I loved him too."

"You aren't competing with Ty."

"I can't. I know that. But I wish we could start out fresh, as if we'd just met, without all the past behind us."

"That's not possible. But I think we could try not to let the past mess us up."

"I'm game."

"Me too."

"Good. Then I'll see you after the next home game?"

"Yes, please." That was two weeks away and would mark the end of the exhibition season and training camp. Neil would be in Phoenix after that except for the weekend trips to out-of-town games. She would see him regularly. The thought both chilled and excited her. She was eager to be with him again, to feel his kisses and caresses. In fact, merely thinking of him sent waves of heat through her. But mingled with the anticipation was a tinge of panic. After Neil returned their relationship would have to run its natural course, which meant that sooner or later she'd wind up in Neil's bed. The idea of so close, so intense a relationship frightened her. Was she ready to get in that deep? Could she really give herself to another man? Would she, could she fall in love again? After Ty's death love had become synonymous with pain and grief.

Yet Stephanie knew that the only alternative to a sexual relationship with Neil was to end it altogether. They couldn't go only so far; they couldn't retreat to their old camaraderie. They had gone past being friends. Either they would become lovers or they wouldn't see each other again. Stephanie knew that she didn't want to take the latter option. She liked Neil too much—and experienced too much shivery delight at his touch. It was scary, all right, but her desire was stronger than her fear.

The last two weeks of camp went by slowly. If she hadn't been involved in her new story Stephanie was sure she would have been a nervous wreck. Fortunately she was able to fly to Los Angeles again for interviews with Julio Rodriguez and the detective who had worked on the second kidnap investigation, the one which had led to the arrest and eventual trial of the real kidnapper. The police detective, still active on the force, was a short, square man with thinning hair, who looked slightly harassed. At first he was reluctant to talk to Stephanie, obviously not wanting to cast bad light on the original investigation, which had turned out to be so mishandled. However Stephanie was careful to avoid all mention of the first investigation and skillfully led Detective Fullmer through the case from the time the maid came to the station to confess that she had helped convict the wrong man up to the day the real kidnapper was convicted.

After her talk with the policeman the interview with Julio Rodriguez was a breeze. He was eager to talk, and though his English was poor enough that his daughter sometimes had to translate what he had said, his story had such pathos and strength that Stephanie was entranced. At times she became so involved with what he was saying that she forgot to take notes and then had to hurriedly scribble down what he had said before she forgot it. It was fascinating, sad, infuriating, frightening—and the more Stephanie listened, the more sure she was that she had a marvelous story on her hands.

She returned home, pleased with what she had accomplished, and settled down to transcribe her notes into more readable form. The work was satisfying, but it couldn't completely keep her mind off Neil, who continued to call her from camp. Much as she enjoyed talking to him, though, it wasn't enough. The sexual tension built in her daily. She dreamed about him at night and fantasized about what his lovemaking would be like during her waking hours.

The next Sunday she watched the Apaches' game on television. It was basically a boring game, full of rookies and mistakes, but when Neil came onto the field Stephanie sat forward in her chair, her heart pounding with excitement. She clasped her hands tightly in her lap, mentally cursing the TV cameras for not showing a closeup of him. When they finally did she hated the helmet for hiding so much of his face. He played only two quarters, but Stephanie remained glued to the screen, hoping that the cameras would catch him standing on the sidelines.

The game ended shortly before eleven, and although Stephanie went to bed soon afterwards she was too keyed-up to sleep. She told herself that she was behaving like a teenager, getting all excited just at seeing Neil on TV, but rational thoughts had little effect on her emotions. She finally fell asleep only to be awakened by the sudden blaring of the telephone on her bedside stand. She fumbled for it and lifted the receiver to her ear. "Hmm?"

"Stephanie, it's Neil." His voice was low, almost a whisper.

"Neil!" Stephanie opened her eyes and struggled to a sitting position. "What time is it?" She groped for her alarm clock and held it close to her eyes so that she could read the face.

"I don't know. Late. Everyone's in bed."

"Three o'clock!" She set the clock down with a clatter and struggled into a sitting position. "Is something wrong?"

"No. I wanted to talk to you. I couldn't sleep, so I sneaked out of bed and came down here to the pay phone."

"Gene'll fine you if he catches you wandering around at this hour. He'll never believe you just got out of bed. He'll think you've been out carousing."

"I know. But I had to hear your voice."

Stephanie melted inside at his words. "I . . . I'm glad. I watched you on TV tonight."

"Not exactly a sparkling performance, was it?"

"Do you feel bad about it?"

"Frustrated. I hate exhibition games. I can't stand hanging around on the sidelines watching everyone foul up."

"You want to be out there fouling up too?" Stephanie teased lightly.

He chuckled. "Yeah, I guess so. You're good for me. You have a way of putting things into perspective so I don't take myself so seriously." He paused. "I wish I could see you tonight."

"I want to be with you too," Stephanie confessed.

"Really?" He sounded inordinately pleased. "Steph, are you coming to the game next Sunday?"

"I hadn't planned to."

"I wish you would. I'd like to see you afterwards. It'd be nice to know you're in the stands."

"Well, I—if you want me to."

"Good. I'll call the office tomorrow and have a seat held for you at the ticket office."

"No, I'd rather buy one. I don't want to sit with the wives and families."

"Why not? They're better seats."

"I know. But I'd rather not sit there. It—I'd feel uncomfortable."

She could sense his tightening on the other end of the line. It was this sort of reminder of Ty that had made him blow up last time. Stephanie was about to agree to sit with the wives when he blew out a breath and said, "Okay, if that'll make you feel better. Will you wait for me after the game?"

"Yes."

"I usually go home after the game and get in the whirlpool. Otherwise my muscles feel like hell the next day. Would you mind coming with me? I'd take you back to your house later."

She smiled. He was carefully skirting the subject of sex, yet telling her that she didn't have to sleep with him. "That's fine."

"Good. Bring your bathing suit if you'd like to get in the hot tub too."

"All right."

"I'm sorry I woke you up. But I couldn't stand not to talk to you. I think about you all the time." His low-toned words were heavy with sensual connotations.

"Neil . . ." She was breathless with a sudden surge of desire.

"If I told you what I'm thinking right now I'd probably get arrested for making an obscene phone call. I better hang up or I'll work myself into worse shape than I was before I called. See you Sunday?"

"Yes."

He was silent for a moment, then said hurriedly, "Good-bye, Stephanie."

Stephanie murmured a good-bye and slowly replaced the receiver. She slid down in her bed and looked up at the ceiling. It would be ages now before she went back to sleep. She smiled. How wonderful it was that Neil had called!

The last exhibition game made up for the others in excitement. It was tight all the way and better played than the previous ones. Neil played the first and fourth quarters, and he ended the game with a fast drive from one end of the field to the other in the last two minutes to score the winning touchdown. Stephanie's seat was in a miserable location high in the second tier and almost in the end zone. But that didn't keep her from clearly seeing every rush the defense put on Neil. She clutched her hands together, heart in her throat, as she watched the opposing players sack him, miss him or slam into him after he released the ball. Recent rules in football had made it illegal to hit the quarterback after he threw the ball, but many times the rushing player's forward momentum carried him into Neil just as or immediately after he let go of the ball. Stephanie winced every time Neil went down and waited, hardly breathing, for him to rise to his feet.

Despite her anxiety when he was on the field

Stephanie couldn't help but be caught up in the game. When she had first met Ty she knew little about football and hardly ever watched it. Over the years, however, both her knowledge and interest had grown as she attended game after game. She now knew enough so that games were interesting, and because Neil was involved she had a stake in the outcome. When Darrell Bliss caught Neil's short pass in the end zone for the winning touchdown she leaped to her feet like everyone else in the stadium and cheered, clapping till her hands were red.

The other team was unable to score in the few seconds remaining, and the game ended. Stephanie sank back into the molded plastic seat and let her breath out in a rush. This was too much for her nerves, she thought grimly. The game had been exciting enough, but her anxiety over Neil's safety had sent her adrenaline pumping way out of control. She watched the players run off the field, then glanced around at the fans streaming out of their seats and toward the exits. She hated the jostling and pushing that went on after a game, but she had plenty of time and could afford to wait for the crowd to thin out.

When it did she rose and made her way to one of the restrooms, where she put on lipstick, brushed her hair and once again checked her reflection. It had taken ages to decide on the sundress she had worn to the game today. She had wanted something eye-catching yet casual, and had rejected nearly everything in her closet in her search for the perfect outfit. Finally she had settled on a golden-yellow sundress splashed with huge green and white flowers. It was strapless and the waist was encircled by an extremely wide yellow cumberbund. It had a cool, casual look, but the wide sash set off her slender waist to perfection and the bared shoulders added a hint of sexiness. Neil would like her in it, she reassured herself, then grimaced. Why was she worrying about whether Neil would like her clothes? She was acting like an insecure high school girl.

Straightening her shoulders, Stephanie strode almost pugnaciously out of the ladies' room. It was a long walk down the ramps from the second tier and around the stadium to the players' entrance, but when she arrived Neil still hadn't come out. After that touchdown pass the reporters would no doubt keep him longer than anyone else. Other players passed her and smiled as they ran the gauntlet of fans. Finally Neil emerged and was immediately engulfed in a wave of admirers. Good-naturedly he grinned and signed autographs, all the while trying unobtrusively to scan the area for a glimpse of Stephanie. When he located her he stared straight at her for a long moment, his pen motionless in his hand and a slow smile curving his lips. He liked the dress, Stephanie thought, and her own grin grew wider.

The fans were like glue. Neil thought he'd never get through them. Stephanie was radiant in that dress. How could she look even lovelier than his memories? The excitement of the game was still coursing through him, rendering almost painless the sore muscles and bruises that would plague him tomorrow. Now the sight of Stephanie, so cool and enticing, heightened his excitement to an unbearable level. He signed autographs mechanically, nodding, smiling as he worked his way through the crowd toward her. Finally he was free of the well-wishers, and he hurried across the few remaining feet of pavement.

Stephanie watched him approach, his long legs eating up the ground between them. Gene Cheyne, strict in many ways, was lax in regard to the players' attire coming to and leaving the games, so Neil was dressed casually in tan slacks and a gray-blue polo shirt that followed the powerful lines of his shoulders and arms. His face was taut and his bright black eyes glittered. "Stephanie." His arm went around her shoulders, pulling her tightly against his side, and he swept her on to her car without breaking stride. Stephanie felt his tension in his arm muscles; he was squeezing her so tightly she could barely breathe. She knew he was whisking her out of everyone's sight so that he could greet her as he wanted to. He didn't trust himself to do it in front of the fans.

"Neil!" she protested, laughing a little. "You're cutting off my air."

"What? Oh, I'm sorry." He relaxed his hold and bent his head to rest his forehead on her hair. "God, I want you. I think I could have stripped you right there in front of everyone." He brushed his lips against her hair, nuzzling softly.

"I'm glad you didn't," Stephanie retorted, trying to keep it light despite the sparkling sensations his lips were sending through her. "It might have been a trifle awkward with all your fans there."

"I don't know. Might have made me a folk hero." He glanced back and could no longer see the knot of people waiting at the players' entrance. He pulled her into the shelter of one of the gigantic concrete pillars supporting the stadium, and his arms went around her, lifting her up and into him. His mouth captured hers, seeking, twisting, pressing avidly as his fingers sank into her hips and ground her suggestively against his rigid body. His skin scorched her wherever it touched, and his mouth was a cave of heat. He broke the seal of their mouths to rain kisses over her face and neck, slowing to soft, nibbling caresses over her bare shoulders and chest. His tongue traced moist patterns along the hard line of her collarbone, then paused to explore the vulnerable hollow of her throat.

Stephanie's head fell back as she arched her neck and chest to receive his nuzzling lips. She was on fire, electrified, helpless. She clung to his shirt as if to anchor herself to reality. Neil sucked in a deep breath and leaned back against the concrete pillar, eyes closed. Stephanie felt the rapid pounding of his heart through

his shirt and saw the sheen of moisture on his face and
neck. His chest rose and fell quickly, gradually steady-
ing. He braced his legs slightly forward and wide apart,
and let her slide down the length of his torso and come
to rest intimately between his thighs. He swallowed. "I
can think of several very lewd and quite possibly
debauched acts I would like to commit with you right
now."

"Here?" Stephanie responded breathlessly.

He grinned. "I think I better get you home first."

They left the shelter of the huge square pillar and
started again for Stephanie's car. Neil clasped her hand
loosely and walked carefully apart from her, but the
heat of his palm told her of his desire. When they
reached her small foreign-make sedan Stephanie held
out the keys to Neil in a questioning gesture. "Would
you like to drive?"

"No, you do it. I want to look at you."

Stephanie blushed. "You'll make me nervous."

She started the car and turned it toward the freeway.
Neil lounged in the bucket seat beside her, his tall, hard
body incongruous in the small car. He watched her just
as he'd said he would, but rather than making her
nervous his gaze filled her with a liquid heat. Stephanie
felt a flush rising up her throat and cheeks and she
sought desperately for trivial conversation. "You were
very good today."

He shrugged. "We won. But I've had better days."
Carelessly he analyzed the game, his play and that of
the other players. They talked easily all the way out to
his home on Camelback Mountain, but Stephanie
suspected that only a fraction of his attention was on
their words. She wondered what he was thinking, then
decided that it was better she didn't know. She had
never imagined such a sensual nature lay beneath his
unruffled exterior.

When she reached the turnoff to his house she
slowed down and watched intently for the treacherous

potholes and bumps which infested the road. "Every time I come up here," she complained, "I swear I'm never coming again."

"I may have to resurface the drive, then."

They drove through the rough desert terrain of cacti and boulders, climbing the barren mountain until the modern buildings of Phoenix lay scattered below them. Stephanie stopped in front of his house and stepped out, taking in the scene before her. "I always forget how beautiful it is up here," she breathed.

"You should be here during a thunderstorm. It's magnificent. You can see the lightning all over the valley and on the mountains beyond. It's like a gigantic fireworks display."

Stephanie turned away from the view and started toward Neil's house. It was a one-story structure that sprawled across the face of the mountain. Made Pueblo style, with rough round timbers thrusting out of the roof in the front, it was tan adobe and blended in with the landscape around it. Plate-glass windows ran the length of the side facing the valley. Stephanie knew that the view at sunset must be breathtaking. Hidden by a high wooden fence, the pool and spa lay to one side of the house.

Before they reached the front door a dog barreled out from around the side of the house, his hind legs fishtailing in the gravel. He managed to straighten out before he fell, and came at them with undiluted fervor. Stephanie hastily backed away from his eager greeting. She'd had experience with Neil's Irish setter, and she had come away from all their encounters covered with muddy pawprints. "I see you still have Goofy."

Neil chuckled. "Yeah. Down, Red-dog. Good boy." He bent to scratch the setter's head, and the dog writhed with delight. Neil gripped his collar and muttered, "Come on inside, kid; you're heading for a night in the utility room." He glanced back at Stephanie. "Otherwise he'll be all over us in the pool."

"I know."

Neil unlocked the door and they stepped inside. Stephanie liked his house. Though obviously expensive, it shared none of the ostentation Ty's home had had. The entry and living area were floored in rough red-brown quarry tile, its harshness softened by multicolored Navaho rugs. The room was sparsely furnished with roughhewn furniture, and the walls held only a single muted sand painting. The decoration in this room was its view, and nothing detracted from it. There were few rooms in the house, but all were large and airy, bringing the spacious outdoors inside. The house had an Indian flavor, accentuated by the paintings, rugs and wall hangings. There was a minimum of furniture and lots of open space.

"I have to change to my bathing suit and hit the whirlpool," Neil said. "Did you bring a suit?"

"Yes."

His face broke into a smile. "Good. I was afraid I was going to have to choose between duty and you. I have to soak for a while or these muscles will tighten up on me so that tomorrow I'll be stiff as an old man." He started toward his bedroom and motioned toward a bathroom off the hall. "Here's the bathroom where you can change. But I guess you know that."

With a wave of his hand he was gone. Stephanie moved more slowly to the bathroom. She closed the door and began to remove her clothes. Goosebumps popped out on her arms although it wasn't cold. She pulled on the suit she had brought along in her massive purse. It was modest in comparison to many, but alluring nonetheless. The one-piece black suit was strapless and cut high at the thighs. A purple band encircled the neckline. On the left side a design of long-stemmed purple flowers swept up, ending beneath her breast. The dark suit hugged her figure, and the sweep of flowers accented her slenderness as well as bringing the viewer's eye to her breasts. Stephanie gazed at her image in the mirror and wondered if she should have bought this suit.

Not that it really mattered. Neil didn't seem to need anything to excite him this evening. Her fate was rushing down on her like a freight train. There was no way she could avoid it. And though it was a little scary, the tingling throughout her body told her that she didn't really want to avoid it. There were no thoughts of Ty in her now—or of anything except the effervescing excitement in her chest and the heavy ache in her abdomen. She wanted Neil. She wanted to feel his hands and mouth on her, to see his firm naked body and hot black eyes, heavy-lidded with passion. Stephanie blushed and turned away. Her hand shook as she opened the door and walked out to meet Neil.

He was kneeling beside the bubbling hot tub on the deck outside, adjusting the various knobs. When he heard the sliding glass door open behind him, he turned and went still as a statue. Stephanie shifted under his gaze. With the clinging blue trunks he wore, the effect of her swimsuit on him was obvious. Neil rose slowly from his knees, his eyes devouring her. "Stephanie," he murmured huskily. He came toward her and stopped only inches away. Slowly, his eyes never leaving hers, he raised his hands to encircle her neck, then smoothed them down and across the bare expanse of her shoulders and chest. Stephanie could feel the faint tremor of his fingers as they traveled over her flesh. Almost reverently his hands moved down her back, rounding over her hips, and slid back up her front, coming to rest on the soft mounds of her breasts. Neil closed his eyes, his breath rasping in his throat, and he rested his forehead against hers.

"I don't . . . want to rush you. But, oh, Stephanie, I want you here with me tonight." He gathered her hair in one hand and lifted it from her neck, twining it around his hand and arm. "Is there any chance I can persuade you to stay?"

Stephanie smiled, tilting her head back to look at him. "Why don't you try?"

His eyes widened slightly at the invitation in her words and smile. He bent and grazed his mouth against hers once, twice, then his lips hovered just above hers as the tip of his tongue traced the shape of her mouth. His fingertips moved down her body, retracing their earlier path. They touched her as softly as moth wings, inviting without demanding, teasing, arousing. Slowly, Neil reminded himself. Slowly. Stephanie's intimation that she would make love with him made him pound with desire. He wanted to sweep her up in his arms and carry her straight to his bed. He yearned to see her, touch her, bury himself deep inside her with all the force and hunger of years of waiting. But he must not. She wasn't ready yet for hot, overflowing passion. Neil raised his head and stepped backward, taking her hands in his. Stephanie glanced up at him in faint surprise. He smiled and turned away, leading her to the sunken pool of bubbling, frothing water.

Chapter 9

NEIL STEPPED INTO THE HOT TUB AND SAT DOWN IN FRONT of a pulsating jet of water. Stephanie sat across from him out of years of habit, unaware that she did it because they had always sat that way—she and Ty on one side, and Neil and his girl across from them. Neil noticed and knew the reason, but he banished the thought from his mind. That was past. All he could possibly have with Stephanie was the future. He was not going to spoil it by bemoaning what had happened before.

Neil stretched out his legs, ankles crossed, feet on the seat beside Stephanie. Steam rose around them in the evening air, which was cool here in the desert after the sun went down. He leaned back his head and closed his eyes, concentrating on the soothing action of the water on his muscles. He wouldn't think about tomorrow and the soreness. That was the way he always got through pain, whatever form it took. He would cut it from his

mind, relegate it to another time and place. Unacknow-
ledged, the pain never seemed as great as it was. It was
a special talent, this ability to section things off and lock
them away in his brain, and it had enabled him to play
hurt or scared or unhappy without letting it affect his
game. In college he'd once played almost three quarters after his left arm got hurt, refusing to acknowledge
the pain until after the game. Afterwards, when the
team doctor x-rayed it, he discovered that Neil's forearm was actually fractured. It made a good story for his
college coach to tell to prove Neil's toughness.

Stephanie, surprised by Neil's abandonment of their
lovemaking, relaxed in the heated water, letting the
little aerating jets bubble over her skin. It was soothing,
yet at the same time the tiny spurts of air beneath her
legs set up a tingling in her skin. After a while the water
became too hot for her, and she sat down on the edge
of the tub and dangled her feet in the heated water as
she let the desert air fan her wet body. Neil studied her,
his dark eyes narrow slits. Stephanie's suit clung even
more tightly to her body now that it was soaked, and
the cool air on her skin had caused her nipples to
pucker. As he stared they tightened even more.

Neil stood up and crossed the small pool. Stephanie
watched him, fascinated. Steam rose from his recently
submerged skin, giving him an other-worldly appearance that was both frightening and intriguing. He knelt
on the seat and touched his lips to one of her nipples.
Stephanie shivered and sank her fingers into his damp-
ened hair as he pulled the nipple into his mouth,
material and all. His tongue worked magic on her,
stroking, tickling, lashing the engorged bud until she
was gasping with pleasure, then retreating to let his
lip-sheathed teeth nibble and roll the nipple. Stephanie
groaned his name, and Neil pulled away to begin on the
other breast. By the time he finished with it she was
moving restlessly on her perch, aching to feel his body
against hers.

He looked up at her, his eyes dark pools, his usually impassive face slack and stamped with hunger. He reached up and pulled her into the water with him. Standing in the center of the pool, he wrapped his arms around her and held her high so that her face was level with his. He kissed her hungrily, moving his lips against hers, taking her mouth like a treasure—precious, but indisputably his. Stephanie's tongue met his, welcoming him with a teasing courtship dance until his breath blew hot and demanding on her cheek.

Stephanie wrapped her dangling legs around Neil's waist. The intimacy of their position sent a strong shudder through Neil, and his kisses turned wild and hot. He had wanted her for so long, had fought and denied his hunger so many times, and now she was offering herself to him. Everything he'd dreamed of was in his hands, and the idea sent flames of desire shooting through him, fogging his mind and making him tremble with eagerness. He couldn't get enough of her. His hands were everywhere and his mouth seized hers, fiery and demanding. Stephanie had never felt such urgency, such need. It surprised and titillated her, the very strength of his passion sparking hers.

She clung to Neil, helpless in the face of his strong desire, awash in her own awakening sensuality yet feeling curiously safe and secure because Neil held her. He would never hurt her, she knew. Her fingers worked through his thick hair, kneading his scalp, and he tightened his arms around her, pressing her even more intimately against him. His hands slid down to cup her derriere, circling and caressing, slipping along her wet thighs. He dug his fingers into her hips and twisted her against his body. A groan escaped him and he pulled away from their kiss, burying his face in her neck and shoulder.

"Oh, Stephanie!" His breath came in short, hard gasps and she could feel the quivering tension in his muscles. "I'm too . . . far ahead of you." He nuzzled her tender flesh, his lips moist and velvety soft upon her. "Sweet, sweet girl. I'm already about to explode."

Reluctantly he loosened his arms and set her down on the floor of the tub. She looked up at him questioningly. "It's all right. Go ahead."

"Not yet. I want it to be good for you." His burning black eyes glowed with a promise to her. "Just right. To welcome you back to the land of the living."

Stephanie stared at him, puzzled. She was already as eager and yearning as she had ever been, aching to feel him inside her. "It's okay. I'm ready."

He grinned, his white teeth slashing through the dark. "Oh, no, you're not nearly ready. That was just a warmup. You're not a fast starter. You need a little time and attention."

Hurt, Stephanie turned away and sat down in the water, huddling her legs up against her chest. "Did Ty tell you that?" she asked resentfully. Did Neil know everything about their sex life? Did he know how long it took to excite her and how rarely she reached the glorious high everyone talked about? She'd always heard men talked about their women, even their wives —but how humiliating to think that all the time she was with Neil he knew about her problems.

"No," Neil responded firmly, sitting down beside her. "Ty never said a word to me about your sexual relationship." It was a small lie, for there had been a couple of times when Ty was drunk and had remarked on Stephanie's skills in pleasing him. But it hadn't happened often. Neil hadn't encouraged it because it ripped him apart with jealousy. "It's something I guessed about you. I've known you for a while, remember?"

"Not that way." She let her legs slide back down, though she still wouldn't look at him. "Well, I am slow, I'll admit." She shrugged. "But that's not your fault. There's no need for you to . . . to deny yourself because I can't . . ."

He chuckled. "Believe me, I'm not denying myself. I intend to enjoy every second of it. I simply need to take a breather, that's all." He leaned closer, his breath tickling her ear. "There's nothing wrong with going slow, you know. It's not a race." He rose and started up the steps. "I'm going to take a dip in the pool to cool off. Want to come? It feels good after the hot tub. I promise." He extended one hand to her.

"Okay." She took his hand and climbed out of the tub. Neil flicked a switch on the wall of the house, and lights sprang on beneath the water. Neil dove into the swimming pool and swam toward the opposite end. Stephanie followed more slowly, easing down the ladder. The water sparkled in the slanting western light, deliciously cool after the heat of the whirlpool. Stephanie pushed herself away from the side in a smooth, slow glide and stroked her way across the pool. She swam in a leisurely manner, often pausing to rest beside the rim and idly swish her legs through the water.

Neil, on the other hand, zipped up and down the length of the pool like a swimmer in training. Stephanie marveled at his strength and stamina. When at last he stopped in the deep end of the pool, one hand grasping the rim, Stephanie swam over to him. "You aren't even breathing hard!" she exclaimed accusingly.

He shrugged and grinned, wiping the drops of water from his face. "I was just working off some excess energy. I swim about three miles every morning."

"Jocks!" Stephanie shook her head in bemusement.

He touched the tip of her nose with his forefinger. "But for some reason you're attracted to us. Isn't that right?"

"It seems to be," Stephanie agreed, assuming a puzzled look. "I'll never understand why."

"Oh, no?" He moved closer, one eyebrow lifting in a leer. "Maybe you go for staying power."

"Don't be crude."

"Can't help it. I'm a jock, remember?" His large hand cradled her cheek, one finger tracing the lines of her face. "You're so beautiful. All during camp I'd lie awake at night and think about you." The timbre of his voice lowered and his lips seemed fuller. Stephanie's gaze was drawn to his mouth. She couldn't look away. She wanted to feel his mouth on hers again. "I want you, Stephanie."

His forefinger grazed her lower lip and involuntarily her mouth opened to allow his finger access, then closed over it, trapping his finger in a velvet clamp. Neil's lids fluttered and his chest began to rise and fall rapidly. Stephanie knew what to do to tempt and please Neil. She had been good at arousing Ty—a sort of compensation, she guessed, for her frequent failure to reach satisfaction. But this time she wanted to tantalize and inflame Neil's senses for her own pleasure. Every heated glance, each melting of a taut line in his face, added to the liquid fire in her abdomen. She wanted to touch him, to experience him in every way possible.

Stephanie ran the tip of her moist tongue along the side of his finger, her lips sucking at it ever so lightly. His skin tasted of salt and was coarse against the sensitivity of her tongue. Stephanie smiled and opened her mouth wider to take his finger between her teeth, worrying it as her tongue made swirling designs on his flesh. Neil murmured hoarsely and closed his eyes, gripping the rim of the pool so tightly that his knuckles whitened. Finally Stephanie released his finger, but she took his hand in hers and with slow, aching deliberation brought each of his other fingers to her mouth to give them the same treatment. When she finished Neil's arm lashed out to pull her tightly against him and his legs wrapped around her like steel cords. He shoved them away from the edge and with one powerful arm stroked down the pool. Stephanie lay pressed intimately against his body, pulsatingly aware of each cord, tendon and muscle, and of the heated throbbing of his desire.

When he reached the shallow end of the pool Neil stood and swung her into his arms like a child, then climbed the steps and strode across the cement to the hot tub. Gently he set Stephanie on her feet. He hooked his thumbs into the top of her swimsuit on either side and rolled it down over the swelling white flesh of her breasts, scraping the sensitized nipples. He stopped when she was naked to the waist and gazed at her breasts as if he would memorize them. Gingerly he covered the full mounds with his hands, dark and hard against her soft white skin. He cupped them, seemingly weighing them in his hands. He pushed the quivering globes together, lifting them, and bent to circle the pink-brown aureoles and center buds with his supple tongue. Stephanie moved restlessly, unsettled by the wild, fluttering sensations he caused in her lower torso. He lifted her, his arms beneath her hips so he could more comfortably take her nipples in his mouth, and suckled first one and then the other. When he set her back down Stephanie wasn't sure her legs would hold her, they felt so weak and watery.

Neil peeled her bathing suit down past her hips, smoothing it over her slender thighs. It fell to her ankles and she stepped out of the wet suit, blushing. A flush crept up Neil's throat and face, darkening his tanned skin, and his tongue crept out to moisten his lips. He looked at her, she thought, like a starved man at a feast that had suddenly been set before him. The thought made her knees even weaker.

At last he moved, quickly stripping off his form-fitting swimming trunks. Stephanie watched him, glanced away, then back, unable to keep her eyes off his powerful form yet embarrassed to stare so openly. He stepped into the whirling pool and reached back to help her in. Again he seated himself before the pounding jet of water, but this time he pulled Stephanie onto his lap, facing him. She drew in her breath at the feel of his legs between hers, his skin touching her most private flesh. The bubbles of air tickled her naked body, startling and delightful. Neil kissed her over and over, loving her with his mouth as his strong fingers played with her breasts, rolling the nipples between thumb and forefinger, stroking and squeezing lightly.

A hot bar formed in Stephanie's abdomen, expanding with every touch, every kiss. His fingers roamed her body masterfully, callused fingertips evoking responses Stephanie had never known she had. His mouth explored her ears and throat and shoulders, nibbling, nuzzling, teasing with his tongue. Stephanie moaned and moved helplessly, yearning to ease the throbbing ache inside her. She rose on her knees, her mouth seeking its mate, and his hand slipped between her legs to press the mound of her femininity. Stephanie gasped, and Neil chuckled deep in his throat. He cupped her in the palm of his hand and his fingers teased at the satiny folds until Stephanie writhed against his hand, seeking release.

She pulled her mouth away to whisper raggedly, "Please, Neil, I want you. I want . . . to feel you inside me."

He groaned and buried his face in her hair, his hands clenching behind her back. Finally he sucked in a long breath. "No, not quite yet, sweetheart."

"Neil!"

"Shh. I'll show you." He slid one arm around her torso and pulled her around so that she arched over his arm, her head resting against the rim of the hot tub. Her breasts broke through the surface of the water, the nipples proud and taut. Neil bent to scoop off the drops of water with his tongue. His lips closed around one button of flesh and he tasted her tenderly. His other hand moved to her soft inner recesses and he eased a finger inside. Stephanie twisted and moaned as his finger and tongue stroked simultaneously and his thumb pressed and released. He maneuvered her lower body a little higher, and she felt the jet of water gushing over his hand and her flesh.

Stephanie whimpered. She had never felt anything like the fire running rampant through her body. The ache between her legs was enormous, uncontrollable, and she moved her hips wantonly against his hand, seeking, begging. She was aware of nothing except Neil's hands and mouth. He was driving her crazy with his slow, sure lovemaking. In another moment she was certain that she would start to scream. Desperately she sought the fulfillment of his body, gasping out his name.

He eased her back to a sitting position astride him, this time deftly positioning her so that he moved inside her. Stephanie closed her eyes at the exquisite pleasure of his possession. Perspiration dotted his forehead and upper lip, and his breathing was shallow. His fierce control was almost exhausted. "Oh, my love, my love." He rested his face on the soft pillow of her breasts, his fingers digging into her hips. "Take me there."

Stephanie began to move, slowly at first, then harder and faster as she gained confidence and her desire grew. Every nerve in her body seemed to have gathered into a fist in her abdomen, and with each movement the fist drew tighter and tighter until Stephanie was sobbing for release. Neil began to thrust, lost in an instinctive drive for fulfillment. Stephanie clung to him, quivering with the force of her need, and suddenly the knot of longing within her exploded, washing outward. She cried out, digging her fingernails into Neil's back, and felt the primitive shudder of Neil's body as he found his own blissful surcease.

They melted together, limp and exhausted. But the temperature of the water, unnoticed in their excitement, was almost unbearable now to their sensitized nerves. Reluctantly they parted and climbed the steps. Neil wrapped a large, fluffy towel around her, and

Stephanie leaned against him, dazed and glowing, content to let him do with her whatever he willed. He dried off haphazardly with another towel and lifted Stephanie into his arms again. He caught the handle of the sliding door with his elbow and pushed it open, then stepped inside. Stephanie reached out and closed it after them. He smiled and kissed her lightly on the forehead before he walked down the hall, cradling her against his chest. It seemed to him that he carried his world in his arms. When he reached his room they tumbled into his bed, happily intertwined, and slid into a deep sleep.

Stephanie was awakened the next morning by light kisses being feathered over her face. Her eyelids fluttered open and she focused on Neil's tanned face, inches away from her, relaxed and smiling. "Hello, sweetheart." He straightened, picking up her hand and turning it over to kiss the palm. "Sorry to wake you,' but I didn't want you to think I'd stolen away in the night."

"What time is it? Where are you going?"

"Practice. It's eight o'clock, and it takes me thirty minutes to get to the practice field." He rose and tucked in his lightweight cotton shirt, preparing to leave.

"Practice? On Monday? That's your day of rest."

"Not anymore. They decided we got too stiff taking Monday off, so now we have a light practice on Monday and take Tuesday off. Will you be here when I get back?"

Stephanie blinked. "I don't know. I hadn't thought about it. I . . . I guess I'll go home and work."

"Then I'll drop by your house after practice. We can go out to dinner." He leaned over her, one sinewy brown arm on either side of her. Softly, almost nervously, he asked, "Are you okay? I mean, do you have any regrets?"

Maddeningly, Stephanie felt herself blushing. "No," she breathed. She put her hands on his arms and slid them upward, loving the crisp feel of his hair under her hands. "I never felt anything like it. It . . . was never like that with Ty." Now why had she blurted that out? Stephanie turned her gaze away, chewing on her lower lip. Neil didn't like to be reminded of her relationship with Ty.

"Oh, baby." Suddenly he sat down on the bed, his arms going under her, and he nestled his head against her breasts. Rubbing his cheek against her smooth skin, he murmured, "I don't want to go away even for a few hours."

"Cheyne would fine you. What is it now? A thousand bucks?"

"Mmm." He paused. "It'd be worth it, I think."

Her breath caught. "Then . . . then you enjoyed it too?"

He chuckled and sat up. "My God, yes. Couldn't you tell?"

"I wasn't sure. You—you did so much for me, and I hardly did anything for you."

"Everything I did to you excited me just as much as it did you. Touching your body is an unbelievable pleasure."

"Really?" Stephanie gazed searchingly into his eyes.

"Really." He bent to kiss her deeply. When he pulled away at last Stephanie was shaken, and Neil's breath was decidedly uneven. "Shall I skip practice?"

Reluctantly Stephanie shook her head. "No. I don't want you to get stiff." Her eyes sparkled mischievously. "That might cramp our . . . uh . . . leisure activities."

Neil laughed. "I certainly wouldn't want to do that." He gave her a quick, firm kiss and stood up. "See you this evening."

"Good-bye."

"'Bye."

Stephanie listened to the sound of his footsteps in the

carpeted hall and then on the hard quarry tile. She linked her hands behind her head and contemplated the ceiling, her lips curving into a smile. She had never experienced anything like last night. Much as she had loved Ty, his lovemaking hadn't come close to doing what Neil had done to her. She closed her eyes, remembering the sweetness, the surging, turbulent need, the blissful swirl of oblivion. Neil had coaxed her, caressed her, played her until she had writhed in an abandon totally unlike herself. Ty had touched her and kissed her, but never with such a wild, sizzling effect, and he had never taken the time and trouble to arouse her as Neil had. No wonder Neil always had plenty of available women.

She felt a stab of guilt. It seemed disloyal to Ty to enjoy herself so much with another man. She had loved him, she really had. So why hadn't sex with the man she loved been as good as it was last night with Neil, whom she didn't love? Neil was her *friend,* for Pete's sake. Ty had been her beloved husband! It didn't make sense. Stephanie swung her feet out of bed and went into Neil's bathroom. She stopped dead at the sight of her reflection in the mirror. Her hair stuck out wildly in all directions because she had slept on it wet. She looked positively electrified. How could Neil have kept a straight face as he told her he'd enjoyed their lovemaking when she looked like an absolute witch!

She searched Neil's cabinets and found a plush towel and washcloth. After setting them on the counter she stepped into the huge glassed-in shower. There was a showerhead high on one marble wall, obviously meant for the 6'3" Neil. The one in Ty's house had been the same way, and it was a real nuisance. But here, on the wall directly across from that showerhead, there was a much lower one, obviously meant for a woman. How convenient for a bachelor, Stephanie thought grimly and turned on the spray. It was instantly warm and she stepped under it, letting the drops drive away the annoying thoughts of what other women had shared Neil's shower.

Thirty minutes later, her hair washed and dried, her clothes of the evening before back on her body, Stephanie let herself out the front door. She hadn't eaten any breakfast. It had seemed too strange to go through Neil's kitchen cabinets looking for something to eat without him there. She felt almost guilty being in his house by herself. She jumped into her car and headed for Phoenix. During her shower she had decided what to do that day. First she was going to beg her way into an appointment at her hairdresser's. She hadn't done anything to her hair in months, and suddenly it seemed terribly drab. Next she would shop for a new dress. She supposed she ought to work, but she was too giddy with the remnants of the previous night's pleasure to get anything constructive done. All she could manage to keep her mind on was looking the best she could for Neil.

Fortunately her hairdresser found a cancelled appointment. In fact, from the horrified expression on his elegant face she suspected that he had made up the cancellation just to keep one of his clients from providing such bad advertising for him. Robert cut her hair slightly and layered it into a light, frothy style that looked good either straight or curled. Then he used a curling iron to turn it into a lovely mass of crushable curls, and discreetly lightened a few strands. Stephanie smiled at her reflection. It was a definite improvement on what she had looked like coming into the shop.

From there she went to the Biltmore Fashion Park, a new mall of exclusive shops. In Saks she found a pair of pale pink shorts, crisp and temptingly short, and in a small boutique she matched them with a crepe blouse of hot pink that had an off-the-shoulder peasant neckline and puffed sleeves. Pleased with her finds, she stopped at a small eatery that faced onto the mall. She was really very hungry, although she hadn't noticed it before. She hadn't eaten any breakfast, after all, and here it was past two in the afternoon.

As she sat there, watching the people pass, she saw a familiar, tall woman approaching. It was Jill Byerly. Neil had been dating her before Ty died. The woman swerved out of her path and stepped up to the counter to purchase a drink. Stephanie kept her eyes on her plate, hoping Jill wouldn't notice her. The last person she wanted to see today was one of Neil's old flames. Her luck had run out, however, for she heard her name exclaimed across the narrow room and she was forced to look up.

"Jill!" Stephanie pasted a pleasant smile on her face.

Jill came toward her with that long-legged model's walk of hers that Stephanie had always envied. "Fancy meeting you here."

"I've been shopping. Uh, would you like to sit down?"

"No, thank you. I'm on my way to work, actually. I'm modeling now at the Clotheshorse."

"Oh, I see." Stephanie was puzzled by the other woman's cool voice and expression. She had never felt that Jill particularly liked her, but Stephanie couldn't see any reason for the downright hostile look in her eyes now. "I understand it's a lovely store."

Jill shrugged, indicating disinterest in the subject. Her eyes were hard and bitter as she went on. "Karen Randall came into the store a couple of days ago. She told me that you and Neil have a thing going now."

Stephanie's stomach sank. It hadn't occurred to her that Jill might know anything about her and Neil. Well, that explained Jill's coolness. No doubt she still harbored an interest in Neil, and she was jealous of Stephanie. "Well, I . . . it isn't anything serious."

Jill made an inelegant snort. "Maybe not to you. Actually, I'm surprised Neil waited long enough for Ty's corpse to get cold."

Stephanie gasped. "What in the world do you mean?"

Jill shot her a scornful look. "Oh, come on, don't tell me you still don't know."

"Know what?"

"That Neil is in love with you. He's been in love with you ever since you met."

Chapter 10

STEPHANIE STARED AT JILL FOR A MOMENT, THEN EX-claimed, "Don't be absurd! Neil's not in love with me!"

Jill's lips thinned into a vicious line. "No? Ask anybody. Everyone who saw Neil look at you knew. The only ones who didn't figure it out were you and Ty. Neil always wanted you, but he was too noble to tell you. I never had a chance with him!" Her eyes flared with anger. "Not a chance. No matter what I did or how I looked. I couldn't get to first base just because I wasn't you."

Stephanie couldn't pull her thoughts together enough to say anything. It was crazy! How could Neil have been in love with her and she never picked up a clue? Jill was lashing out in bitterness and hurt because Neil had rejected her. That was all. Stephanie wet her dry lips and groped for something to say. "Neil and I were good friends. Maybe you blew that out of proportion."

Jill laughed humorlessly. "No. You've been blind."

She turned to leave, flinging a parting shot over her shoulder. "I hope Neil's happy now that he's gotten what he always wanted." Her tone indicated the exact opposite of her words.

Stephanie watched the woman walk down the wide hall, then looked back down at her food. Her appetite had vanished. She piled the containers together on the tray and swept them into the trash. Shakily she gathered her packages and purse and left. As she walked through the mall and out to her car she ran over Jill's assertions in her mind. The idea that Neil had been silently in love with her for years was ridiculous. He and Ty were good friends, so the three of them had been together a lot. Perhaps that had started rumors. Or maybe Jill wanted to believe what she had said so that it wasn't her own fault that Neil hadn't loved her. Neil had been Stephanie's friend. Their attraction to each other had started only recently, over a year and a half after Ty's death.

Surely if Neil had felt anything more for her he would have revealed it at some point. Or would he? Stephanie had to admit that it would fit Neil's personality to love her without letting on. He was too loyal to hurt Ty and too kind to saddle her with the burden of a hopeless love. He was also the only person she knew who had the iron will it would take to love someone without ever expressing it. Now that she thought about it, Stephanie remembered a few occasions when she had caught Neil watching her with a dark, pained expression. There had been other moments—the time he had danced with her and in the middle of the dance pulled away suddenly as if he were angry, and then stalked out of the room; his tirade the other day after the game when he had berated her for still loving Ty; a remark he had once made when he was more than a little drunk, hinting that he envied Ty; his care and trouble last night to make sure their lovemaking was the best it could be for her. And there was the time Ty had slapped her.

It had been in the beginning stages of Ty's illness,
when the growing tumor had started to affect his
personality, though at the time they hadn't known the
cause of the change. Ty had turned moody and sullen,
often lashing out at friends for no reason or storming
out of the house in a rage. Stephanie didn't know what
had precipitated his fury that particular evening, but he
had begun striding around the room, bitterly complain-
ing about football fans. Stephanie, irritated by his
recent moodiness, had answered sharply, and he had
turned his anger on her. She wasn't one to back down
from an argument, and soon they were in the middle of
a full-fledged fight. Finally, in a paroxysm of fury, Ty
had lashed out and hit her open-handed, flinging her
backwards. She had crashed into a wall, and for a
moment they stared at each other in blank surprise.

Then Ty had groaned and raised his hands to his
head, digging his fingers into his scalp. He had closed
his eyes and sat down heavily on the couch. Stephanie,
thoroughly frightened and enraged, had run outside to
her car, grabbing her keys on the way. She had driven
the miles up to Neil's mountainside home in furious
haste, blinded by tears of anger and pain. Her first
instinct had been to seek safety, and Neil had automatically come to mind.

When she reached his house she had beaten wildly on
his front door. Moments later Neil had answered,
frowning with irritation at the noise. When he saw her
tear-streaked face, already swelling and bruised where
Ty had hit her, his expression had turned to shock. He
had pulled her in, pouring out questions, and Jill had
appeared in the front hallway, her eyes wide with
astonishment.

"Ty hit me!" Stephanie had cried out, and Neil's face
twisted, his dark eyes blazing with an unholy fire.

"I'll kill that son-of-a-bitch," he'd grated, and
pushed past her, striding toward his car.

Stephanie had gasped and run after him, Jill not far

behind her. The two women had grasped his arms, one on each side, and managed to slow him down long enough for the red rage to clear. Then he had gone back inside and gently applied an ice pack to Stephanie's swollen cheek while they discussed what was wrong with Ty. It was then that they decided Ty had to visit a doctor.

Had that moment when Neil charged out into the night, intent on getting revenge for Stephanie's injury, been an indication of his love for her? Had sudden stress ripped away the mask of friendly calm?

Stephanie worried the thought in her mind like a dog with a bone, unable to let go of it during her drive home or the rest of the afternoon. Neil was coming by after practice, and she vacillated between eagerness to find out the answer to her questions and dread of what would happen next. This morning she had been blithe and happy with their new relationship, but this news changed everything. If Neil had been in love with her all this time, their lovemaking last night was based on a foundation entirely different from what she had imagined. How could she be easy with him, knowing that he was different from the man she had thought she knew? And how was she to treat him, knowing that his own feelings ran so much deeper than hers? She was poised on the edge of something, but Neil was already far down the path.

Stephanie wasted most of the afternoon in fruitless wondering and barely got dressed in time to be ready for Neil's arrival. She had decided to put off wearing the new outfit she'd bought. Instead she dressed in a colorful, full Mexican skirt and a white, embroidered peasant blouse, clothing Neil had seen her wear many times before. The doorbell sounded with Neil's distinctive double ring and she went to open it, noticing that her palms were sweating with nerves. She would have to deal with this issue soon or she'd be a wreck before the evening ended.

Neil lounged against the wall of her small front porch, arms folded across his chest and one booted foot hooked casually over the other. His eyes were snapping with life. Stephanie's nerves set up a strange tingling. She suddenly felt as giggly and excited as a schoolgirl. "Hi." Her voice was almost shy.

He grinned and unfolded himself, covering the ground between them in one huge step. He seized her upper arms in his steel grasp and pulled her up into a long, breathless kiss. Stephanie's heart tripped into a fluttering beat, and by the time he released her she was dizzy. She stepped back in confusion, amazed at her immediate response to him. What kind of power did Neil have over her, anyway?

He released her and followed her into the house. Stephanie's heartbeat steadied and her breathing returned to normal. She searched for something innocuous to say. Now that he was here, she didn't know how to broach the subject. "How was practice today?"

He groaned comically. "Like it always is the day after a game. Painful." His eyes twinkled at her. "I didn't pay proper attention to my whirlpool last night."

To her dismay Stephanie felt a blush rising in her cheeks. Neil sat down on the couch and tugged at her hand, indicating that she should sit down beside him. Stephanie pulled back. "No, I better fix supper."

His eyebrows went up. "It's only four o'clock. Besides, why don't I take you out?"

"Oh, no, I'd rather cook tonight." She cleared her throat. "How about a drink?"

"Nothing, thanks. Just sit down and talk to me." Again he pulled her hand, and she sat down, fitting all too easily against his side. "How was your day?"

"I didn't do much of anything. I couldn't settle down to work. And don't grin at me like that."

"Sorry." He pulled the suggestive smile from his face, but his eyes twinkled more than ever.

"You're impossible."

"So what did you do instead of working?"

"I shopped at Biltmore Park." The introduction to her subject was suddenly there, staring her in the face. Stephanie chewed on her lower lip. She had to know. She would have to ask him and the sooner the better, no matter how much she hated it. "I ran into Jill Byerly there."

"Oh?" He stiffened almost imperceptibly. If Stephanie hadn't been pressed against his side she wouldn't have noticed it. "How is she?"

"Bitter, I think."

Neil sighed. "Jill knew where she stood from the start, but she refused to accept that I didn't love her. I didn't want to hurt her."

"She told me she never stood a chance with you. Is that true?"

"More or less. I knew from the beginning that I wouldn't fall in love with her."

"Why?"

Neil shot her a wary glance. "What does it matter? It was over a long time ago. My relationship with Jill has nothing to do with us."

"That's not what Jill said."

His face was still, almost resigned. "What did Jill say?"

"She . . . she said you've been in love with me ever since we met. Is that true?"

"You make it sound as if it were a crime."

"Of course not. But it's important."

He regarded her for a moment. "All right. Yes. I fell in love with you a long time ago. If Ty hadn't been my friend I'd have done my best to break you up. There, does that satisfy you?"

Stephanie shook her head wonderingly. "I never knew. I really didn't have any idea."

"I didn't mean for you to. It wouldn't have helped

matters for you and Ty to know it." He took one of her hands in his. "But Steph, that doesn't affect what you and I have now."

"Doesn't it?" she asked distractedly, pulling her hand from his and rising to her feet. She walked away to look through the sliding glass doors at the backyard. "I feel as if I've known you all this time under false pretenses."

"You think I'm a liar? I can't be trusted?"

"No, of course not. I mean, not exactly."

"Stephanie, what good would it have done to tell you? We couldn't have been friends any longer. It would have been too awkward. Not knowing didn't hurt you and Ty."

"But *you* must have hurt!"

"I have only myself to blame. If I chose to do it, what's wrong with that?"

"I feel guilty somehow, as if I'd hurt you. As if I were responsible for coming between you and Ty."

"You didn't come between me and Ty. If anything, he was between you and me. You'd have been mine a long time ago if it hadn't been for him. You didn't hurt me. We weren't unfaithful to Ty. Where's the harm?"

"I don't know. Maybe there was none. But it makes me feel uneasy." She looked at Neil, her eyes dark with pain. "I'm so sorry."

"Don't pity me," he cut her off sharply. "I don't need or want that, especially not from you. I chose to love you, and I chose to conceal it in order to remain friends with you and Ty. There's nothing you could have done and no reason for you to feel bad. I made my decision. I lived with it. There's no place for pity."

"I'm not being condescending. I'm not pitying you. But I feel hurt for your hurt. Sympathy isn't bad, Neil."

"Neither is loving you. I don't think there was ever any evil in it."

Stephanie sighed. "I'm sure there wasn't. But don't you see how it puts us in an awkward situation now?"

"No, how?"

"Now I know. Now if you get hurt, it *will* be my fault. I don't want to cause you grief or pain. I like you far too much."

"Believe me, you aren't causing me any grief by letting me make love with you. Just the opposite, I'd say."

"Maybe right now. But there's an inequity there, and someday it's bound to hurt you. Don't you see? Maybe now a physical relationship seems enough to you, but after a while you'll start to think about how much more you're giving me than I'm returning. You'll want a more equal relationship. You'll want love."

Neil was silent for a moment, studying her. In a low voice he asked, "What makes you think I won't get what I want? Do you plan never to fall in love again? Was Ty the only mate for you?"

She blinked. "No. I imagine I'll fall in love again someday. At least, I hope so. But . . ."

"But it won't be with me?"

Stephanie blushed. "I didn't mean that. It—I might fall in love with you. But the point is, I don't know! What if I don't? Then you'll get hurt. You can't count on my falling in love with you!"

"I'm not." He rose and walked toward her, his hands jammed in the rear pockets of his jeans. "Steph, do you know what makes me a successful quarterback?"

Stephanie started at his sudden change of topic. "What in the world are you talking about?"

"I'm talking about my personality. I have pretty average talent for pro football. But I'm determined. I can concentrate on my goal and not be distracted. And I'm patient. I work for things. I don't try to win in one glorious play. That's why I think I'll get you someday. I'm willing to wait, but I won't ever forget what I'm after." He stopped in front of her and withdrew one hand from his pocket to tilt up her chin. "I love you, Stephanie, and I'll do everything I can to make you love me. But I won't push. I won't pressure you into committing yourself. I'm not about to put any demands on you or expect your immediate love." He paused. "There's another thing I do well. I roll with the punches. I've learned how to deal with defeat. It's not something I enjoy, but I'm able to go after something with all my heart and at the same time accept the fact that I may not get it."

"And that applies to me as well?"

He smiled. "Does that upset you?"

"Comparing me to a football game? No, why should it?" she replied tartly.

His smile broadened into a chuckle, and he took her hands in his. "I'm not comparing you to a game. You're far more important than that. You're the most important thing in my life. I'm just trying to show you that I can love you, try desperately to win your love and yet realize that I might not get it. I can deal with the situation, Stephanie. Trust me."

Again she pulled away. "I don't know. This is so unsettling."

He caught her wrist before she could get beyond his reach and pulled her around to face him. "Look, I don't expect you to love me. I won't pressure you. I can't promise that I won't be hurt if you don't return my love, but I can promise that I'm aware of the possibility and I've *chosen* to get involved with you in spite of it. I'm not a child. I'm going into this with my eyes wide open. I've wanted you for longer than I care to remember. I thought I'd never have even a portion of what we had last night. Stephanie, I want some happiness. And I want to give you some as well. It's that simple. That easy."

Stephanie frowned. "I don't think things are ever as simple as you make them sound."

"You'd be surprised how unnecessarily complex I make them sometimes. After Ty died I felt horribly guilty for loving you, as if my love had somehow killed him. I thought about all the times when I had wished him out of the way so I could make you mine, and I hated myself because those wishes had come true. It was awful. My feelings for you were tainted with guilt and remorse. That's one reason I stayed away from you. I was punishing myself for loving you, for thinking bad things about Ty, for coveting my friend's wife— God, how I coveted you!"

Neil sighed and closed his eyes briefly. "Finally I saw that I was ruining my chances for happiness out of some idiotic need to pay for Ty's death. I was letting the past make my present and future just as gloomy as it had been. That's wrong, Stephanie. You can't let the past interfere. Now is what counts, this moment. Please, don't let the fact that I loved you in the past make you throw away what we have now."

His thumbs began to draw slow, steady circles on the backs of her hands, a caressing invitation, a beckoning to return from the chasm of her thoughts. It was a small gesture, not overpoweringly sexy, yet it stirred the desires Jill's revelation had banked. She wanted Neil. Last night he had made her feel as no other man had. The prospect of his lovemaking started a low, throbbing heat in her. Why throw that away? Why not enjoy what she could have with Neil and let nature take its course? Neil was right. He was a grown man. He made his own choices. Who was she to protect him by denying him something they both wanted? It seemed idiotic when she thought about it from that point of view.

She looked up at Neil and a smile crept across her face. She thought of his joy in their lovemaking, of the satisfaction he must have felt after years of denial. His pent-up longing made it even more incredible and sweet that he had taken such time with her last night, putting her pleasure before his. Suddenly Stephanie knew she wanted to please him, to give Neil all the fire he'd wanted from her for so long. "Why are we standing here talking?" she asked in an injured tone. "I'd think you'd have had me in the bedroom by now."

"An accomplished stud like me?" His grin was wide and relieved. "Maybe my reputation exceeds my ability."

"I don't think so." Stephanie turned her hands so that their palms fitted together. "Come on. I have a surprise for you."

"What?" She dropped one of his hands and tugged at the other, guiding him from the room. He followed with gratifying alacrity.

"How about a massage? I thought you might like one after working out and discovering all those stiff muscles."

"Mmm. Sounds good."

They reached her bedroom and Stephanie motioned him toward her bed. "Then take off your clothes and lie down."

"All my clothes?"

Stephanie chuckled. "Yes, *all* your clothes."

Neil joined in her laughter. After last night, his comment had sounded peculiar. But there was something in his brain that couldn't quite adjust to the fact that Stephanie was now his lover. "Sorry. I'm just naturally shy," he quipped and began unbuttoning his shirt. Stephanie ducked into the bathroom and searched the cabinets for the unscented oil she had always used for Ty's rubdowns. It had been so long since she used it; it was bound to be at the back—if she hadn't thrown it away when she moved. She breathed a small sigh of relief when she found the small bottle.

Neil had made quick work of undressing and was already lying face down across her bed when she returned to the bedroom. Stephanie slipped out of her shoes and outer garments and pulled off her ring, laying it atop her dresser. Rings could scratch when one gave a massage. She settled down cross-legged beside Neil on the bed, clad in only her flesh-colored lace underpants and brassiere. She dug her fingers into his thick black hair and began to work. Neil made a contented noise and his body relaxed all over. Stephanie smiled and continued her ministrations, moving down to his neck. Then she turned and poured a bit of oil into one palm. She held it in her hand, letting it warm as her eyes moved down the length of his body. A bruise the size of a softball marred the muscled skin of his back just below the left shoulder blade. When Stephanie saw it she drew in her breath sharply. "Neil! What happened!"

"What?" His head came up and he glanced around. "What are you talking about?"

"This bruise." Stephanie reached out tentatively to touch the edge of it.

"Oh, that." Neil shrugged. "I don't know. I got it in the game sometime."

Of course. How could she have forgotten? Ty had always been cut and bruised after a game. She grazed the purplish stain with her fingertips, remembering the time when Ty's chest had been half covered with an ugly creeping bruise that seemed to have expanded each day. Her eyes skimmed over Neil's back, looking more attentively this time. She touched a small scar low on his back. "What's this?"

"I got cut by a cleat in high school."

Stephanie closed her eyes, remembering the tape around Ty's ribs after he had cracked them. It had hurt him to breathe and laughing had been an agony. She thought of the scars that had etched his fair skin, the knob on his collarbone where he had broken it and it had reknit poorly, the deep bruise on his thigh. She opened her eyes and found the scar on Neil's elbow where they'd done the surgery. She looked at the bruises dotting his hips and legs. She knew that if he rolled over she'd find them all over his front too. The little finger of his passing hand was permanently bent at an unnatural angle above the second knuckle because it had been broken so many times. "Why do you guys do it?" she breathed, fear and sickness clutching at her stomach. What was she getting herself into? Life with another man who did his best to get bruised and torn and battered every Sunday?

"Goes with the territory."

"I wonder if the territory's worth it," Stephanie retorted sharply.

"Sometimes I wonder that myself." He cocked his head to grin up at her. "Maybe I'm a masochist."

"That thought has crossed my mind."

"But aren't things better when you have to struggle to get them?"

"Struggle I can understand. Mutilating yourself I can't."

"It's just a ploy to get your sympathy. Didn't you know that?" Stephanie grimaced at him and he went on teasingly, "Hey, what happened to that massage? Were you overcome by the sight of my magnificent body?"

She rolled her eyes and smiled. "Just letting the oil warm up." She rubbed the oil between her palms and set to work on his back muscles, carefully avoiding the painful-looking bruise. She would have to get accustomed to this rough-and-tumble world again.

Her fingers dug in deeply, working out the soreness in Neil's corded muscles. She moved down his back, then did each arm in turn, supporting it as she kneaded the warmed oil into his skin. Neil sighed blissfully, and groaned now and then as she soothed a particularly sore joint or muscle. "Can I arrange for this after every game?"

"We might be able to work something out. Do you like it?"

"Yes. Except you're turning me on so much that I

don't know if I can last long enough for you to get out all the kinks."

"Really, Neil," she said with mock sternness. "I have *not* been giving you a sexy rubdown."

"No? You could have fooled me."

"I'll show you a sexy one." Stephanie's hands slithered over his oiled back and dug into his buttocks, eliciting a muffled groan from Neil. She stroked and smoothed, kneaded and lifted, letting her thumbs drift into the dark joinder of legs and torso, teasing at the sensitive, hair-roughened flesh. Neil writhed and moved his legs restlessly. Stephanie's fingers moved over his thighs, still rubbing the tense muscles in a professional way but also teasing with her fingertips. She worked her way down his legs, bending over to kiss the tender skin behind his knees. Neil jerked involuntarily and murmured her name. Stephanie took his foot in her hand and firmly massaged it, then slid off the bed onto her knees and ran her tongue lightly across his toes.

"Stephanie! What are you trying to do to me?" Neil rolled over on his back.

"Looks like I've already done it," Stephanie remarked, glancing significantly at his body's unmistakable message. "Didn't you like it?"

"Like isn't the word for it."

"Then lie still. I haven't finished yet." She continued to kiss and caress his feet and moved her mouth up one of his legs until her breasts were pressed against the soles of his feet, pricked by her thrusting nipples. She stretched her arms up his legs, her fingers tickling their way through his coarse, curling hair.

"I never knew feet were so erogenous," Neil gasped as he dug his fingers into the bedspread.

Stephanie slid sinuously up his body, her flesh skimming over his at every point. Neil's breath rasped in his throat, his chest rising and falling unevenly. Finally he grasped her shoulders and pulled her up to the level of his face. Fierce black eyes blazed into hers as he raised his head to kiss her, blotting out everything else. Stephanie clung to him, their mouths greedy on each other, tongues mingling, teeth hard and sharp beneath the velvet cover of lips. Neil wrapped his legs around hers as his hands went between their bodies to cover her breasts.

He turned over, pinning her beneath him, and ended their kiss. He rose to his knees to look down at her, his legs like iron around hers. The sprinkling of hair on his legs rasped teasingly against her skin. His widespread fingers caressed her breasts, and he watched with heavy-lidded hunger the pointing of her nipples beneath his thumbs. Stephanie's breath came hard and fast. She felt as if each whorl and line of his thumbs were raking across her nipples sending shivers of violent pleasure through her. With extreme gentleness he rolled the pink-brown tips between his thumbs and forefingers, glorying in the way his touch made Stephanie arch her back and moan with longing.

"Neil. Oh, Neil. Make love to me."

He closed his eyes and forced his legs to relax around her. "Not fair," he said, rising. "First I have to return the favor."

"What?" Her mind was dazed with pleasure.

"I'm going to give you a massage. Turn over."

Stephanie groaned but did as he bid, anticipation blossoming in her abdomen. He didn't disappoint her. He unhooked her brassiere and slid it from her, then insinuated his fingers beneath the sheer silk panties and tugged them down her legs. He dropped the gossamer garments onto the floor and his hands returned to her body. His touch was light as a feather, exploring her everywhere, not massaging so much as teasing and arousing. He traveled up and down her back and legs, coming close to, grazing but never quite touching the hot, throbbing locus of her senses, even though she moved her legs apart slightly, inviting his hand.

Still not caressing her there, he began to kiss her, making wet, intricate patterns on her hips and thighs and the tender sides of her breasts. Stephanie writhed under his mouth, aching, longing for the satisfaction only he could bring.

Finally his hand slid between her legs, and the long-awaited contact was electric. Callused flesh touched moist smoothness. Heat melded to heat, and pressure answered ache. Stephanie squeezed her legs together, capturing his fingers, urging him to finish his delightful torment. She twisted, moving her hips to match the rhythm of his fingers. Neil's face was flushed, his skin damp with sweat. His hand left her and she turned over on her back, her eyes liquid with passion. Neil positioned himself between her legs and Stephanie encircled him eagerly. Sliding his hands beneath her hips he poised at the gate of her desire, then slowly pushed into her welcoming warmth. Stephanie moved in counterpoint, luxuriating in the fullness of his deep thrust. She felt as if she could go on this way forever, yet the budding need deep within wanted more . . . and speed . . . and now.

Neil was trembling and breathing shakily as he buried his face in her breasts, his mind fixed on the small pinpoint of sanity remaining in him. His body was taking over, rushing to the prize, panting, lunging, past all reason and knowing only the scent and feel of his beloved. Stephanie wrapped her legs tightly around his back. Suddenly he cried out and his face contorted as he shuddered under the onslaught of unstoppable passion. The force of his rapture swept Stephanie along to her own explosion of joy. Sparks showered through her body, setting off a wild, tingling fire all over her. She buried her face in Neil's shoulder to muffle the sounds which were torn from her innermost being.

Quivering, they lay together, not daring to speak, hardly daring to breathe. Finally Neil rolled from on top of her and pulled her against him, her back to his front. One of his arms looped around her waist, and the other pillowed her head. Stephanie could feel the faint brush of his breath against her hair. Neither spoke, for they had experienced something past words. The loving nestling of their bodies held the moment close, and they drifted to sleep in utter peace.

She had known it for only two nights, but the lack of Neil's body warmth awoke Stephanie. Sunlight pierced the cracks of the miniblinds, bathing the room with a glow indicating that it was late morning. Stephanie blinked and pushed back her tangled hair with one hand. Where was Neil?

Then she spotted movement in the mirror of the tiny bathroom adjoining the bedroom, and she turned in that direction. Neil stood at the sink, clad only in his underwear, his lower face lathered in pink foam. He tilted back his head so he could shave under his throat, wincing as the razor pulled. "Damn!"

Stephanie giggled, and he turned to shoot her a dirty look. "What is it that women have against sharp razors? A guy could kill himself with this thing."

Stephanie sat up in bed, propping a pillow behind her. "It's meant for shaving legs, not faces. It's perfectly adequate for that." He grimaced and continued to shave. Stephanie smiled. "The pink shaving cream looks nice with your hair."

Neil made a mock growl. "It smells to high heaven."

"It's 'delicately scented—for a woman's touch,'" Stephanie quoted with high good humor.

A grin quirked his mouth through the pink foam. "That makes about as much sense as pink lather."

Stephanie leaned her head against the headboard of the bed and watched him shave. There was something comfortingly masculine about the ritual. She was suddenly aware of how much she had missed a male presence in her home and in her bed. The past few months had been unbearably empty and lonely. She hadn't realized what a desert she lived in until now, when Neil had brought life back into it. Tears stung her eyes, but it was from the pleasant ache of being filled to overflowing.

She left her bed and went into the bathroom to wrap her arms around his waist from behind and kiss the outthrust of his shoulder blade. Neil smiled at her in the mirror and reached behind him with his free arm to press her against him. She kissed him again, then left him reluctantly. She stepped into the shower and turned on the faucet. Moments later she was surprised to hear the shower door open, and she turned to see Neil joining her. Playfully he took the soap from her hands and lathered her body, his play rapidly becoming a sensual game. She returned the favor, and soon they were making love, her legs gripping his waist and the cold tile wall against her back, the shower spraying over them warmly.

Later they dried each other off, and Neil pulled on his jeans to go out to the front yard for the newspaper. "I can tell I'm going to have to bring a few things over here," he joked, "or I'll have to live in one set of clothes and have a bloodied face." He stopped abruptly and shot her a slightly wary glance.

Stephanie realized that he was waiting for her permission to fulfill his humorously worded request. She smiled, her heart swelling with joy. How wonderful it would be to have Neil living there! "Of course. I wouldn't want you to bleed to death."

He grinned and winked, then strolled out of the room, whistling under his breath. Stephanie slipped on underwear and the shorts and blouse she had purchased the day before. She fastened a set of earrings in her ears and reached for her wedding ring on top of the dresser, where she had put it the previous night before

giving Neil his massage. Her hand paused in midair.
She studied the ring for a moment. Then her fingers
curled around the cool metal, enclosing the ring in her
palm. She slid open a tiny drawer of her jewelry box
and placed her wedding ring in the satin-lined drawer.
Stephanie closed the drawer and walked out of the
room.

Chapter 11

STEPHANIE SHIFTED THE OVERFLOWING FILE WHICH LAY IN her lap. It contained all her correspondence with the various people involved in the Willoughby kidnapping and subsequent investigations and trials. It had taken her quite a few letters to relatives, friends and employers to track down some of the people. After she found them she had written to them. In some cases she had gotten no reply whatsoever. In others she had received letters full of suspicion or reticence or just plain lies. But there had been some who granted interviews and others who had written concise, readable accounts of their roles and observations in the case. These were invaluable.

She was going through the file, weeding out the useless letters and getting the rest into some sort of order, while Neil watched a college football game on television. She lifted her eyes from her task and glanced across the room at him. He lay on the sofa, feet up on

one end and head on the other. One arm rested on his
chest, and his opposite hand was raised, propping up
his chin, his forefinger in a thoughtful pose across his
lips. He was utterly absorbed. Stephanie shook her
head in amused disbelief. She had thought that she was
good at focusing on something to the exclusion of all
else, particularly when she was reading, but Neil made
her concentration seem laughable. His limbs and face
were perfectly still. Even his breathing was relaxed and
slow. He could have been asleep except for his wide-
open, piercing eyes.

She studied him, a smile hovering on her lips, her
eyes warm. The past two weeks had been close to
perfect. Since she and Neil had been friends for years,
there had been little of the discovery period, often so
irritating—even horrifying—which usually accompanied the beginning of a relationship. Stephanie had not
had to face the shock of learning that Neil splattered
Louisiana hot sauce on his scrambled eggs. Neil hadn't
been disillusioned by Stephanie's disinterest in the
physical activities he liked so much. They had long ago
adjusted to Stephanie's lying in a lounger reading while
Neil swam laps up and down the pool, and Stephanie
knew to avert her eyes from his gruesome eggs as she
ate her breakfast of toast and fruit.

They already knew that they loved to talk and that
their senses of humor matched. Each was warmly
familiar, yet delightfully new and interesting too. And
whenever they were together sexual excitement bubbled just beneath the surface. Neil was an inventive,
thoughtful lover, and his sheer hunger for her was more
seductive than anything Stephanie had ever known.
She had always thought of herself as a warm person,
but not an especially sexual one. But with Neil she
discovered that her warmth was not limited to her
emotions. She had a deeply passionate nature which
only he had been able to bring to the surface. She

looked forward to their lovemaking with no less eagerness than he did, more than once meeting him at the door when he came in from the practice field and twining herself around him. Much to her delight, he never failed to be more interested in taking her to bed than in resting his weary body or filling his empty stomach.

They had spent every night together except for the Friday and Saturday of the previous week, when the team had flown out of town for a game. Stephanie had missed Neil those two days more than she would have dreamed possible. Funny . . . with Ty she had preferred the out-of-town trips because she didn't have to endure his pregame nerves and bad temper. She frowned and studied Neil more sharply. There wasn't a sign of nerves in his whole limp body. She closed her book and sat forward with interest. "Say," she began, "Neil . . ." She cleared her throat ostentatiously. "Mr. Moran."

Neil broke his stare at the television and glanced over at her questioningly. "What?"

"Aren't you nervous or are you just good at hiding it?"

"Hiding what?" He frowned, puzzled.

"The tension, the fear, the excitement—you know, about the game tomorrow."

"Oh." His brow cleared. "I'm as excited as you can get about an ordinary game after ten years of playing. Tomorrow morning sometime I'll start pumping adrenaline. No point in wasting it today."

Stephanie chuckled. "You're the only person I know who can turn off your adrenaline because it's pointless."

"Pretty cold-blooded, huh?" Neil grinned and sat up, bracing his elbows on his knees and spreading his hands as he tried to explain. "It's not that I don't get excited. I do. I love football. But I've learned to channel the excitement and tension into something more constructive than jumping with nerves the day before a game. When I was in high school I'd get so high on anticipation that I couldn't sleep the night before a game. I'd charge through Friday like a bull and not remember a thing I learned that day. It was okay in high school, but in college I couldn't pour out that much energy and still compete on the field. Everybody else was too good. One day, when I was all charged up before a game, I slammed my fist into a metal locker and broke my little finger and a bone in my hand. I couldn't play the next day. That's when the coach took me aside and explained that I was killing my own game by acting that way. After what I'd done I had to accept that he was right, so I learned how to relax."

"You mean deep breathing and all that?"

"Yeah. Focusing my mind on something else. The excitement was still there, but I'd bundle it up and set it aside until it was useful."

Stephanie shook her head. "You're amazing. Are you able to get rid of the fear that way too?"

"What fear?" Suddenly his face cleared of its faint puzzlement. "You mean, why am I not pale and sweating and tossing up my lunch like Ty?"

"Yeah. He was awful to be around the day before a game—grouchy, nervous, sick. One minute he'd tell me how he'd run this cornerback into the ground last time they played each other, then the next minute he'd worry that the other guy had gotten better or that he himself had lost his speed . . ."

". . . or a hundred other things," Neil finished for her. "Sure. That was Ty. He had a real love/hate relationship with football. He was a dazzling player, but he was filled with insecurities. I don't need to tell you that. You knew him as well as I did. I have some of that fear—I suspect anyone who performs does. Actors, singers, athletes. Don't writers have it? You know—what if I fail? What if they hate me? What if

I've been fooling myself all these years and I don't really have any talent?"

"Yeah," Stephanie admitted. "Sometimes when I sit down at the typewriter to begin writing I'm absolutely frozen with fear, and I think of a hundred occupations I should have pursued instead."

"It's natural. I have it, but not to the extent Ty did. I learned to relax and ignore negative thoughts, and I have a calmer personality. I had a coach once whose favorite saying was, 'Some of you guys are racehorses, and the rest have to accept the fact that you're drays.' Ty was a racehorse. He was high strung, nervous, insecure and supremely talented. He was a superb player, but he couldn't quite believe it. He never achieved enough for his father. You know how his old man was."

"Yeah, I know."

"Football was all that counted to his father, and being best was all that was acceptable. Ty never simply loved football the way I did. He didn't feel the sheer excitement of playing, of pitting yourself against the other team. It wasn't a game for him, but a way of proving himself over and over. He was afraid he wouldn't measure up."

Stephanie considered Neil, her head tilted to one side. She had assumed that Ty's feelings about football were natural, that Neil, too, looked on the game more as an enemy than a friend. She understood now that it wasn't true. Neil genuinely loved it. His eyes lit up when he spoke about the excitement and the competition. "It's a big part of your life, isn't it?"

"Sure. I've played since I was eleven years old. I've gone to practice every fall and spring for twenty-one years. From high school on it's been my career. Oh, I have other interests. I've invested in some businesses. Computers fascinate me. But they're not the same as football. There's no danger, no charge from winning. I'll do okay when I retire. I'll put the game behind me and go on. But I'll keep playing as long as I can. I don't have any desire to retire."

"Then I hope that day's a long, long way off." Stephanie crossed the room to kneel beside the couch and nestle her head against his chest. His arms curled around her. He bent his head to kiss her hair. He would have liked to tell her that as long as he had her at home, retirement wouldn't seem too bad, but he didn't want to scare her. He'd promised her that he wouldn't talk of love or pressure her.

Neil tugged gently at her hair until she lifted her head to look at him. "Are you coming to the game tomorrow?"

"Yes."

"And you'll use my ticket?"

Stephanie hesitated. She dreaded sitting with the wives. She'd be uncomfortable under all their speculative gazes. But it was obviously important to Neil that she sit there. It represented some kind of commitment to him, she guessed, an open avowal of their relationship. She ought to be willing to give him that much—it was rather silly not to. "Yes, I'll use your ticket."

He grinned. "Good. And will you come to the party?"

"What party?"

"You know, the opening party. The one they have every year for the whole team."

"Oh." The management gave a huge party after the first regular season home game. It was *the* social event of the year for the players and their wives, the one occasion when coaches, players, clerks, management and even the owners mingled freely. The rest of the time everyone pretty well stayed within his own sphere. "I'd forgotten. I . . . yes, of course I'll come." Personally she found the annual party boring, but again there was a look in Neil's eyes that said it was important to him.

He smiled and drew her to him for a long, eloquent kiss.

When Stephanie arrived at the stadium the following day her palms were sweating despite the air conditioning in the enclosed dome. She walked down the wide concrete steps toward her section as she had so many times in the past. Her stomach was jumping. Why was she nervous about sitting down with a bunch of women she'd known for years? It was crazy. They wouldn't jump up and condemn her for dating Neil when her husband had been dead for a year and a half. What was it about her sitting there that upset her? Maybe it was the same as the reason she suspected Neil wanted her to sit there. It represented a commitment to him. Her mind skittered away from the thought.

She hesitated at the entrance to her row, her eyes scanning the seats given to the players. She spotted Karen Randall in the row in front of her. And there was Quentin Hill's wife, Tonya. Stephanie gave a faint smile to the woman at the end of her row, whom she didn't recognize. The woman turned aside to let Stephanie through, and she edged down the row to her seat. The woman on the other side of her empty seat looked up. It was Ruthie Pendleton. Stephanie smiled genuinely. Ruthie was exactly the opposite of her little-girl name. The black woman was tall and pencil thin, and her clothes and hairstyle reflected her modeling background. She was cynical, intelligent and possessed an acerbic wit. Stephanie had always enjoyed her company.

Ruthie's eyes widened in surprise and she jumped up, holding out her hands. "Stephanie! How are you?"

"Fine. How are you?" Stephanie squeezed the other woman's hands.

"Me? Great. I'm giving up my career, such as it is."

"Really? Why?"

They sat down as Ruthie grinned and patted her abdomen. "I'm going to have a baby."

"Ruthie! Oh, that's wonderful!" Stephanie remembered a meeting of the Wives' Association when she had sat beside Ruthie. Ruthie had been glumly reading a newspaper article concerning a premature baby. She had jabbed her finger at the article, her liquid dark eyes suddenly hard and flashing. "Look at that," she'd commanded bitterly. "That baby's mother is only fifteen. A little fifteen-year-old dropout without any money or prospects or sense, and she'll probably continue producing a baby every year—and I can't have a kid!" Stephanie had tried to reassure Ruthie, reminding her that she was young and had plenty of time to have children, but Ruthie had been embittered by a miscarriage only two months before and had ignored Stephanie's words of comfort.

"You look radiant," Stephanie told her truthfully.

"Thank you. I *feel* radiant. You should have seen me two months ago. I was sick as a dog. But I'm past the third month now—no miscarriage and no more morning sickness."

"Stephanie!" Stephanie glanced up and saw Julie waving to her from a seat three rows down. Stephanie smiled and waved back. During halftime she'd make her way down to see Julie. At Julie's exuberant greeting several people turned to look at her, and she saw surprise, speculation and pleasure on several faces. Ruthie introduced her to the rookie's wife on the other side of her. She turned out to be from southern California, and Stephanie delightedly engaged her in conversation about their common home state.

Before she knew it the players were on the field and lining up for the kickoff. It hadn't been so bad, she thought with surprise. She'd been nervous over nothing. No one had asked her about Neil or said anything about Ty. And she had been amazed to discover how happy so many of the wives were to see her. She had always thought of herself as something of an outcast among them, but now she realized that she had been wrong. She was different from a lot of them, true, but now she sensed a certain admiration for her differences. She wondered if they respected her for the fact that she had made a name for herself apart from her husband's fame.

More relaxed, she settled down to enjoy the game. She felt a niggling worry, a fear every time Neil passed the ball and was rushed by the defense, but she was able to submerge it in the excitement of the game. When the Apaches won she was as happy as everyone around her. The wives gathered their belongings and prepared to leave. Ruthie turned toward her. "Are you coming to the party tonight?"

"Yes, I'll be there. Are you?"

"Are you kidding? Of course. It's the one night I can get Joe dressed up enough to go someplace where I can wear an evening gown." Ruthie laughed. "I'd never pass up an opportunity like that."

Stephanie trailed out of the stadium with Julie chattering excitedly beside her. She didn't wait for Neil this time, but drove straight home to bathe and get ready for the party. Neil came in after six-thirty. His tanned face was flushed with excitement and he picked her up in a rib-cracking hug and whirled her around, laughing. She protested, and he set her back down on her feet, then kissed her soundly. Stephanie laughed aloud with sheer pleasure at his exuberance. His skin was warm, his hair still wet from the shower he had taken after the game. "You look delicious," she told him.

Neil threw his head back and laughed. "I look what?"

"Good enough to eat."

He wiggled his eyebrows suggestively, and she threw a mock punch at his arm. "Would you get serious? I have to get dressed for a very important date."

"They'd probably like you better that way." He

indicated her low-cut brassiere and ankle-length, side-slit slip.

Stephanie made a face and moved beyond his reach. She pulled a robe from the closet and slipped it on, saying, "I'll make us a light supper before we go."

"Haven't got time," he replied. "I just stopped by to see you before I went out to my house. I have to spend my time in the whirlpool, then get dressed. Besides, they'll have a lot of food at the party. They always do."

"Well, if you're sure . . . I figured you'd be starving."

"I am. I'll fix a couple of sandwiches when I get home." He kissed her again, softly and more lingeringly. "You're beautiful. You know that?"

Her breath quickened. Just his low words and the faint brush of his fingertips under her chin were enough to stir the familiar longings inside her. "Neil . . ."

"Maybe I'll skip the whirlpool."

Stephanie put her hands between them, palms flat against his chest. "No. You'll start stiffening up in a couple of hours, and then you won't dance with me. And I want to dance tonight."

"All right. All right." He did his best to sound disgruntled.

Stephanie walked with him to the door, where he kissed her again, leaving her flushed and smiling. Dreamily she wandered around the kitchen, making a supper of cold cuts and a salad. Then she returned to her bedroom and finished getting ready for the party. She put on an ankle-length white sheath, long-sleeved and very simple in design. In the back it was slit up to the knees to allow easy walking. The collarless neckline dipped down in a narrow vee between her breasts and ended in a diamond-shaped decoration of white beading. It was a beautiful dress, very understated but elegant, and it looked especially good with the French-braided coronet in which she had styled her hair.

However, it definitely needed something to set it off

at the neck, and Stephanie was digging through her jewelry box and trying on necklaces when she heard Neil return to pick her up. He strolled into the bedroom and Stephanie turned around, modeling a chunky gold necklace. "What do you think about this necklace with this dress?"

He stopped in his tracks as if stunned and swept her slender figure with his eyes. "Gorgeous. Not the necklace. You."

"Thank you."

He held out a flat, hinged box. "But I think this will look better. Lucky you chose tonight to wear that dress."

Stephanie took the box curiously and opened it. Inside, nestled on dark brown velvet, was the pale pink, rock crystal jewelry she had admired that day long ago in Sedona. "Neil, it's beautiful!" She set the box on her dresser and almost reverently lifted out the necklace to slip it around her neck. The cool pink shells adorning the ends of the gold circle nestled against the hollow of her throat. Stephanie fitted the bracelet around her wrist and fastened the nearly transparent shell-shaped earrings in her ears. One look in the mirror assured her that the jewelry went beautifully with her dress. She couldn't have asked for more perfect accessories.

She touched the glassy stones. "Neil, I . . . they're beautiful. When did you—I mean . . . I probably should say, 'You shouldn't have,' but I'm awfully glad you did." She turned to him, eyes warm and loving. "I'll treasure them always."

"Just treasure me." He held out his arms and she stepped into them eagerly. For a long moment they clung to each other, lost in a warm glow. Reluctantly they pulled apart and started for the car.

The party was held, as always, in one of the meeting rooms of the Biltmore, the prototype of the Phoenix resorts. The large room had a portable bar in each corner, a small stage set up for a band, a dancing area, small round tables for eating and long, cloth-covered tables loaded with appetizers. The Ingrams stood by the door to meet the players and their wives personally, a nice touch made possible by the fact that Gene Cheyne and his wife were beside them greeting everyone by name, thus clueing the owners in. They had no difficulty in remembering Neil's name, though, and were delighted to see him. Stephanie's heart swelled with an unexpected rush of pride. It was silly, she knew. She had made no contribution to Neil's popularity or ability, yet she was as pleased and proud as if they had remembered the names of her books—and praised them.

They walked through the room, stopping to chat now and then. Stephanie noticed that Neil kept his arm possessively around her waist and that he introduced her to people with a note of pride in his voice. The thought warmed her. They settled down at a table with Bobby "O," so nicknamed by his teammates because of his hard-to-pronounce Greek surname beginning with an "O." Pete Cherneski, a linebacker, joined them a few minutes later and proceeded to demonstrate a complicated magic trick which required several minutes of explanation and preparation, then failed. Pete had a bizarre sense of humor, and Stephanie was always uncertain how to take him. Neil reassured her under his breath that Pete was simply crazy like all linebackers. Strange as he was, it was hard to keep from laughing around him, and Stephanie had to admit that she enjoyed his company.

The dancing started at nine, and from then on Stephanie made sure they spent most of their time on the dance floor. Neil didn't seem to mind, although he made token protests about his lack of dancing ability. In fact he was a fair dancer, and Stephanie enjoyed the time in his arms, their bodies brushing against each other. Her nipples tightened at the contact, and her mind went automatically to their lovemaking and the feel of his skin on hers with no clothing in between. From the way Neil gathered her closer in his arms with each dance, his head drooping down to rest on her hair, it was obvious that he was recalling the same thing.

Once when they left the floor Pete Cherneski asked Stephanie to dance, and Neil watched her walk away from him. A faint smile hovered about his lips. Cherneski had two left feet on the dance floor— although it never seemed to keep him from getting out there—but Stephanie was floatingly graceful. Neil enjoyed watching her like this, unobserved. He was able to drink in the tender line of her throat, the glossy spice of her hair, the exquisite angles and curves of her body. Lord, but she was beautiful!

Neil couldn't remember ever being this happy. It was as if everything he'd always wanted had been suddenly dropped at his feet. Stephanie was as lovely, as warm, as passionate as he'd always dreamed—and more. Once he had believed that he loved her as much as it was possible to love anyone, but now he knew he'd been wrong. Every moment he was with her he fell more deeply in love with her. There were aspects to her personality that he had never guessed at—secret desires, fears and hopes—and he was discovering them daily, peeling away the layers of her as one would open a rose until the soft, sweet center was revealed. And everything he found out about her made him love her all the more.

There was only one imperfection in all his bliss: Stephanie didn't love him. She enjoyed his company and his lovemaking; she was fond of him. But she didn't love him in the all-consuming way that he loved her. Neil chewed thoughtfully at his lip. He wasn't used to not winning. Whatever he wanted, he went after and usually got. It would be the same here. It had to be.

What use were all his other victories if he couldn't obtain the single most important thing in his life—Stephanie's love?

He watched the dancers stop as the song ended. Stephanie smiled at Pete, and they walked back toward Neil. Stephanie's steps quickened as she neared Neil, and the smile she directed at him was soft and glowing. He rose to meet her, his pulse speeding up. Someday she would love him. He'd make sure of it. He'd do whatever it took. He had to.

They left long before the party ended, more anxious to be alone than to enjoy the good food, drinks and conviviality. As Neil drove home Stephanie snuggled against him, resting her head on his arm, one hand spread across his thigh. She felt warm, sleepy, content and atingle with anticipation. "Mmm. I'm very happy tonight. How about you?"

He chuckled. "I think you could safely say that."

"I wish everyone could be as happy as I am right now. Like Claire. She always winds up with turkeys." She frowned, her mind suddenly racing. "Say, maybe I ought to fix her up with somebody."

Neil groaned. "Oh, no! Don't tell me you're going to turn into a matchmaker."

Stephanie shrugged. "Normally I'm not. But Claire's luck is so bad."

"Maybe it's her taste in men."

Stephanie ignored him. "And you know what? I met someone tonight who'd be perfect for her. Ray Cooper!"

"The defensive line coach?"

"Why not? He's the right age for her, early forties, I'd say. He's nice-looking, quiet and very pleasant. And he's a widower. Don't you like him?"

"Oh, yeah, I think Ray's a good guy. But Claire didn't strike me as the type who went in for 'quiet and very pleasant' guys."

"That's because they're hard to find. I know she'd like Ray."

"Well, I'm not going to ask him to go out on a blind date with your friend."

"No, that wouldn't be a good idea," Stephanie agreed, unperturbed by his recalcitrance. "We'll have to make it seem natural, not like a blind date." Neil groaned. "I'll invite Claire over for supper one evening. I won't tell her about Ray or anything. Then you can just walk in with him. Let's see. You can bum a ride home from him. I'll drop you off at practice that morning."

"Stephanie . . ."

"Can't you do that?"

"I could. Ray doesn't live far from your house, so it would seem natural. But, honey, are you sure you really want to get into this?"

Stephanie grinned. "Yes, for some crazy reason I do. I've never arranged a blind date before, but I feel so good and happy that I'm almost overflowing. I want to share it with someone. I want to give someone else a chance at what I've got right now. Does that make sense?"

His smile was slow and stirring. "Yeah. It makes sense. And it makes me very happy."

Looking back on it, Stephanie realized that she should have known her arranged meeting between Claire and Ray Cooper had all the ingredients for disaster. But she was too happy and cheerful to consider that. She simply assumed that everything would turn out as she had planned. She invited Claire for Wednesday evening, and Claire accepted eagerly, elated at the chance to learn more about Neil Moran. Stephanie drove Neil to the practice field that morning, setting the stage for Ray Cooper to bring him home. She quit working two hours early so she could tidy the house and start dinner, being careful not to fix anything too elaborate. It was, after all, supposed to be an ordinary dinner with a close friend. Stephanie didn't change out of the casual shorts set she had worn all day and plaited her hair in a single thick braid down her back. When the doorbell rang she went happily to answer it—and received her first indication that the evening might not go as she had planned.

She hadn't told Claire about Ray, feeling that it would make her more at ease and spontaneous. It had never occurred to Stephanie that Claire, not knowing the importance of the evening, would not dress up. Claire usually took care to look her best, even if she were just driving down to the grocery store. But now Claire stood on her doorstep without makeup, her hair limply tucked behind her ears, and dressed in sneakers, faded denim cutoffs that were ragged around the bottoms and a faded blue workshirt pulled up and tied around her waist.

For a moment Stephanie couldn't speak. Claire walked past her, not noticing the stunned expression on her friend's face, and flopped down on the living room couch. "God, what a headache!" she exclaimed, rubbing her temples. "To tell you the truth, I almost cancelled tonight, but my curiosity was stronger than my headache. I decided, what the hell, Neil won't be interested in looking at me, so I'll go like I am. It's been one hell of a day. I took four aspirins this afternoon, and they haven't made a dent in my headache. Do you suppose it's a migraine?"

"I don't know. I've never had one. Could I fix you a drink? Or will that make it worse?"

"Who knows? I'll risk it. Maybe it'll stop the pain."

Stephanie returned to her kitchen and mixed two quick gin fizzes. She came back with the drinks and sat down across from Claire. Claire took a sip and sighed. "At least it tastes good, even if it doesn't cure my headache. You wouldn't believe the problems I had today." She began to recount the multitude of things that had gone wrong at the theater and at home as she took out a package of cigarettes from her purse and lit one. "Ah, I'm beginning to feel a little better. Maybe another couple of drinks and I'll feel human . . . or be under the table."

Suddenly Stephanie jumped to her feet. "Oh, my God, the casserole! I forgot what time it was." She ran to the kitchen and glanced at the clock as she opened the oven door. Fifteen minutes overdone. She pulled out the dish, burning one finger where the hot pad had gotten thin. She sucked on the burned finger as she lifted the lid and peered inside. Not burned, thank heavens, but definitely scorched around the edges. Well, with the vegetables and salad, maybe no one would notice. She took a pan from the cabinet and had started toward the freezer for a package of frozen vegetables when she heard the slamming of car doors. Neil was home. She wet her lips and went to the front door, arriving just as Neil stepped inside, Ray Cooper behind him . . . and right behind Ray was Pete Cherneski. Pete Cherneski!

Stephanie, stepping forward to kiss Neil hello, froze in her tracks. "Hi, Steph," Neil began a little stiltedly. "I invited Ray and Pete in for drinks. Hope you don't mind. Ray gave me a ride home."

"No, of course not," Stephanie managed to get out. "Hello, Ray, that was awfully nice of you. Pete. Come in and sit down." She led them into the living room where Claire sat. "Claire, this is Ray Cooper, one of the coaches of the Apaches. He gave Neil a ride home. And this is Pete Cherneski. He's a linebacker."

Claire looked up and smiled charmingly. "Hello, so nice to meet you."

"Claire's a good friend of mine," Stephanie explained. "She runs a new theater here."

"Movies?" Pete asked, irritating Stephanie by plunking himself down on the couch beside Claire, leaving Ray to the chair. Pete wasn't a bad guy. He was even good-looking in a rough, athletic way. But at the moment he was fouling up Stephanie's plans royally.

Stephanie started to answer Pete, but Claire had already turned to him and was explaining her work. Stephanie smiled at Ray. "What can I get you to drink?"

"A light scotch and water, please."

"I'll take bourbon, honey," Pete volunteered. "And don't make it light."

"Neil, would you help me?" Stephanie asked in her sweetest voice.

Stephanie marched into the kitchen and straight across to the farthest corner of the room. She turned. "What is going on?" she whispered indignantly.

Neil shrugged, turning his palms upward, and replied in an equally hushed voice, "I'm not cut out for intrigue. I asked Ray to drop me off, and Pete was standing there to one side. He heard me, and when Ray said yes, Pete asked if he could bum a ride too. What could I say? 'No, you can't come because Stephanie's trying to lure Ray into a trap'? I figured you'd rather have Ray with Pete along than not at all, so I went ahead and invited them in for a drink."

Stephanie sighed. "You're right. It's better than nothing. I'll ask both of them to stay for supper and hope I can keep Pete from monopolizing the conversation."

Neil mixed the drinks, giving Pete a walloping dose of bourbon. Putting on her best smile, Stephanie followed Neil into the living room. There she found Claire staring at Pete Cherneski in amazement as he crushed her half-smoked cigarette out in the ashtray and started a lecture on the evils of smoking. Fortunately the arrival of the drinks diverted his attention.

Stephanie fixed a bright smile on her face and asked,

"Won't you two stay for supper? There's plenty of food."

"Sure," Pete agreed enthusiastically.

With a sinking heart Stephanie watched Ray Cooper shake his head. "Nope, 'fraid I can't. I have to prepare something for the coach by tomorrow morning, so it'll be a quick sandwich at home for me."

Stephanie didn't think the evening could go any further downhill, but it did. Ray left fifteen minutes later, and Stephanie hauled the rest of them into the dining room, figuring that there was no point in delaying dinner. Then she discovered that in her astonishment she had forgotten about the frozen vegetables. By the time they were ready the casserole was rather cool as well as burned around the edges. Only the salad was tasty, although she realized after they'd eaten it that she had forgotten to add tomatoes.

The conversation was as bizarre as the food. Claire went into her litany of complaints about the day again, and Pete described in detail how she could fix her broken garbage disposal without her having to wait for the plumber. Pete and Claire continued to knock back the drinks, and by the time dessert came around Claire was beginning to giggle as she described her headache.

"All your nerve endings are in your feet!" Pete exclaimed, and Claire giggled harder. Stephanie burst out laughing. Neil remained unaffected by Pete's statement, merely reaching for a second helping of chocolate almond mousse. Obviously he had heard it before.

"I'm telling you the truth," Pete protested, and promptly slid off his chair. For a moment Stephanie thought he had passed out, but then she realized that he was untying Claire's sneakers and pulling them off her feet. "Every nerve in our bodies ends somewhere in our feet. You can get rid of headaches, backaches, anything, by massaging your feet. I know. I've studied it." He pulled off the white terrycloth tennis sock on Claire's right foot, felt the pads beneath her toes for a

moment and began to press with his thumbs. Claire
came several inches up off her chair and let out a yelp.
Pete shifted his fingers and she collapsed into giggles.

Stephanie covered her face with her hands and
contemplated the headache that was starting to sprout
in her own head. Neil watched Pete's performance with
mild interest. Claire, when she stopped laughing, announced that her head was amazingly better. Stephanie
thought to herself that after the number of gin fizzes
Claire had consumed, she doubted that Claire could tell
if she had a head at all. Claire, now revived, lingered
for another hour, and Pete showed no signs of leaving.
The crowning blow came when Claire rose to leave.
Pete stood up too, and turned to Claire. "Say, would
you mind running me home? That way Neil won't have
to go out."

"Of course not."

Neil and Stephanie walked their guests to the front
door and watched them get into Claire's BMW. As
Claire pulled away from the curb Stephanie gave her
friend a final wave. She walked back into the house and
Neil followed her, closing the door behind him.
Stephanie let out a shriek of pure frustration. "I could
just strangle Pete Cherneski! Why tonight of all nights?
He ruined everything. My God, massaging her feet to
cure her headache at the dinner table! Lecturing her
about smoking. Giving us all a course in unstopping
your garbage disposal. And then he had the gall to bum
a ride off her."

A smile hovered around Neil's mouth. "Come on,
Steph, don't get so excited about it. It wasn't that bad.
In fact, I thought it was kind of funny."

"Funny! I was humiliated. Claire will probably never
speak to me again," she fumed, hands balled into fists
and planted pugnaciously on her hips. "How dare you
laugh? Neil, stop that." Neil had gone from a smile to
chuckles to outright guffaws. In a fury Stephanie
grabbed a sofa pillow and hurled it at him, striking him

on the shoulder. He simply laughed harder, dropping onto the edge of a chair and supporting his head on his hands. Stephanie glared at him. Against her will her lips twitched. She smiled. It grew. And then she was laughing too.

She dropped onto the floor beside Neil and gave way to her mirth, recalling every comical mishap. They leaned against each other, howling until their sides hurt and tears ran from their eyes. When at last they calmed down Neil pulled Stephanie up from the floor and into his lap. She leaned against his chest, utterly warm and at home. "I think I'll give up matchmaking."

"It might be a wise idea."

She sighed and snuggled closer, exhausted by her anger and subsequent hysterical laughter. But she'd never felt happier in her life. No matter what had happened, everything was all right. Nothing too major. Nothing too horrifying. Nothing too silly or frustrating or boring. Because Neil was there. It came upon her softly, with no bolt of lightning or clap of thunder. There wasn't even a sizzle of excitement through her nerves. Quite naturally Stephanie nuzzled Neil's neck and murmured, "I love you."

Chapter 12

THE FOLLOWING WEEKS WERE HALCYON. STEPHANIE AND
Neil spent every minute together when he wasn't at the
practice field or a game. They talked about her work,
his fascination with his computer, his interests outside
of football. Neil described the summer camp he and
Asa Jackson planned to establish for underprivileged
children and took her to the location in the mountains
around Flagstaff where they planned to set it up. They
talked about everything, yet it seemed as if they never
ran out of things they wanted to say or grew tired of
listening.

Stephanie's work thrived. Her interviews went well,
as did the rest of her research. Rodriguez and his
former attorney had sent her copies of their papers and
notes, and she had obtained a transcript of the trial and
of the brief the attorney presented on appeal. She
pored over the faded documents, examining the deposi-
tions of everyone involved, as well as police reports,

interviews and the attorney's notes. The story seemed
to come alive for her in the jumbled papers, and soon
she had a working outline for most of the book. It was
as if her creative juices had dried up during the flat,
sterile months after Ty's death, but now her brimming
emotions filled her with energy and creativity. Neil was
interested in her work and often asked about it, occa-
sionally offering suggestions. She was amazed and
impressed by his insight. He even told her he would try
to arrange an interview with the Willoughbys for her.

Stephanie stared at him. "What? Are you feeling all
right? The Willoughbys never give interviews."

He grinned. "I wouldn't be so sure. It seems Bernard
Willoughby is a football fan, more particularly an
Apaches fan. And Russell Ingram knows him. I'm sure
I can wangle an introduction, maybe a little chat with
him, and I'll ask about the interview, if you'd like."

"If I'd like! That'd be the greatest thing in the world
for my book." She ran to throw her arms around him
and kiss him, and their conversation ended, as so many
did, in Stephanie's bed. Their lovemaking was one of
the most blissful elements of those almost perfect
weeks.

But there was a serpent in Stephanie's Eden, and it
took the form of Neil's profession. He loved football,
and she knew he would never give it up until he
absolutely had to, but she was growing to hate it. No
matter how exciting or enjoyable each game was,
Stephanie was a mass of nerves all through it because of
the danger to Neil. Every time he was hit she cringed
inside, and she would grip her hands together so tightly
that her nails bit into her flesh until he was up on his
feet again. It had been bad enough when she was
married to Ty, but it was worse now. She got to the
point where she dreaded the games. She hated going to
them, but she couldn't stand not to see them either.
Hours before the game her stomach would begin to

knot, and as the weeks passed the time of her nervousness extended, so that before long she was a basket case all day Saturday as well as Sunday.

It was midway through the season when Stephanie's worst fears materialized and Neil was hurt in a game. Stephanie came to the game, as always, in the grip of nervous fear. Several of the women and children in the players' section looked up and smiled at her as she sat down. Julie waved cheerfully from her seat a few rows in front of Stephanie. Stephanie tried to respond with equal calm and lightheartedness. She wondered whether the other wives and girlfriends felt the same fears she did inside and hid them just as she did. She glanced at Tonya Hill. The petite black woman seemed utterly carefree as she joked with Chanelle Perkins beside her. Yet Quentin's shoulder had separated each of the last two seasons. The doctors had told him that if he injured it a third time he would have to give up football or face irreparable damage to the joint. Stephanie wondered how Tonya handled her fear that it would happen again. Did she somehow put it out of her mind? Did she pretend it wasn't her husband down there on the field? Or did she simply sit, like Stephanie, with her stomach churning and breathe a heartfelt sigh of relief when the game ended?

The players trotted onto the field. Stephanie lifted her field glasses and focused them on Neil. He crouched down to bounce on the balls of his feet, limbering up. Then he sat spraddle-legged and bent his head to each knee several times. Stephanie watched his serious, set face. She knew him well enough to realize that he wasn't thinking anything, wasn't psyching himself up by building anger against the other team or by pumping up his ego. He wasn't even going over Cheyne's game plan. He had told her one day that during warmup he blanked out his mind and went into a relaxed, unworried state similar to meditation or hypnosis. It was his method of purging negative messages from his mind and getting rid of the mistake-causing tension.

He must have transferred all the tension to her, Stephanie thought wryly, aware of a rushing desire to chew gum, pace, smoke, snap her fingers and do a thousand other nervous things. She'd never get used to it—never. Especially before the game. At least after the game started she could get at least partially caught up in the action and her desire for Neil to do well. She brought down her binoculars and set them in her lap, then took three deep breaths and closed her eyes.

She waited patiently as the players finished their exercises and trotted back to the tunnel. Julie came over to squat down on the stone steps and casually converse with her across three children and two women. When the players returned to the field Julie hurriedly returned to her seat. It was an important game. The opposing team was their chief division rival and was out for blood, since the Apaches had beaten them in the season opener. They had a reputation for hard hitting, not finesse, and their forte was sacking the quarterback, which they managed to do with sickening regularity. Their defense had been given the nickname the "Sack Pack" by the press and fans. In terror Stephanie watched the huge linemen and linebackers charge at Neil, while he stood there, waiting to throw, unintimidated by their rush. Boojie Randall was fond of saying that Neil wouldn't be intimidated by a freight train.

They flattened him twice in the first half, and each time Neil rose without any sign of harm, dusted off his hands and waited for the other team members to join him in the huddle. But late in the third quarter he went down under the brutal rush of one linebacker just as he released a pass. Even from where she sat Stephanie could see Neil's head snap back as he fell, and she cried out, then clamped her teeth down on her lower lip. Asa Jackson caught the pass and the crowd roared, but

Stephanie didn't even glance toward the wide receiver. Her eyes were fixed on the two bodies behind the line. The linebacker, Tony Nowak, lurched up and extended a hand to pull Neil to his feet. Nowak, two years younger than Neil, had gone to the same university as Neil and was one of that strange group of "friendly enemies" which existed in football. Neil didn't move, and Nowak bent closer.

Stephanie's throat was choked. Neil wasn't thrashing about as players did when they had the wind knocked out of them, nor was he simply recovering before he rose. His body was limp. He was unconscious. Stephanie rose to her feet, one hand clenched over her heart. Her face was blanched. Beside her Ruthie slipped her hand into Stephanie's and squeezed encouragement.

On the field other Apache players and a referee went to stare down at Neil, and Tony Nowak returned to his side of the line. The team doctor and head trainer hurried onto the field and knelt beside Neil, blocking Stephanie's view of his head and torso. But she could see his feet and legs, and they didn't move. After another minute the doctor turned and motioned, and two assistants came onto the field with a stretcher. Carefully the four men lifted Neil onto the stretcher, and the assistants picked it up and carried him off the field. Stephanie realized that she was standing and forced herself to sit down. She watched the sidelines as play continued on the field. Again the doctor worked beside Neil, waving a small tube under his nose and checking his eyes. A motorized cart trundled down the outside track and stopped near Neil's inert form. The assistants picked up the stretcher and placed it carefully across the cart. Hal Mintner, the trainer, climbed into the cart to steady the stretcher, and the little vehicle buzzed along the track to the dressing rooms.

Stephanie crawled over the people between her and the aisle and raced up the cement steps. She took the down escalator on the run, and when she reached ground level she tore around the stadium to the dressing room tunnel. An ambulance stood there, back doors open. Stephanie stumbled when she saw it and grabbed at a concrete pillar to hold her up. She braced against the huge column, gasping for breath, and fought to control her fear. An ambulance at the tunnel did not mean Neil was dead. It didn't even necessarily mean they were taking him to the hospital. It could be just a precaution.

Stephanie pushed herself away from her support and approached the tunnel. She met two men coming up the stairs with a portable gurney between them. Neil lay strapped down on the narrow padded table. His eyes were closed and his normally olive skin was sallow. Hal Mintner followed the stretcher up the stairs. Stephanie swallowed and wet her lips. "Hal?"

He glanced up. "Mrs. Tyler! Now, don't you worry. He's okay."

"Where are you taking him?"

"St. Anthony's." Stephanie paled, and he hastened to assure her, "It's all right. That's where we always take them."

Stephanie knew he meant that simply because St. Anthony's Hospital was where Ty had gone, it didn't mean that Neil was dying too. "I know."

"It's a good hospital."

The two attendants wheeled the shaky gurney to the ambulance and lifted it in, collapsing it flat. Mintner turned to her. "I have to ride with him. Team rules. Can you follow in your car?"

Stephanie nodded. Team rules. She couldn't even ride with Neil to the hospital. With a shiver she realized that she didn't really want to. Neil looked too awful for her to want to sit and stare at him for the whole ride. He looked too . . . dead. She wanted desperately to be with him, yet it terrified her. She swung around and walked toward her car, her legs too weak to let her run now. She spent the time calming herself down enough to drive. It wouldn't help Neil any if she got in a car wreck. Oh, Neil, Neil!

She opened her car door and jumped in, heedless of the searing heat. She whipped out of her slot and zoomed through the unpopulated lot, taking the expressway north. Her driving was mechanical. She gripped the wheel tightly but her mind couldn't stay with it. Coherent thought was gone, she realized. She seemed capable only of instinct. It was a ten-minute drive to the hospital. She pulled around to the emergency entrance and parked illegally, then hurried into the emergency room. The attached lounge was large and filled with uncomfortable plastic chairs. A round nurses' station dominated the center of the room, and doors lined the walls. Stephanie didn't stop at the nurses' station, sure they would make her sit in the waiting area away from Neil. Instead she walked along purposefully, glancing into the open doors of the treatment rooms. She found Neil in the third one. He was sitting up on the examination table, his long legs, still in uniform, dangling over the side. They'd removed his jersey and shoulder pads. Two doctors, a nurse and Hal Mintner huddled around him. He leaned heavily on Hal, but at least his eyes were open. He was awake.

Stephanie stepped into the room and Neil saw her. A sickly grin spread across his face. His usually sharp black eyes were dull and cloudy. "Hey, Steph, how are you? What are you doing here? Where's Ty?"

"Ty!" she repeated in shock, her eyes widening.

"Pretty pass, wasn't it?" he went on, not noticing her stunned expression. "Nobody but my man could catch it, huh?"

One of the doctors motioned to the nurse, and she hustled Stephanie out of the room. "I'm afraid you'll have to leave, ma'am. Mr. Moran is being examined."

Stephanie let the woman drag her along. "What's the

matter with him?" she asked. "He's talking about Ty as if he were alive!"

"Mr. Moran is a little confused right now. It's very common for a concussed patient to exhibit some disorientation." The nurse spoke calmingly as she placed Stephanie in a chair. "If you'll wait here, the doctor will let you know Mr. Moran's condition as soon as possible. Are you his wife?"

"No, he's not married. I'm his—" She paused. "Girlfriend" sounded so sophomoric. "We're close friends. We've been friends for years."

The nurse smiled to herself and returned to the examining room, closing the door firmly. Stephanie stared out the plate-glass window at the end of the room. Ty! Why was Neil talking about a man who'd been dead for a year and a half as if he were alive? As if he'd just thrown a pass to him? Stephanie glanced down at her hand. It was trembling on the arm of her chair.

She raised her head at Hal's approach. She started to rise, but he motioned her back down. "They kicked me out too." He sat down across from her and linked his hands, frowning. "What Neil said just now . . . I wouldn't think anything about it, if I were you. I've seen it a lot. They get hit, and sometimes when they come to they think they're somewhere else. In some other time. Neil thinks it's the Minnesota game three years ago when he threw that unbelievable pass to Ty. Neil had a concussion then too, and was out for ten minutes. He's not losing his mind. He'll straighten it all out in a while. Neil's tough, the least fragile quarterback I've seen."

Hal's words reassured her slightly, but she couldn't shake the fear. Neil had sounded too much like Ty had when he was dying. There had been times when Ty thought Neil was his father or that a nurse was Stephanie, or Stephanie a nurse. Nothing had been as sharp as the pain of Ty's looking straight at her and not recognizing her. Of course she knew Neil's confusion was a result of being knocked out. It wasn't caused by a tumor. It didn't mean he was going to die. But knowing it in her head didn't ease the awful feeling in her stomach and chest.

What if Neil died? What if she lost him? She didn't know what she would do, how she would live. With a shock Stephanie realized that she would be much less able to deal with Neil's death than Ty's. She loved Neil so much—more than she had Ty. Ty had been a very special person, a free spirit. She had always had the vague feeling that he was merely visiting her life. But Neil was a part of her. He was entwined in her life, threaded into the warp and woof of the fabric that was Stephanie Tyler. That was why she had been more scared that he would get injured in a game than she had been with Ty. If Neil were hurt, she hurt also. And if she lost him she would lose a big chunk of herself.

Stephanie jumped up, her heart pounding, and began to pace. But when the white-coated doctor emerged from the examining room and walked over to Hal she scurried back to her seat to hear what he said. ". . . a concussion," he was saying as she came up. "He seems to have only the usual symptoms—dizziness, confusion, but I'd like to keep him under observation for a couple of days. He'll be better off here if signs of intercranial bleeding or fluid pressure should occur. Merely a precaution, you understand. Knowing these guys, he'll want to play next Sunday."

The doctor answered Hal's questions and turned to go. Stephanie jumped up to stop him. "Doctor, may I see him now?"

"What? Oh, yes, if you wish. They're taking him to the fourth floor. Ask one of the nurses at the desk for his room number."

When she tiptoed into his room a few minutes later Neil was lying in bed with his eyes closed. His face was still pale, but when he opened his eyes the dullness was gone. He smiled weakly. "Hi, Steph. Good thing it was my head that got hit, huh? Otherwise it might have hurt me."

Stephanie grimaced and took one of his hands in both of hers. "You don't have to play the hero with me."

"I don't? Good. Then I'll admit my head hurts like hell." He paused. "When I first woke up I didn't know where I was. I thought it was the Minnesota game where Ty made that super catch. You know, when I got my first concussion."

"Yeah, I know."

"I'm sorry if I acted weird. It was a strange thing. For just a few minutes there Ty was alive again in my head. I hope it didn't upset you."

Stephanie forced a bright smile onto her face. "It didn't upset me," she lied. "I just thought—well, that's Neil. Doesn't know what's going on."

"Don't make me laugh. My head is killing me."

"I'm sure it is. I'll go and let you get some sleep."

"That's exactly what I'm *not* supposed to do." His mouth turned up in the closest thing to a real smile he'd given yet. "You need to keep a person awake when he's had a concussion."

"In that case I'll sit down."

"How'd the game come out?"

"Honestly!" Stephanie made an exasperated noise. "You're right—your skull's too thick to damage. Why would I have listened to the score when you were lying unconscious on the stretcher?"

"I thought you might have heard after you got to the hospital."

"I was worried then too."

"I shouldn't be glad you were worried, but I am." He smiled, and she returned it tremulously, barely fighting back the tears. It was difficult to act calm and cheerful when inside she was a wreck, but she forced herself to handle it, staying another hour before one of Neil's teammates sauntered into the room and she was able to say good-bye and slip away without feeling guilty.

She felt drained, as if she had been working hard for days. She trailed slowly down the hall and into the elevator and strolled out to her car with equal lassitude. She got in her car and turned on the engine, then sat, the air conditioner blowing over her and the engine idling. She rested her forehead on the steering wheel. Driving home suddenly seemed a monumental task. She wasn't sure she was up to it. Finally she raised her head, put the car in gear and backed out. Afterwards she would barely be able to remember the drive home.

When she reached her house she went straight to the bedroom and flopped onto the bed, one arm thrown across her eyes. She felt so tired that she had thought she would go to sleep at once, but she didn't. There was an overload of adrenaline coursing through her body. Her mind was active, buzzing around, jumping from thought to thought, with one thing clearly repeating itself over and over: I can't do it. Day in, day out. I can't do it.

Slowly her thoughts settled into more coherent lines. Neil was too stubborn to retire. He was in great physical shape. Even though he was thirty-two, he might stay in the business another three or four years. Every Sunday for sixteen regular, four exhibition and however-many playoff games, he would be out there risking his neck. And she would be watching, consumed by fear, praying that he'd make it through one more game. Whenever he was tackled she'd feel the crash and agonize for him. More than that, she'd know the heart-stopping terror that this time he wouldn't get up. That this time when she reached the hospital he wouldn't be sitting up, smiling at her. She couldn't stand it. She simply couldn't.

Stephanie lay there through most of the evening and night, the same thoughts running over and over in her head, interrupted now and then by the heartbreaking thought of what her alternative was. If she couldn't take it, she would be out of Neil's life. She couldn't bear that either! Finally, in the middle of the night, she made her decision. Then she broke down and cried, sobbing out her fear and anguish.

Stephanie woke up early the next morning and struggled into the bathroom to wash her face. After a glance at her image in the mirror she decided that she looked as dead as she felt inside. Her eyes were puffed and red from her long bout of tears, and her skin was waxen. She showered, dressed in a crisp white linen shift and braided her hair in one thick rope, which she wound into a coronet on the crown of her head. Makeup helped her eyes and skin, and a cup of coffee raised her spirits a little, but she rejected the thought of food.

It took her almost thirty minutes to reach St. Anthony's, and by the time she got there the ache in her head had increased and her resolve was wavering. She rode the elevator to Neil's floor and met him as he was emerging from his room. He was dressed in slacks and a sports shirt, still a trifle pale, but other than that looking much his normal self. "Stephanie! You barely caught me. I was leaving."

"The hospital? Are you crazy?"

"Hey, keep it down, would you? I feel like I've got about five hangovers this morning."

Hal Mintner stepped out of Neil's room and Stephanie glared at him. "Are you responsible for this?"

The unfortunate man stopped and stared, amazed at the fury glittering in Stephanie's usually warm blue-gray eyes. "Wha—" he began to stutter.

Neil came to his rescue. "Don't blame him, Steph. He just happened to be here when I checked out. Otherwise I'd have gone home in a taxi."

"The doctor wanted to keep you here for two days, in case you developed some kind of seepage of blood or fluid—although in your case apparently there's more danger of your brain leaking out."

He chuckled, then winced at the effect it had on his head. "I'm okay. Honest!"

"Did the doctor say it was all right for you to leave?"

"Well, he didn't advise it, but he said I didn't have to stay."

"More likely he said he couldn't keep you from killing yourself if you were bound and determined to do it." Stephanie was seething. How typical it was of football players—playing with injuries as if it were something to be proud of. They considered themselves too tough to be downed by broken bones or illness, as mere mortals were. Neil would leave the hospital before he was supposed to, and no doubt he'd manage to play in the next game too. It was foolish. Idiotic. All for some silly game, for winning, as if that was all there was in life. But, no, she was wrong there. Winning *was* the only thing in their lives. Wives, children, other careers were mere sidelines, to be loved when there was time off from their first choice: Football. *The Game*. WINNING.

Stephanie's doubts of the night before vanished. She had made the right decision, the only choice a woman with any self-respect could make. She released a long sigh. "All right. I give up. You'll do exactly what you want, no matter what the risk. Come on, I'll drive you home. Hal won't have to go out of his way."

Neil turned to Hal with a smile. "Sorry, pal, I just got a better offer."

"Can't say I blame you," Hal returned jokingly. "See you tomorrow."

Tomorrow! Stephanie thought, enraged by Neil's careless attitude toward his own health. He was going back to practice tomorrow! He didn't care how she worried about him. He'd go back to playing despite the doctor, despite her, despite everything. Stephanie whirled around and stalked off to the elevators, where she crossed her arms and waited for Neil. Behind her he raised his eyebrows expressively at the trainer, and Hal shrugged as if to say there was no figuring women. Neil smiled to himself. It was obvious that Stephanie was mad at him. He wasn't sure exactly how to handle it. But the reason for her anger was concern over his health, and it warmed him to think she had so much feeling for him. She wanted to protect him. It was funny and sweet.

When he reached her he slid one arm around her shoulders and bent to whisper in her ear, "I'm all right. Really. This happened to me before, and I know what I can and can't do. I promise I won't hurt myself."

"It's pointless to argue the issue with you." Stephanie looked up at him. His face was so familiar, so dear, so beloved. How could she follow through with her decision? How could she not? The love and pain were clear in her eyes, and Neil caught her to him, wrapping both arms around her. "Don't look at me like that. There's nothing to be concerned about."

That's what Ty had always said too. Shoulder and ankle taped, yellow and purple bruises on his back, a shot of painkiller. He always went out on the field no matter how hurt he was. Neil would do the same thing. He wouldn't admit he was too hurt to play until it was too late. The only bad injury was the final one. Stephanie pulled away, turning her head so he couldn't see the sparkle of tears in her eyes. The elevator door opened and she stepped inside. Neil followed, frowning. Stephanie seemed more upset than mere concern over his health warranted.

She drove Neil to his house, where one of the coaching assistants had left his car after the game. It was a long drive, and the silence Stephanie maintained became uncomfortable. She knew that Neil was wondering what was the matter with her, but she didn't want to discuss it until she was at his house and didn't have anything else to deal with. She wasn't able to keep up pleasant chatter until then. After a few conversational attempts Neil gave up. With his headache he really didn't feel like talking anyway. Besides, there was a steadily growing knot of dread in his chest. He didn't want to know what was on her mind.

Stephanie turned off the highway onto the uneven road leading to Neil's house. She drove slowly, mindful of the dips and bumps that could destroy her car's axle—not to mention hurting Neil's already painful head. She pulled up in front of his house and stopped, then turned in her seat to face him. Her insides were icy, but she knew that now was the time. She'd never have more courage or more certainty than she did right now. "Neil, I've been thinking."

Suddenly his heart began to beat faster. The ache in his head grew perceptibly. "About what?"

"Us. I love you, but I don't think it's going to work out between us."

"What? How can you say those two things in the same breath?"

"Maybe it sounds illogical, but it's true."

"Why won't it work out for us?" His face was still and taut, his eyes opaque.

"Because I can't take it anymore. I can't love another football player!"

"Stephanie . . ." He reached out for her, but she pulled back sharply.

"No, I mean it, Neil. It's too much for me."

"You mean the notoriety?"

"No. I got used to that with Ty. I don't enjoy it, but I can live with it. What I can't live with is the worry. I worry when you fly off every other week. What if the plane crashes? I worry before and during every game. I've reached the point where I'm sick all through the game, wondering whether this will be the day you get hurt. Yesterday, when you were knocked out, I nearly went crazy.''

His frown deepened. "That's no reason to—"

"It is! I simply can't stand it. I refuse to be a widow again, Neil.''

"Stephanie, that's ridiculous.''

"Football players don't die?''

"Of course they do, but not from playing football.''

"The other day I read about a boy in Tempe who passed out in football practice, and by the time they got him to the hospital he was dead. He'd had a heart attack.''

"That was a kid. Sometimes that happens. He doesn't know how to pace himself, or the coach doesn't know. Nobody's aware of the fact that he has a weak heart. It's a freak thing, and by the time you get to the pros you know you don't have a heart condition. It's entirely different.''

"Even if you don't die, I know you'll be out there playing when you're hurt, trying to get your head bashed in again or your elbow rebroken or your shoulder dislocated. I can't take the anxiety! Don't you understand? I love you too much! I hurt when you're hurt. I'm scared silly that something will happen to you. Every week it gets worse. I have to stop it. I went through it all with Ty, and I can't do it again. Please, try to understand the agony of sitting in the stands watching someone you love getting hit and thrown to the ground, of seeing him lie there motionless or writhing in pain. I realized Sunday that I love you more than I ever did Ty, and I can't bear the pain.''

His eyes were blazing and his mouth was a thin line. "Damn it! How can you sit there and claim you love me more than you loved Ty and yet tell me you're going to walk? It's senseless. Won't you hurt when you leave me?''

"Yes, of course." She couldn't meet his eyes. "But

the pain will go away in time. I won't feel it every day for the rest of my life."

"No? Then it must be easier for you, Stephanie, because I'll feel it every day for the rest of *my* life. You're lying, you know, even to yourself. You aren't dropping me because you're scared I'll get hurt on the field. I'm healthy and resilient. I have fewer injuries than most quarterbacks my age. And how many more years will I play? Maybe three. My football career is almost over. You won't be facing it 'for the rest of your life.' It's not because I'm a football player. Ty didn't die because he was a football player. He died from a brain tumor. He could have been an accountant or a lawyer or anything else, and he would have died just the same way."

"How do you know? They don't know for sure that repeated trauma might not be the reason for the cancer starting in you. Think of how many athletes get it."

"You're talking out of your head." Neil's hand shot out and wrapped around her wrist. "I'll tell you why you're leaving. You're still too bound up with Ty. You feel guilty because you love me instead of mourning away your life for your dead husband. So you're going to punish us both by running away."

"That's not true!" Stephanie protested automatically. "Please, Neil, don't make this any harder than it already is."

He flung her arm away. She sneaked a glance at him and a thrill of fear darted through her. His nostrils were pinched and white and his eyes glittered ferally. His mouth was thinned almost to nothingness. He was barely keeping a lid on his boiling rage. "Oh, no, I mustn't make it any harder on you, must I?" he asked caustically. "Not fragile little Stephanie, who can't bear to take life as it is. The good *and* the bad. God, what a sap I've been all these years—wasting my heart on someone who isn't woman enough to accept her love, no matter what it entails. Good-bye, Stephanie." He threw open his door and lunged out, slamming the door behind him.

Stephanie watched him stride across the yard and into his house, frozen by his harsh words. The loud click of the front door closing released her from her paralysis and she began to shiver. Neil was gone. Gone. Out of her life forever. That was what she wanted, wasn't it? No, not what she wanted. What had to happen for her own mental well-being. Slowly she put her car in gear and started off down the long, rutted driveway.

Chapter 13

STEPHANIE HAD EXPECTED PAIN AND LONELINESS AFTER her breakup with Neil, but she had never imagined that they would be as bad as they were. There wasn't the shock there had been with Ty or the agony of witnessing his suffering, but the sheer loneliness and sorrow were greater. The knowledge that she had chosen this course made it even harder to bear. Many times during the next few days she told herself that it was for the best, that the worst of the pain would soon pass and that before long she would be happy with her decision.

It didn't help.

She missed Neil physically, emotionally, mentally—every way possible. She missed his warm presence in her bed at night, the sensitive, knowledgeable touch of his fingers on her body, the exquisite pleasure of his lips. Sometimes she woke up sweating and throbbing with passion after a dream about his lovemaking. At those times she ached so much that she would reach for the telephone, but she always managed to put the receiver down before he answered.

It wasn't only the sex she yearned for, wonderful as it had been. Her life was empty without the warm companionship, the shared laughter and thoughts. It was depressing to face each day without Neil's presence at her dining table, barefoot and shirtless, his hair disheveled. She pictured in her mind the way he drank his coffee and yawned until his jaw popped, the way he'd reach out to pull her into his lap as she passed by. The memories made her silent house unbearable. Stephanie found herself storing up thoughts and discoveries about her book to relate to Neil at the end of the day, and it was always a shock to realize that he would not be there to hear them. What had she done before Neil? Who had she laughed with? Where had she gone? It seemed now as if her life were utterly empty.

She had built her love on the solid foundation of friendship. The amazing things he did to her in bed had been an unexpected bonus, another thread that had woven them more closely together. Her love was so strong, their lives so intertwined—how had she ever believed she could simply cut him out of her life? It was ridiculous, crazy. Could her worry about his safety for the next few years be worse than this agony? Her resolve would begin to crumble, and she would think longingly of returning to him.

But what made her think she could return to his arms and be welcomed? she asked herself. Neil had been cold, hard and angry when he left her car. He had accused her of lacking real love and the ability to be a woman. He had sounded as if he hated her. There was no reason to think he wouldn't feel the same now. She had ruined herself in his eyes by being afraid to stick with him. She couldn't go back. He wouldn't want her.

Besides, she had to stick to her position. It was the only way she could save herself from even more misery.

She had to remember that, no matter how hard it was to do without Neil.

The only thing that kept her going, it seemed, was her work, and she was thankful for that. The story of the kidnapped child and reclusive woman who was Marianna Willoughby still held her interest. After several days of moping around the house and office she decided that it was a good time to interview the remaining participants in the drama. She needed to talk to the policeman in charge of the investigation that had resulted in the arrest of Rodriguez, as well as to some of the Willoughbys' former servants. There was also a former character actor, now living in New York, who claimed to have known Angela Drake well during that period. Though Stephanie had her suspicions about the validity of his information, she had to investigate the lead.

She had put off these interviews because she had been reluctant to leave Neil. Now there was no reason to stay in Phoenix, and the change of scenery might relieve some of her unhappiness. She spent most of the next two weeks out of town. The interviews forced her to step outside her own problems, but when she wasn't actually interviewing someone she felt as bad, if not worse, than she had at home. Stuck in a hotel room with nothing to do but watch TV, read or think about Neil, she invariably wound up tearful and miserable.

On Sunday afternoon she was drawn to the television set. The Apaches were playing a Florida team, an important game for both sides. Before the game started there was an interview with Neil which had been made the preceding day. Stephanie watched him hungrily, her eyes taking in every detail. He was his usual assured self. There were no signs of grief or unhappiness about him. Not that she wanted him to be unhappy, Stephanie reminded herself. That was the last thing she wanted for Neil. If there were any way she could have ended it without hurting him, she would have. If his hurt was less than she had expected, that was all to the good. But she couldn't stop the sharp thought that he couldn't have loved her very much if now he could look so calm and natural.

Angered by her selfishness, Stephanie turned off the television and stalked away to stare out the motel window. Children frolicked around the swimming pool, shrieking and jumping in. She decided against going for a swim in the afternoon sun. After all, what could be the difference between Florida heat and Arizona heat? Almost involuntarily she was drawn back to the TV set. She flicked it on and settled into one of the uncomfortable motel chairs to watch. The other team had already scored, and the Apaches seemed unable to get a drive going. Neil's play was erratic—brilliant on one long pass, then lousy on the next two plays. More than once he threw far over the head of his receiver, and every time he walked back to the huddle his face was grimmer and his eyes shot angry sparks.

His concentration was lousy. Stephanie knew it as certainly as she knew her own name. Neil's unswerving concentration was his greatest asset, but this afternoon it was slipping and sliding all over the place. After a controversial call by an official he marched over to the referee, arguing and obviously furious. That wasn't like Neil. Stephanie clenched her hands. Had she done this to him? She'd never dreamed that she might damage his game. That was one area that nothing seemed to affect. She was torn with guilt and sympathetic pain, and for a moment she considered going back to him. She couldn't let his career be wrecked over her.

But, no, that was crazy. She couldn't let her life be wrecked either. She was just looking for an excuse to return to Neil's arms. It wasn't guilt. It was weakness. Neil was having a bad day. It happened all the time. The whole team looked flat today. Next week he'd be back on top.

The show cut to a commercial. There was Neil, a

white towel wrapped around his waist, extolling the
merits of the disposable razor he held in his hand.
Stephanie leaned forward, swept with longing as she
studied his broad tanned chest, lightly covered with
black hair; his muscled arms; his long, sinewy hands.
The black eyes twinkled with suppressed merriment as
he talked, and the unexpected dimple on one side of his
mouth popped in. Stephanie realized that she was
trembling, and she jumped up to turn the television off
again. This time she picked up her purse and headed
out the door, determined not to be lured back to Neil's
image. She'd get in her rented car and drive all
afternoon if necessary.

It was a miserable day and Stephanie was glad to fly
home to Phoenix the following morning. She was
almost finished with her interviews. She needed to pull
her rough outline into better order and start writing.
The first thing she did after she entered the house was
check the answering machine she had recently bought.
There were a few calls: one from her parents, one from
her editor and two from Claire. Nothing from Neil.
Well, that was for the best. He was getting over her just
as she should be getting over him. Only it didn't seem
to be working too well with her. Stephanie threw
herself down across her bed, burying her face in her
crossed arms. She would have to pull herself together
soon. There was a whole life waiting for her. A whole
empty life. She began to cry.

The phone rang and she sat up, hastily wiping away
tears and gulping back her sobs. She couldn't answer
the phone sounding hysterical. Finally, on the third
ring, she lifted the receiver. "Hello?"

There was a fractional hesitation on the other end of
the line. "Stephanie?"

She thought for a moment that her breath had
stopped. She swallowed and forced out his name.
"Neil?"

"Yeah. I—uh, tried to get you a couple of days ago, but your answering machine was on."

"I was out of town doing some interviews for the book." She hoped her voice wasn't trembling the way her hands were.

"That was what I wanted to talk to you about. I have a dinner invitation from Bernard Willoughby. He's willing to meet you and listen to your plans for the book, and to let you meet his daughter. Then he'll decide whether he'll let you question him and Marianna further."

It was the best news she could have received, but strangely Stephanie's heart sank. Was this all Neil had called her about? "Why, that would be terrific, Neil," she forced herself to say, striving for as cool a tone as Neil's. "When?"

"Friday evening. Is that too little notice?"

"No. It'll be fine."

"He expects me to come along." Neil paused. "Like I said, he has a thing about football. I think the main reason he agreed to consider you was because you're Ty's widow. He had a lot of respect for Ty's ability. Anyway, he wants me along. I couldn't get out of it gracefully."

"That's . . . uh . . . all right with me." She had trouble speaking past the tears gathering in her throat. He didn't even want to be around her for an evening! He must hate her for breaking off their relationship—or he'd found out that he hadn't really cared for her as much as he'd thought.

"Good. I'll see you Friday. I'll come by about five-thirty. We're expected at eight."

"I'll be ready."

"Good. Good-bye, Stephanie."

"Good-bye," she whispered, but he'd already hung up the phone.

* * *

Stephanie was dressed and ready to go an hour before Neil arrived on Friday afternoon. After much debating she put on the same dress she had worn to the ceremony retiring Ty's number. She didn't like the memories it carried of that afternoon and Neil's angry kisses, but it looked professional and ladylike, both of which were probably important to Bernard Willoughby. She wondered what he would ask her to determine whether to let her interview his daughter. The thought of answering such important questions turned her palms ice-cold. She wasn't sure whether she were more nervous and scared about meeting Willoughby or seeing Neil again.

Finally the doorbell rang, heralding Neil's arrival, and Stephanie went to answer the door, smoothing her skirt and swallowing her nervousness. Neil was turned away, looking out across the yard when she opened the door. He pivoted back slowly, almost reluctantly, to face her. He was dressed in a tailored three-piece suit of an indeterminate gray-green color that on anyone else would have looked flat and mousy. With his size and distinctive coloring, however, he was able to carry it off. In fact, it was in muted clothing that Neil looked his best. Anything very colorful on Neil was like waving a red flag.

Stephanie forced a smile. She felt as if her face might break. "Hello, Neil."

"Stephanie. Ready to go?"

"Yes. Just let me get my handbag." He waited for her on the doorstep. Stephanie felt a press of pain in her chest. He wouldn't even come inside the house. Her thoughts skittered around as she picked up her purse and returned to the front door. He was as handsome as she remembered, no signs of stress or strain on his smooth face. No sign of anything. He was as blank as ever. More so. There was no friendliness, no liking on his face. They might never have met before for all the warmth in his eyes. How could he treat her like this? How could she expect anything else, after cutting herself off from him?

Stephanie closed the front door behind her and Neil escorted her to his car, opening the door for her but never touching her, even on the arm. Stephanie settled into her seat and closed her eyes, willing herself not to feel the way she did. It was silly. Crazy. Wrong.

Neil backed out of the drive and started for Interstate 10, the highway to Tucson. The silence was thick between them. Stephanie looked across the seat at Neil's profile and wondered what he thought of her now. Would he take her back if she asked him? Or was he closed to her forever? But, no, she couldn't ask. She had known it would be hard without him at first, but later it would be worth it. Soon the pain would ease, and she would be grateful for the rest of her life that she'd had the courage to break up with him.

Stephanie jerked her gaze back to the road. "Thank you for getting me the invitation," she mumbled lamely.

"You're welcome. It was no trouble." They were polite, stilted words, something he might have said to any stranger who'd asked him for his autograph. They were also the last words spoken in the car for almost two hours. After a few minutes of grim quiet Neil switched on the tape deck and shoved a cassette into it. They listened to music the rest of the way. Stephanie leaned her head back against the seat and closed her eyes. She often fell asleep while riding in a car, and though she was certain she would not today, at least she could pretend. It made their enforced closeness less awkward.

Neil glanced over at Stephanie. She was asleep. It eased the tension, but he couldn't understand how she could relax enough to drop off like that. Personally, he was so wound up that it would be hours before he could fall asleep after he got home. No doubt he'd spend half the night wandering around, pacing the floor or lying rigid in bed, trying not to think of Stephanie. When she had first left him, he'd been furious with her for the hurt she'd caused him. At times he had hated her. Why had she let him get close, only to drop him? He felt used, wronged, rejected. She still loved Ty. He would never be able to compete with him, never win her love. He had taken his anger onto the field with him, and most of the time it had hurt his game. The anger gave him drive and energy, but the emotion hurt his accuracy. His passes were often overthrown or thrown so hard the receivers couldn't hold on to them. He was erratic, something he had rarely been in his career.

Gradually the anger had passed, leaving him drained and full of pain. There was no reason to be angry with Stephanie. She had warned him, tried to stop the affair as soon as she found out how deeply he was involved. And he had blithely told her that he could handle it. How naive he'd been; he had thought he'd already felt all the hurts love could dish out. But he had found out that this was far worse than his earlier unknown, unrequited love for Stephanie. He'd never imagined how sharp the pain would be, how much he'd miss her, how his body would ache for hers. He couldn't sleep; he was tense and irritable; he could think of nothing except Stephanie and how miserable he was without her. Yet through all the emotions, rage and pain, there was the lingering hope that she would regret what she had done and come back to him. But after weeks went by without hearing from her, even he had to admit she wasn't going to.

So when Willoughby called and gave him the opportunity to see her again he'd been so excited that he'd literally trembled as he dialed Stephanie's number. Then she hadn't been home, and he had phoned her again and again, going out of his mind with worry and jealousy, picturing her dead, injured, moved or seeing other men. When she finally answered he'd wanted to rage at her and question her, but he managed to keep enough common sense not to. He wanted to see her again—had to see her—and jealous anger would only alienate her. He had kept calm and given her the invitation with all the cool casualness he could muster, and he had been rewarded by her acceptance.

Now he wondered if he'd done the right thing. Stephanie seemed utterly disinterested in him. Lovely as ever, she didn't look as if she had spent any sleepless nights or had any nagging regrets over leaving him. She was cold, and he felt so stiff and awkward that he could think of nothing to say. All he wanted to do was grab her in his arms and kiss her until she let him back into her life. He managed not to, but it took every bit of his willpower and left him feeling drained, remote and unbearably out of place. He could have been with a stranger for all the closeness between them.

Neil's bitter thoughts continued all through the drive south. Just north of Tucson he had to start looking for the exit he was to take, and when he left the wide, smooth interstate and turned onto a small local road Stephanie opened her eyes immediately and glanced around. On either side of the road was rough desert terrain, empty except for cacti and rocks. Now and then the flat land was broken by a wash or gulley. Neil slowed the car, his eyes flickering over the landscape.

"What are you looking for?" Stephanie's words broke the long silence.

"A road. Mr. Willoughby said the turnoff was on the right after that big red boulder."

Stephanie joined Neil's search, shielding her eyes against the glare of the setting sun. It was hard to see anything against its brightness. Finally Neil decided that he'd gone too far and turned around to retrace their route. This time he spotted the faint indication of a dirt road and turned the sturdy vehicle onto it. For the first two or three miles the road was bumpy but adequate. After that it practically disappeared. Neil drove slowly, constantly looking for evidence that they were still on the right path. They crossed a wash which had been graded slightly so cars could cross it.

"Boy, you'd be stuck out here if it rained," Stephanie commented.

"I think that's the general idea. Willoughby used every natural barrier he could as well as manmade ones."

After the wash the huge house materialized in the distance, only the upper stories visible beyond a high fence. Stephanie breathed a little easier. At least now they wouldn't have to search for the road. It was a straight shot. And it was a good thing too, she added mentally, since the road had completely vanished. They bounced over rocks and sand to the high electric fence. A sour-faced man in a brick sentry box came out to meet them. He looked them over carefully, checking something on a clipboard in his hand, then inspected their car before he opened the electronic gates and waved them through. From that point the road was noticeably improved. Closer to the house was a high brick fence with ornate black iron gates set into it. Here another guard emerged from his enclosed box to check them out and open the gates.

Now the road became an asphalt drive which ran through extensive grounds before curving to a stop in front of an imposing brown-brick house. Neil parked close to the front door, a massive affair set with narrow bands of leaded glass. Stephanie stepped out and glanced around her, awed. She had seen pictures of the house in the article she'd read, but its reality was still overwhelming. It was ponderous and somber, despite the carefully tended lawn and the elaborate fountain amidst a trim garden. Stephanie tried to imagine what it would be like to spend almost your whole life in its environs. She couldn't suppress a shudder. The fact that the doors and windows were wired to a sensitive burglar alarm and the lower-level windows were barred on the inside didn't relieve her gloomy impression of the house. It seemed like a very expensive prison.

Neil started up the low set of stairs leading to the double doors and turned back to her questioningly. Stephanie shook off her hesitation. She joined him on the steps and he put an impersonal hand under her elbow to politely guide her to the door. Stephanie reminded herself that it meant nothing. It was a gesture any man might make. Neil rang the doorbell. Moments later a picture-perfect butler opened the door and ushered them into the sitting room.

Bernard Willoughby was waiting for them, seated in a heavy, green velvet chair which even Stephanie's inexperienced eye recognized as an antique. A half-empty highball glass stood on the spindly legged table beside him. He rose, an unforced smile creasing his features as he extended his hand to Neil. "Neil! Good to see you again. I was certainly relieved to see you guys pull out that game in the last quarter."

Neil smiled. "Not as relieved as I was. Mr. Willoughby, I'd like you to meet Stephanie Tyler. Stephanie, this is Bernard Willoughby."

"What's this Mr. Willoughby stuff?" the man protested jovially. "I told you to call me Bernard. You too, Stephanie. Glad to meet you."

He held out his hand and Stephanie slipped hers into it. His handshake was firm and warm, and Stephanie felt a twinge of liking for the man. She hadn't expected to. But then, she had expected a pale, grave paranoic, not this craggy-featured, bluff, heavyset man. His hair was iron-gray, not the salt-and-pepper it had been in the photographs taken at the time of the kidnapping. He had not been handsome in his photographs, but his face hadn't yet acquired the thickening and roughening of age.

"Thank you for allowing me to come," Stephanie replied, managing to cut off the "Mr. Willoughby" but unable to call him Bernard.

"My pleasure. Could I offer you a drink?"

Neil requested his usual whiskey and soda. Stephanie took a glass of white wine. Willoughby went to an unobtrusive wet bar in the corner and poured their drinks, returning with them on a small silver tray. Stephanie's wine was in a fragile crystal wine glass that looked as if it might break if she breathed on it. He indicated that they should sit down, and Stephanie perched on a small straight-backed chair close to Mr. Willoughby.

"I apologize for my daughter. Marianna is running a little late tonight. She'll be down in a few minutes." Stephanie suspected that the girl had received clear instructions to leave the visitors alone with her father for a while. Willoughby turned toward Stephanie. "Your husband was one of the finest athletes I've ever seen play."

"Thank you."

"I wish I'd met him. He had tremendous talent. I enjoyed watching him. I was an all-Ivy league halfback at Yale, you see. Football's one of my favorite pastimes."

"Yes, I learned to enjoy it after I met Ty."

"Moran here tells me you want to do a book on my little girl."

"Yes."

"I've read your other books. Didn't care much for the one you ghosted for Blonsky's wife. You write well, don't get me wrong. I just didn't like the subject matter. But that last one, the one Neil gave me, it was well done. You write fairly, no preaching or slanting the facts. I like that. Plus you're not sentimental—clean, straightforward. If I approved of anyone writing the story, I'd take you. But we've made it a point to live quiet lives since the kidnapping. I don't know that I want Marianna's life made public."

Stephanie refrained from pointing out that he had nothing to say about whether the book was written or not. Instead she leaned forward and presented her case. "It's quite a story, the kind of thing a writer can't pass up. The kidnapping and the two trials are already public. The Rodriguez case was a significant event in American judicial history. I'll touch on that, of course, but primarily I want to delve into the human issues. The first part of the book will be almost a detective story covering the actual kidnapping and the searches for the kidnappers. But the last section will focus on how the lives of everyone involved were changed by that event. What happened to Rodriguez? To the detective who was wrong and the one who was right? What about the maid who lied for her boyfriend, then turned him in? What happened to Marianna and her family? That's what really fascinates me: your daughter's life since the kidnapping."

"It hasn't been at all sensational."

"I realize that. But it's been most unusual. I think it would fascinate readers."

"I'm sure it would. But why should I allow that invasion of our privacy?"

"To insure that the facts are straight. To make certain that people will get a proper picture of Marianna and her life."

He watched her with narrowed eyes. "You're telling me that you'll write the book whether or not I wish it."

"Yes."

He was silent for a moment, studying her. "I'd rather you didn't. I've fought hard to keep Marianna from being exposed to the public."

"I realize that, and I respect your wish for privacy. I certainly understand it, having been married to someone famous. Unfortunately, your position, your wealth, the kidnapping, your ex-wife's fame—all make your daughter a public figure whether you like it or not. Even if I don't write it, someone else is bound to pick up on this story. You can't keep it from being written.

But I can promise you that I won't invent anything, and I'll get my facts as straight as possible."

"And it's much more possible to get the facts straight if you talk to us?"

"Naturally."

Bernard sighed and strolled over to a large table, where he opened a wooden box and extracted a cigar. He offered Neil one, then went through the ritual of snipping the end off the cigar and lighting it before he turned back to Stephanie. "Young lady, you intrigue me. I have to admit I had my mind set against your doing the interviews. I invited you here solely as a favor to Neil Moran, whom I admire greatly. However, you've interested me in this book of yours. I like your writing and your approach. Tell you what, I'll let you do it as long as you follow my conditions. First of all, I won't talk about my business affairs, but I'll tell you about the kidnapping or anything else. Secondly, you're not to question Marianna about the kidnapping. I don't want her reminded of it. With her you'll stick to her present life, her life since the kidnapping. Do you agree?"

"Yes, certainly. I have no desire to bring up unpleasant memories for your daughter."

"All right. You can see Marianna whenever she wishes. As for my interview . . . I'll be out of town for the next two weeks. I'll set up an appointment when I get back." He paused, musing, puffing at his cigar. "You know, I think it will be good for Marianna to be around you."

Stephanie covered her surprise. "Why, thank you."

Willoughby sat back down and began a discussion with Neil about the next week's game. Stephanie stayed out of the conversation, hugging her joyous knowledge to herself. She could have danced and sung with sheer excitement. Never had she expected to pull off an interview with Marianna Willoughby herself. That alone would push her book's quality and interest level several notches higher.

There was the sound of footsteps on the marble entry, light, eager steps, and a young girl entered the room. She was dressed in a deceptively simple outfit of straight-legged blue trousers and a white blouse with sheer double sleeves edged in bands of red, yellow and blue. Stephanie could tell at a glance that it was a designer creation and had probably cost an outrageous sum. Marianna Willoughby was small, the fragility of her appearance enhanced by large, liquid brown eyes, a heart-shaped face and a mass of long honey-blond hair tumbling down her back. She wore no makeup on her golden-toned skin, only lipstick and mascara. She seemed much younger than twenty-four, more like eighteen—although Stephanie doubted that you could find an eighteen-year-old today who had quite that innocence in her face. She looked as unspoiled and untouched, as timid and glowing as a Victorian maiden.

Marianna hesitated at the threshold of the room, a shy smile on her lips. "Hello. I'm sorry I'm late."

Neil rose to his feet, a sort of hushed wonder on his face, and Stephanie's heart twisted with jealousy. She had to remind herself that Neil did not belong to her and that she had to get along with Marianna. She soon found out that that particular task would not be difficult. Marianna was naive enough not to dissemble, but she wasn't the child she looked, either mentally or emotionally. The result was a woman who didn't hide how she felt, said exactly what she thought, was engagingly frank and curious yet surprisingly intelligent and well informed. Stephanie couldn't help but enjoy her company.

The meal was delicious, the talk lively and Stephanie's spirits should have been high as a kite. But the strain between herself and Neil turned the evening bitter. It was a relief when, after the meal, Bernard pulled Neil away to the small theater to show him

treasured films of early football games. Stephanie and
Marianna were left alone, smiling at each other tenta-
tively. "Would you like me to show you the house?"
Marianna asked.

"That would be nice."

"You've seen the dining room and sitting room, and
Papa's study is off-limits. I'll show you everything
else, though. Let's go to the library first. It's my
favorite."

"You read a lot?"

"All the time. That's the only way I learn, because
I've never really seen anything, you know." Her soft
voice was tinged with regret. "I mean, since I've been
old enough to remember."

"Your father gave me permission to interview you
for the book I'm writing."

"Did he?" Marianna beamed at Stephanie. "I'm so
glad. Papa can be very stuffy about things like that. But
I'll enjoy talking to you. You're different from anyone
I've ever met before."

"How?"

"You're the only woman I know who works for her
living but isn't a servant or a tutor. One of my cousins
dabbles in the theater, but it isn't really a job. She
doesn't depend on it for food. She just does what she
wants. But you—you're independent. I think what you
do is fascinating. I've read your books. I admire your
writing, but I think I admire your lifestyle just as
much."

Stephanie glanced at her questioningly. "Really? I'm
pretty ordinary."

"Not to me. I've never been anywhere or done
anything like you have. I have a lot of possessions, but
I'd be lost if I had to leave this house."

"Is that why you stay here?"

Marianna nodded. "Papa is scared for me to leave,
so I stay partly for his sake. But I'm scared to leave too.
Why, do you know, I couldn't even drive a car! I

wouldn't know how to buy food or find a place to live or anything that everyone else can do."

They finished the tour of the enormous first floor and moved up the grand staircase to the second floor. Marianna showed Stephanie the vast playroom where her childhood toys still sat, and the study next to Marianna's bedroom where she had taken lessons from a succession of tutors. The more Stephanie saw, the more fascinated she became. Marianna's life really did have the ring of a fairy tale. Of course the *Alice in Wonderland* hair and pretty young face encouraged that impression, but even if Marianna had been old and had dark, cropped hair she would still have been charmingly, frighteningly ignorant. When they touched on the subject of her marriage she spoke guilelessly about her distant cousin Wesley, indicating what seemed to Stephanie a very tepid response to him.

"Do you love him?" Stephanie asked bluntly, amazed to find herself genuinely concerned over the girl's happiness.

Marianna considered the question seriously, her lovely brow wrinkling. "I'm not sure," she said finally. "I know that must sound silly. But, you see, I'm not sure how love feels. I mean, I love my father and Aunt Sally and Mother, most of the time, but that's not the same feeling, is it? I like Wesley. He's very nice to me. But I've never been around other men. Only Papa's friends and members of the family. I don't know what most men are like. I don't know how I'm supposed to feel about my fiancé. There are so many things I haven't experienced. I think my emotions must be rather shallow because of that. Don't you?"

Stephanie stared at her helplessly, wishing she could deny the girl's candid assessment. But how could she? If Marianna had never known pain or despair or joy or any of the thousands of emotions people dealt with daily, how could she be expected to know what she felt or whether any of her emotions were strong? "Perhaps you should find out some of those things before you commit yourself to your cousin."

Marianna turned a troubled golden-brown gaze on her. "I know. But Papa would be very disappointed. He wants so much for me to be protected after he dies, just as he's protected me. I don't want to displease him. Besides, Wesley knows me. He understands me. He's not scary. I wouldn't know how to talk to a man like your Neil." Stephanie started to protest the girl's characterization of Neil as hers, then shut her mouth. Despite her naivete, in some ways Marianna was quite perceptive. "I'm better off with Wesley."

"Safer," Stephanie corrected.

"Yes. Safer." Marianna gave her a small smile. "I must seem very dull and cowardly to you. You deal with life head-on. I can't imagine you hiding."

Marianna's innocent words burned through Stephanie like acid, and her mouth twisted into a wry smile. "You'd be surprised just how cowardly I am."

Chapter 14

SATURDAY MORNING STEPHANIE WENT OVER HER NOTES IN preparation for her interview with Marianna Willoughby. It would take a complete knowledge of the material as well as some cleverness to ask only questions which had nothing to do with the kidnapping. However, she had difficulty keeping her mind on the work at hand. Her thoughts crept back to Neil and the evening before. It had been nerve-racking being around him. She'd been far too aware of his appeal, too hungry for his touch. Being away from him was bad enough, but being around him without any closeness between them was refined torture. She was sure she would gladly have flung herself into his arms if he had shown the slightest interest in having her back. But he hadn't.

Neil hated her. She was certain of that now. It had showed last night in every taut line of his carriage, in the way he'd avoided touching her or even looking at her. Well, she ought to be glad of that. If Neil were able to hate her, he'd have an easier time getting over her.

And she wanted things to be easy for him. She didn't want him to hurt as she was hurting.

She'd made the right choice. She was better off without him. Safer . . . safer! Good heavens, now she sounded like Marianna Willoughby. Stephanie frowned, but before she could turn her mind to the implications of that thought the telephone rang. She jumped up and answered it almost gratefully. "Hello?"

"Stephanie, how are you? This is Claire. I've been trying to get you for over a week."

"I've been out of town on interviews. I'm sorry I haven't gotten in touch with you sooner. . . ." She'd neglected Claire ever since that disastrous dinner and she felt guilty for it. At first she'd been too happy to want to get into an apology for the fiasco and another long session about Claire's miserable love life. Then she'd been too sad.

"Don't worry. Truthfully, I hadn't realized how long its been till last week. How about lunch to make up for the long absence?"

"Not today," Stephanie demurred quickly.

"Next week. Whenever."

"Why don't you come over for a visit? I'm not big on going out right now."

"I wondered why I hadn't seen you at the games. What's the matter?"

"*You've* been going to the Apaches games?"

"Sure. You mean you don't know?"

"Know what?"

Claire laughed. "Boy, you really have been out of touch with the Apaches' wives."

"Well, Neil and I . . ."

"That's the reason I want to take you out to lunch. I owe you for the favor."

"What favor?"

"Introducing me to Pete."

"Cherneski?" Claire must have meant to be sarcastic, though she wasn't carrying it off well. "I'm really sorry about dinner that night. It was a fiasco. I hadn't planned for it to go like that."

"Well, I was pretty upset that I hadn't dressed up when Neil and Pete arrived. But the result was great."

She wasn't being sarcastic, Stephanie decided. "You . . . uh, you mean, Ray called you after that?"

"Ray? Who's he?"

"Ray Cooper, the coach."

"Oh, the one Neil and Pete caught a ride with. No, why should he call me?"

"Then what worked out?"

"Pete and me. What else? Honestly, Stephanie, I'll be eternally grateful to you for having me over that night."

"You and Pete?" Stephanie repeated, stunned. Surely Claire couldn't be serious. Pete was attractive in his own rugged way, of course, and he could be fun to be with, but he was also several years younger than Claire, pulled crazy stunts and was far too physical for a person with Claire's artistic bent. Wasn't he?

"Why do you sound so astounded?" Claire's voice sounded hurt. "Do you think I'm too old for him?"

"No, of course not. But you two are so different. Claire, you aren't joking, are you? To get back at me for the dinner?"

Claire burst out laughing. "No! No, no, no! Why should I want to get back at you? I'm the happiest woman in Phoenix, Arizona. Pete is absolutely wonderful. He came home with me that night to fix my disposal for me—you remember how I was having trouble with it. Then he stayed, and we drank coffee and talked for a long, long time and, well, it went on from there. I'll admit Pete's a little strange sometimes, but most of that is an act he puts on. It's part of his linebacker image."

"But he's such a jock!"

"I know. Isn't it crazy? I also know he's eight years younger than I am. But I'm in love with him anyway. He makes me very, very happy. So how important can the rest of it be? I figure you have to take some risks or you're never going to have anything. Pete's a risk, I know, but I intend to get all the enjoyment I can out of this thing, even if I lose him in the end."

Stephanie listened as Claire continued to rave about Pete's good qualities. Finally Claire wound down and Stephanie agreed to meet her the following week for lunch. After she hung up Stephanie flopped down in her easy chair and crossed her arms above her head. Imagine that! Ironic, when she thought about it, how she had cursed Pete for ruining her matchmaking dinner for Claire—and then Claire had fallen for him! A smile twitched across her face. Maybe it was the foot massage that had gotten to her.

There was a sharp rap on her office door, and Stephanie sighed. She was never going to get any work done at this rate. She opened the door to find Julie Koblitz there, her arms crossed and her eyes blazing with anger. "Julie?" Stephanie began tentatively, taken aback by the other's expression.

"Honestly, Stephanie!" Julie exclaimed, uncrossing her arms and setting her fists firmly on her hips. "You haven't got the sense of a . . . a turtle! Why did you drop Neil Moran?"

Stephanie moved back into her office. "Please, Julie, let's not talk about that."

Julie followed her relentlessly. "*That* is exactly what I came over here to talk about. I could just choke you with my bare hands. What is the matter with you? How could you let a wonderful guy like Neil go?"

"Because I couldn't stand to sit around year after year watching him bash in his brains! I don't have your calm acceptance, Julie. I've already lost one husband, and I refuse to worry myself sick about losing Neil too. I don't have the makeup for a football wife!"

"You mean you're making Neil choose between you and football?"

"No, of course not."

"That's what it sounds like to me."

"I didn't say that. I never thought it. Neil loves football. He won't quit until he's too old and tired and broken to stay on the field. I know I can't compete against the game. But that doesn't mean that I have to stick around and watch it happen to him."

"Don't try that excuse on me. It might have worked on Neil, but I know better. It's not football or Neil's getting hurt that you're afraid of. You'd be scared silly even if Neil were a stockbroker. What frightens you is being in love. It hurt you so much when Ty died that you'll do almost anything to avoid getting hurt like that again. You're not afraid of football. You're terrified of loving Neil and maybe losing him because you'd have to endure all that hurt again."

"Worse," Stephanie murmured.

"What?"

"I said 'worse.' The pain would be a lot worse. I loved Ty, but nothing like I love Neil." Stephanie sighed and stood up. "Maybe you're right. Maybe I am scared of love, not the dangers of football. What difference does it make? I have to protect myself. My love for Neil could end up tearing me apart. He was becoming the center of my life. How could I live if I lost that?"

"Why should you lose Neil?"

"Someday I will!"

"Well, yes," Julie countered sarcastically. "He'll die of old age. Do you plan to live the rest of your life without loving anyone just so you won't get hurt? What kind of a life would that be?"

Stephanie stared at her. Finally she murmured, "A life like Marianna's."

"Who?"

"Somebody I know. I . . . I pitied her because she'd been so protected from everything for years that she's experienced almost nothing. She doesn't know what love is. She's been kept safe, but at what a price! Last night I felt sorry for her. I thought how terrible it must be to live in such a wasteland of feelings." Stephanie's eyes widened and her voice vaulted upward. "But that's exactly what I'm doing to myself! I've cut out the love in my life because I was scared of the consequences."

"Hallelujah!" Julie threw up her hands in exaggerated relief and flopped down on the nearest chair. "She's finally come to her senses."

Stephanie stared into space. It was so clear suddenly, so obvious. Why hadn't she realized it before? But she knew the answer to that—because she hadn't wanted to. She had been too scared. And now she'd waited until it was too late. "What am I going to do?"

"What do you mean? Go to Neil, of course. What else?"

"You don't understand. Neil doesn't care about me anymore. He . . . he hates me, I think."

"Have you lost your mind?"

Stephanie turned to Julie, her eyes wide and dark with pain. "Last night he acted as if he hardly knew me. He took me out to visit the Willoughbys, but it was obvious he did it only because he'd already committed himself to the project. You know how he is about duty. He hardly talked to me all evening. He was stiff and cold, as if he despised me."

"How do you expect him to act? You told him to get lost a couple of weeks ago. My God, Stephanie, the man's loved you for years. Finally he gets you into his bed, and the two of you are as happy as can be. He thinks his dreams have come true. Then you call it off. How do you expect him to feel? Happy? He's hurt. It's only logical that he would be. Of course he was stiff with you. I'm sure he didn't know what to do or say, loving you and knowing you're off-limits again. He was probably trying to decide whether to strangle you or drag you off to bed!"

Laughter spurted from Stephanie's throat, the first she'd felt in days. "Oh, Julie, do you think so?"

"I *know* so. Didn't you watch the game last Sunday? Neil was miserable. His concentration was shot to hell. That doesn't happen to a player like Neil Moran unless he's in a bad emotional state. Maybe he is angry at you for dropping him, but underneath that is a huge amount of pain. He loves you!"

Stephanie's eyes shone. "I hope you're right. 'Cause if not, I'm going to make a terrible fool of myself."

Neil curled his hand around his cup of coffee and gazed out the wide windows of his living room. It was dawn and the sun was floating up, cresting the distant mountains and washing the city of Phoenix below him with light. Neil hardly noticed the spectacle. His thoughts were turned inward, as they had been most of the night. He had tossed and turned, now and then dozing off, only to awaken with a start and set his mind back on the treadmill.

The evening had been vicious. Stephanie had looked lovely; she had sparkled and laughed with Bernard Willoughby, and on the drive home she had bubbled with enthusiasm over the prospect of interviewing Marianna. Once she had reached over and squeezed his hand, beaming, and thanked him for getting her the invitation. At her touch desire had pounded in him, hot and hard, temporarily obliterating the pain. He wanted her, wanted all of her: her body, her smile, her bright mind and quick tongue, her inquisitive, eager sexuality. Frustration flooded him. Even after he dropped her off at her house and drove up the mountain to his home his entire being surged with thwarted love and passion.

He wanted Stephanie so much that he ached in both mind and body. But he couldn't have her. She refused to let him. It was an impossible situation, like pushing at a stone wall. He'd never given up before, never accepted defeat. No matter how many times he failed at something or lost what he was striving for, ultimately he'd succeeded because he wouldn't take loss as an ending. He kept on until he won, no matter how difficult or painful. He worked, he traded off, he did whatever had to be done. But this time . . . He was hemmed in, stymied. He couldn't force her to love him, couldn't make her take him back. There was no one to fight, to defeat, except the woman he loved, and if he did that he'd lose her just as surely as he was losing her now.

His turbulent thoughts had kept him awake most of the night, and finally he had given up and left the bed to shower, dress and fix himself a cup of coffee. He drank the coffee, staring sightlessly out at Phoenix. When he finished the cup he jumped into his car and drove to the practice field. The team had its usual light Saturday morning workout. The mood he was in, he welcomed the work. He only wished it were harder. By the time they quit and showered he had worked out only a fraction of his frustration. He would have liked to sweat the previous night out of his system, but he knew that was impossible. He would never be able to get Stephanie out of his system. He'd lost that battle long ago, before Ty died.

Suddenly he froze, staring at himself in the mirror as he toweled his hair dry. He was wrong when he thought he'd never been defeated before. He had accepted defeat with Stephanie long ago. She had been Ty's wife, and there had been no way to win. He'd given up. And now he saw that that was his whole problem. He expected to lose Stephanie. He'd never really believed she was his—had just enjoyed their affair in a kind of stunned wonder without believing it would last.

He thrust his hands in his pockets, his mind racing. Why was it impossible for them to be together? Because Stephanie had told him so? When had he ever let that stop him? The word impossible was normally just a challenge to him. But he had accepted it from Stephanie because he was accustomed to losing with her. His eyes took on a fierce light. Damn it! He wasn't going to give up. He would get Stephanie back. He tossed the towel aside and hurried to his locker, ripping out his clothes and pulling them on. By the time he left the locker room he was running.

Stephanie hurried into the house and headed for her bedroom, not even saying good-bye to her friend. A perfect scheme had popped into her mind. A few years ago she had received a gag gift from some girlfriends. It was an alluring outfit they had ordered from a risqué magazine. She'd never had the nerve to wear it, but now it seemed the perfect way to tell Neil that she wanted to return to him—as well as the perfect way to insure his acceptance of her offer. She pulled open the bottom drawer of her dresser and dug through the odds and ends of unused clothing until she came upon the plastic sack she wanted.

She pulled out the contents of the bag and spread them across the bed. As she studied the skimpy garments lying on her bedcover a slow smile spread across her face. That ought to do the trick, all right. Quickly Stephanie ran a bath, dumping in a capful of bath oil to scent her skin. As she soaked she planned her strategy. She would drive to Neil's house, slip into the costume and be sitting invitingly on his bed when he came home from practice. No, that wouldn't work. Today was Saturday, and he had only a very light practice this morning, so he might be home. Well, then, she'd have to put on the outfit before she went. After all, she couldn't very well walk in the door, say "Excuse me" and slip into the bathroom to change. If she wore her light raincoat over the X-rated costume she could slip off the coat as she walked in. She giggled, thinking of Neil's face when he saw her, then sobered abruptly. What if he didn't react as she expected? What if he shouted at her for walking out on him? Worse yet, what if he sneered at her pathetic attempt at sexiness and ordered her out of his house? Stephanie shook her

head. No, she couldn't let herself think that way. Neil
might not react as she hoped, but she refused to let the
fear of his rejection stop her. She must remember what
Claire had pointed out—you had to take risks if you
didn't want an empty life. And the last few weeks had
very clearly shown her how empty her life was without
Neil. No matter what happened, it was worth the
effort.

Stephanie piled her hair on top of her head in a
painstakingly careless fluff of curls, allowing a few
tendrils at her temples to escape seductively. After
putting on a touch of makeup she turned to the clothes
lying on the bed. First she slipped on the narrow black
satin panties, cut high on the hips at the side and back.
Next she wrapped the main garment around her and
fastened it with snaps up the front. It was made of black
satin with black lace ruffles across the low-cut neckline
and around the bottom, and it was fashioned to resem-
ble a wasp-waisted Victorian corset. The bra inside the
corset pushed her breasts up so that they seemed about
to spill out. The layer of cloth across the top of the
garment was merely black lace, which served only to
temptingly shadow, not hide, the dark circle of her
nipples. The outfit ended just above her thighs, making
the little panties necessary, and dangling from the hem
in front and back were long black garters.

She sat down on the bed to slip into the black net
hose and fasten them to the garters. For the final touch
she tied a wide black velvet ribbon around her throat.
Then she slipped into black high heels and surveyed her
image in the mirror. She assumed a sexy pose, pursing
her lips into a Marilyn Monroe-esque pout, which she
spoiled by giggling. Well, silly it might be, not to
mention tarty, but it shouldn't leave Neil calm and
collected. And that was the whole point of the costume.

She put on her tan trenchcoat-style raincoat, and
once it was buttoned and belted no one would have
guessed how little she had on beneath it. The black

hose might look a little strange, but they wouldn't show in the car. She went into the den to get her keys and purse, then started out the front door. There was a car parked at the curb and a man hurrying up her sidewalk. She had taken two steps before her brain registered that it was Neil marching toward her, his brows drawn together in a fierce frown. "Oh, no," she moaned under her breath. Her whole plan was ruined.

Before she could move or even think Neil was upon her, and he seized her elbow in a savage grip, whipping her around and back into the house. "Damn it, Stephanie," he began furiously. "I am not going to let you do this to us!"

"What?"

He propelled her into the entryway and slammed the door behind him. "You heard me. I refuse to let you tear us apart because you've got some crazy, freaky notion that I'm going to get killed playing football." He paused, for the first time noticing her attire. "Why the hell are you wearing a raincoat? It must be ninety-five degrees out there and not a cloud in sight."

"Uh . . . well, it's—"

He made an impatient gesture. "Never mind." He grabbed her elbow again and stalked down the short hall into the den. "You're going to sit down and listen to me."

Stephanie perched obediently on the edge of the couch, holding the edges of her coat together over her knees. Neil crossed his arms and began to pace. "I've loved you for four years now. I loved you and wanted you all the time you were married to my best friend. I loved you all through his death and afterwards, holding back until you were ready for another relationship with a man. When you finally came to my bed I fell even more in love with you. It seems impossible, but somehow I desired you more and more every day. I couldn't get enough of you. I still can't." He turned to her, fixing her with his piercing black gaze, carefully emphasizing each word. "I love you. And I'm not about to give you up."

"Neil," Stephanie began, starting to rise.

"No, I want to say the whole thing." He waved her back down. "I won't let you do this to me. To us. At first I thought you'd change your mind, that you were still suffering some kind of emotional backlash from Ty's death. Then I realized you weren't going to. When I called you, you had that damn machine on. I nearly went out of my mind for ten days, wondering where you were and who you were with."

"I was interviewing people for my book."

He plowed on as if she hadn't spoken. "I took you out to the Willoughbys, hoping that if we were together we might talk it all out. But you were so cool, and I felt so stiff and awkward. . . . I didn't know what to say. And I hated like hell the way you could turn your feelings for me on and off."

"That's not true!" Stephanie cried, goaded. "*You* were the one who was cold and standoffish."

"*I* was the one who sat there all night feeling like a fool, wanting you so bad I could taste it and not knowing how to make you listen to me. How to make you love me and want me."

"Neil!" She rose, torn by the pain in his voice and face. "I do love you. I do want you. The last couple of weeks have been horrible for me too."

"Then why did you do it?" he thundered. "Why didn't you come back to me?" He made a frustrated gesture and half turned away. "I couldn't sleep last night. I lay awake wanting you all night long. I can't live this way any longer. Stephanie, I love you and I intend to marry you, even if I have to tie you up and drag you to the church!"

A brilliant smile broke over Stephanie's face and she giggled. "How romantic."

He glowered at her. "Why are you still wearing that raincoat? Take it off."

"Yes, sir," Stephanie replied demurely and stood up, her fingers going to the belt of her coat. Neil continued to talk as she unbuttoned the coat. Then she grasped the lapels and drew it over her shoulders and down her arms, letting it drop onto the ground.

Neil's voice turned into a croak and stopped abruptly. His eyes widened and he stared at her, shock quickly changing to blazing heat. "Stephanie . . ."

Stephanie smiled, sauntering toward him with her hands on her hips, luxuriating in the stunned lust in his expression. She stopped two feet away from him, her head slightly tilted at a challenging angle. "Well?"

He swallowed. "God, you're gorgeous. This wasn't—I mean, you weren't going out to see another man, were you?"

"I was coming to your house."

"Good. 'Cause I think I would have choked the—" He broke off and pulled her into his arms, his mouth seeking hers desperately. She opened her lips to his questing tongue, twining her own around his, exploring the sweet warmth that had been missing for so long. It was a slow, delightful rediscovery which brought with it the shattering realization that they desired each other more than ever. Neil pulled away just long enough to murmur, "I love you."

She didn't even have the time to return his words of love before his mouth captured hers again and his hands began to roam her body. His fingertips massaged her back and hips. He caressed the smooth flesh of her thighs between the tops of the stockings and the hem of her panties, teasing his senses with the different textures of skin, lace and satin. Stephanie could feel the heavy thud of his heart quicken as he traced the outline of the slick undergarment and discovered how scantily it was cut. His breathing was ragged as he released her and stepped back. Slowly he looked her over, his hands sliding over her in the wake of his eyes. He skimmed along the lace-decorated neckline, his fingertips grazing the quivering white flesh of her breasts. His thumbs came back to trace the outlines of her nipples beneath the thin lace, encouraging them to swell and harden.

Stephanie was hot and molten inside, and she squeezed her legs together in an attempt to curb the restless yearning there. Neil's hands drifted across her bare shoulders and chest, creating a sweet torture within her. Stephanie sucked in her breath, her head falling back, her face contorting in a grimace of burgeoning desire. Neil knelt and unfastened the hose from their garters, pausing to kiss and nibble at the white flesh exposed between the black above and below. With infinite care he took off her shoes and rolled down each stocking in a long caress. He stood and swept one hand down the snaps of the garment, popping them open. The satin and lace corset fell from her, leaving her clad only in the seductive panties.

He cradled her breasts in his tanned hands and bent to kiss the sensitive centers. His face was slack with passion, his eyes scorching as his hands slid down her body and edged under the briefs. When he touched the damp warmth at the joinder of her legs he shuddered and cupped his palm hard over the fleshy mound. His touch affected him as much as it did her, Stephanie discovered as she ran her fingers lightly down his front and grazed the hardness pressing against his trousers. Neil drew in his breath sharply. "Shall I undress you now?" Stephanie asked him, and he nodded silently.

She rolled up the pullover shirt he wore, sliding her palms over his body as she did so. He lifted his arms and she drew the shirt off over his head, then returned to tangle her fingers in the crisp black hair of his chest. Delicately she brushed her fingertips over the flat masculine nipples and felt them tense in response. Stephanie leaned forward to outline the small buds with the tip of her tongue, delicately spiraling around them before she pressed her lips to them, drawing each sensitive button into the warm, moist cave of her mouth.

Neil's hands moved over her almost frantically, and his murmurs were incoherent as he rolled his face in the fragrant mass of her hair. Stephanie slipped down his body, her mouth tracing the line of hair which stretched from his chest to his navel and blossomed below. Her tongue dipped into the well of his navel as she knelt before him and unfastened his trousers. Neil crushed her hair in his hands, his fingers working helplessly as she continued her liquid exploration of his midriff. She sat back on her heels and lifted his feet one at a time to pull the shoes and socks from them. Neil watched her from above, entranced by the gentle, fluid movement of her breasts as she worked. At last she pulled his trousers down his legs, skimming his flesh with her fingers as she went. Stephanie removed his underwear in the same manner, turning the process into sensual play.

She explored his lower body as carefully as she had his chest, her fingertips fluttering over his trembling flesh. Neil uttered a groan of pure pleasure and reached down to pull her to her feet, but Stephanie resisted, tugging him down beside her instead. He came willingly, one arm going around her shoulders as he pressed her back onto the floor and covered her mouth with his. He kissed her until she felt so weak and languid that she could hardly move. Then his lips began to trace a trail of fire down her body, consuming her breasts and stomach and the soft expanse of her inner thighs. His tongue moved daringly, insistently upon her, drawing gasps of joy from her mouth. "Neil!" Her word was the merest breath, yet it told him all that needed to be said of her wonder and love. He answered with the continued loving of his mouth until Stephanie twisted and moaned, yearning for release yet unwilling to end the exquisite pleasure.

Neil drew back to look at her, his eyes commanding hers to meet his. Never breaking their gaze he covered her, and her legs moved apart in welcome. He entered her slowly, filling her emptiness with a pleasure so keen, so prolonged, that Stephanie wasn't sure she could bear it. She urged him on, sinking her nails into his skin, lightly scraping them up his back and tangling her fingers in his hair. "Love me," he whispered huskily. "Don't send me away again."

"Never, never."

Neil shivered and surged fully into her. Stephanie matched the sweet rhythm of her body to his pounding demand as he took her higher and higher until at last they crested in a shimmering lightstorm. Slowly, softly they floated back to earth, wrapped in each other's arms, their damp bodies clinging. With a long, satisfied sigh Neil rolled onto his back, pulling Stephanie with him so that her head rested on his chest. She idly smoothed his curling chest hairs, only partially aware of the world around her, her mind still floating in the warm pleasure of their lovemaking.

Neil's hand drifted over her hair and back. Now and again he kissed the top of her head. "I love you," he whispered. "Do you see why I can't let you go?"

"Yes." Stephanie raised her head to look at him, her eyes glowing. "I love you too."

He wet his lips. "I . . . I've decided to retire."

"What?" Stephanie gaped.

"I'm retiring from football at the end of the season. You won't have to face the possibility of my being injured."

"You'd do that for me?"

"Yes," he replied simply.

Tears filled Stephanie's eyes. "Oh, Neil, I don't deserve you."

He grinned. "I know. I'm a hell of a guy."

"I mean it!" Stephanie sat up agitatedly, brushing

her hair back with her hands. "I never dreamed you'd give up football for me."

"It wasn't much of a choice. You're my life."

Now the tears spilled out, trickling down her cheeks, and Neil reached up to brush them away as she spoke. "I didn't think when I said what I did. I didn't mean to make you choose between me and your career. I know how much you love football, how much it means to you. Oh, Neil, please believe me, I'd never, ever ask that of you! You don't need to give up football. You can have us both."

"What?" He frowned, puzzled. "Why the sudden turnaround?"

"I'm sorry. I realize now that I was trying to protect myself from getting hurt. Because you were in the same profession as Ty, it was easy for me to blame my fears on your job. But Julie made me see today that it didn't have much to do with football. I'd have been scared of the commitment even if you'd been a lawyer or a bus driver or . . . anything. I was terrified of loving again, of giving my whole self into your keeping. I couldn't face the pain of possibly losing you."

He frowned. "I don't understand."

"Of course not. You're too strong and capable. You don't understand irrational behavior. Logically it doesn't make sense. Just because Ty died doesn't mean you'll be taken from me too. But my inner fears aren't logical. The thought of you dying or leaving me or stopping loving me filled me with terror. I tried to protect myself by putting you out of my life. You see, when you were injured on the field I realized how much I loved you. I had given myself to you wholly. That meant that if I lost you, I'd lose me too. I was scared, and I ran. But that's not what I want out of life. It's better to risk it all than to play it safe and have nothing."

Neil raised one of her hands to his lips, kissing each

finger tenderly. "I promise to take very good care of your love—and of myself. I'm determined not to be separated from you again." He paused and added jokingly, "And you know what happens when I set my mind on something."

Stephanie smiled. "Yes. You get it. Good. Because it's my intention to come back into your life and never leave it unless you kick me out."

"A highly unlikely possibility."

"Will you promise not to give up football, then?"

"I'll have to give it up someday."

"But I don't want you to do it for me. That would only make you bitter and resentful in time."

"All right, I promise I won't give up football for you. When the time comes, I'll do it for myself. Agreed?"

"Agreed. And the time won't come soon, will it?"

"Trying to catch me in a subterfuge? No, it won't be soon, unless I get an injury this year that makes it impossible—or marriage makes me so fat and lazy I can't play anymore."

"Marriage?"

Neil grinned like the cat that had gotten into the cream. Stephanie raised her eyebrows coolly. "Do you have a candidate in mind for the bride?"

"Yes. She has to be beautiful, sexy, intelligent and talented. And she has to have experience in marriage, since I won't know what I'm doing."

"A widow, in other words?"

"Or a divorcee," he reminded her. "Fortunately I know a woman who fits the requirements, so I won't have to conduct a long search."

"Oh, really? Local talent, then?"

"Yeah."

"And who might this paragon be?"

His hands went to her shoulders and he pulled her toward him. "You, of course. Will you marry me?"

"I was beginning to wonder if I had any say in the

matter," Stephanie joked. "Yes, I'll marry you. Whenever you want."

"I wouldn't want to rush things. How about Monday?"

"That's not rushing?"

"You have to remember that I've already waited four years."

Stephanie laughed. "All right."

One of his hands went behind her head, holding it firmly as he kissed her. The kiss started out lightly, but the pressure increased and his lips began to move hungrily on hers. With one quick movement he rolled them both over so that his body pressed into hers. He broke off the kiss to nibble at her earlobes, and his hand began a leisurely exploration of her body. "Neil!" Stephanie protested laughingly. "Again?"

"Mmm. I have a couple of weeks to make up for."

Stephanie pulled back to look at him, widening her eyes in mock innocence. "But, sweetheart, it's Saturday. There's a game tomorrow. You can't break training."

"To hell with training," he growled, and covered her mouth with a kiss that promised the future.

If you enjoyed this book...

Thrill to 4 more
Silhouette Intimate Moments
novels (a $9.00 value)—
ABSOLUTELY FREE!

If you want more passionate sensual romance, then Silhouette Intimate Moments novels are for you!

In every 256-page book, you'll find romance that's electrifying...involving... and intense. And now, these larger-than-life romances can come into your home every month!

4 FREE books as your introduction.

Act now and we'll send you four thrilling Silhouette Intimate Moments novels. They're our gift to introduce you to our convenient home subscription service. Every month, we'll send you four new Silhouette Intimate Moments books. Look them over for 15 days. If you keep them, pay just $9.00 for all four. Or return them at no charge.

We'll mail your books to you *as soon as they are published.* Plus, with every shipment, you'll receive the Silhouette Books Newsletter absolutely free. *And Silhouette Intimate Moments is delivered free.*

Mail the coupon today and start receiving Silhouette Intimate Moments. Romance novels for women...not girls.

Silhouette Intimate Moments

Silhouette
Intimate Moments

more romance, more excitement

———— $2.25 each ————

Silhouette
Intimate Moments

more romance, more excitement

Silhouette Intimate Moments